SOMETHING WI...

Kerry Wilkinson's debut, *Locked In*, the first title in the Detective Jessica Daniel series, was written as a challenge to himself and became a UK Number One Kindle bestseller within three months of release.

His three initial Jessica Daniel books made him Amazon UK's top-selling author for the final quarter of 2011. When *Think of the Children* followed in 2013, he became the first formerly self-published British author to have an ebook Number One and reach the top 20 of the UK paperback chart.

Something Wicked is the first book in the Andrew Hunter series. Andrew Hunter appeared as a private investigator in *Playing with Fire*, the fifth book in the Jessica Daniel series, and Kerry liked him enough to create a new series.

Kerry has a degree in journalism, plays cricket badly and complains about the weather a lot. He was born in Somerset but now lives in Lancashire, thus explaining the climate gripes.

For more information about Kerry and his books visit:

www.kerrywilkinson.com or
www.panmacmillan.com
Twitter: www.twitter.com/kerrywk
Facebook: www.facebook.com/JessicaDanielBooks

Or you can email Kerry at kerrywilkinson@live.com

Also by Kerry Wilkinson

The Jessica Daniel series

LOCKED IN

VIGILANTE

THE WOMAN IN BLACK

THINK OF THE CHILDREN

PLAYING WITH FIRE

THICKER THAN WATER

BEHIND CLOSED DOORS

CROSSING THE LINE

SCARRED FOR LIFE

The Silver Blackthorn Trilogy

RECKONING

RENEGADE

KERRY WILKINSON

SOMETHING WICKED

PAN BOOKS

First published 2014 by Pan Books

This edition published 2015 by Pan Books
an imprint of Pan Macmillan
20 New Wharf Road, London N1 9RR
Associated companies throughout the world
www.panmacmillan.com

ISBN 978-1-4472-6209-1

1 3 5 7 9 8 6 4 2

A CIP catalogue record for this book is available from the British Library.

Typeset by Ellipsis Digital Limited, Glasgow
Printed and bound by CPI Group (UK) Ltd, Croydon, CR0 4YY

Visit www.panmacmillan.com to read more about all our books
and to buy them. You will also find features, author interviews and
news of any author events, and you can sign up for e-newsletters
so that you're always first to hear about our new releases.

SOMETHING WICKED

TUESDAY

1

Cheese dripped from the radio presenter's voice as he drawled his way in a put-on American accent over the top of a song Andrew Hunter didn't recognise.

'. . . just in case you're feeling a bit down this morning, we'll be taking you back to the 1980s with "The Only Way Is Up" by Yazz and the Plastic Population – right after the news . . .'

As if that was going to make people feel better a little after nine on a Tuesday morning.

The unknown song ebbed into the opening bars of the far more serious news jingle as Andrew zoned out from the radio, focusing on the road in front of him. As usual, Manchester was gridlocked. Long lines of cars stretched far into the distance in front and behind, rows of blinking brake lights edging forward two or three lengths at a time before the dreaded red traffic light of doom told them to stop. If that wasn't enough, the mustard yellow traffic camera on Andrew's left gazed unmovingly at the road, daring any wayward drivers to sneak through on crimson.

Do you feel lucky, punk?

'. . . a tanker has spilled its load on the M60, leading to large tailbacks heading into, and out of, the city. Police say the motorway will be closed until at least lunchtime . . .'

The female newsreader's voice remained calm as she

told thousands of people their mornings were going to be spent staring at the back of other people's cars.

The cow.

Andrew began drumming his fingers on the steering wheel as the traffic heading across the junction was shown the green light of acceptance. Waiting directly in front of him at the front of this particular queue, a sleek dark grey Audi growled at the morning, tinted windows blocking any indication of who the driver was.

'. . . have arrested seven people in connection with last month's riots in the Moss Side area of the city. Police swooped in the early hours of the morning in a coordinated operation with the Serious Crime Division. Assistant Chief Constable Graham Pomeroy said . . .'

Blah, blah, blah. They'd be back on the streets by lunchtime.

Ahead, the cross-traffic dribbled to a stop and the engines around Andrew grumbled in anticipation, waiting for the green light to twinkle its emerald glow of approval.

As the burn of red was joined by amber, the grey Audi surged forward, before stopping almost instantly with a squeal of tyres. Directly in front of the vehicle, a thin girl wearing jeans tucked into bright white trainer-boots, a checked shirt and a pulled-down baseball cap jumped backwards in alarm. The car's horn beeped furiously with a flailing arm appearing though the driver's side window.

'Look where you're walking!'

Instead of sheepishly heading for the kerb, the girl stepped towards the car, tugging the brim of her cap down further. She slapped the palm of her hand on the bonnet, before pointing an angry finger at the driver.

'You look where *you're* going. Just because you've got a big car, it doesn't mean you own the . . . world.'

The hesitation before the word 'world' let her down a little but there was impressive venom before it. Behind Andrew, cars beeped their annoyance at the lack of movement. The green traffic light had promised so much but was delivering so little.

The Audi driver's arm flapped its way back inside the car, his window no doubt humming back into place. His vehicle was less than a year old and stuck out like a dad at a disco in this area of the city. Andrew could almost hear the driver's thoughts: was the girl part of some gang who would now swoop down and take their vengeance? You never knew nowadays – the scrawniest runt of a teenager could have a dozen tooled-up mates hiding in the bushes eagerly waiting for someone to talk out of turn.

The girl continued to stand in front of the Audi, arms wide in the universal pose to ask 'what are you going to do about it?' The reason the pose was universal was because no one ever stretched their arms out so provocatively unless they knew the person they were taunting was going to do precisely nothing about it. You ended up looking quite the tit if you asked 'what are you going to do about it?', before promptly finding out the person was going to cave your face in.

The girl's cap was covering the top half of her face as a twisting ponytail of black hair wound its way around the curve of her chin.

She wiggled her little finger. 'You know what they say about men with big cars.'

The traffic lights shimmered from green to amber and a long line of drivers behind Andrew began grumbling. Bastarding, bloody council. Stupid, sodding lights. What's wrong with a roundabout? Why are there so many people on the road?

The girl skipped around the Audi towards the driver's window, crouching slightly but not enough to properly try to look through the dark frosted glass. She tapped on the window before continuing around the vehicle, slapping the rear wheel rim hard. After a glance at Andrew, she sidestepped through the gap between his car and the Audi and then dashed away from the road towards a bush on the other side of a set of railings.

The amber traffic light glimmered tantalisingly before blinking back to red.

Thou shalt not pass.

Except that the Audi did pass, roaring forward and turning left all under the watchful eye of the traffic camera.

Andrew edged forward until his car was resting against the white line, waiting for the lights to change.

'. . . and finally, a postcard sent in the early 1900s has arrived at its destination – over a hundred years late . . .'

Royal Mail up to its usual standards then. Try getting compensation for that one.

The vehicles zipping across the junction slowly trickled to a halt again and Andrew grappled his car into first gear, bopping his free hand on the steering wheel.

Around him biting points were reached, car bonnets rising slightly in expectation.

Suddenly, there was a rush of movement from his left. Andrew spun too slowly as the back door of his car was wrenched open and the shape of a baseball cap-wearing young woman flung herself inside, out of breath, ponytail wrapped around her neck like a python choking its prey.

The traffic light switched to green.

'What are you waiting for?' the girl gasped as she pulled the door shut. 'Go.'

2

Andrew took her advice, turning left and reaching the steady heights of twenty miles an hour.

'Was that really necessary?' he asked, focusing back on the road.

He felt the young woman's knees pressing into the rear of his seat as she righted herself. Doof: take that. Wallop: how's your driving with someone kicking you in the back?

Andrew glanced in his rear-view mirror as she removed her baseball cap and began untying her hair.

'Jenny – was that really necessary?'

Her button-like deep brown eyes met his in the mirror as her face folded into a grin. A single dimple curved into her cheek as her lips angled into a smile. Andrew thought she'd probably spent all twenty-three years of her life perfecting that get-out-of-jail-free smirk.

'What?'

'All you had to do was plant the tracker somewhere – not hold up a line of traffic or intimidate the guy.'

Jenny shrugged. 'It had to be authentic, didn't it? Besides, if he didn't leave his car locked away behind those big gates at his work, we'd have got to it before.'

She began wriggling her way out of the checked shirt. Don't look – she's young enough to be your daughter, for

8

God's sake. Well, your daughter if you started having sex at twelve, which definitely hadn't happened – but wouldn't be uncommon nowadays. The twelve-year-olds without kids of their own could be the odd ones out, depending on which newspapers you read.

'He had a suit on,' Jenny said in among a thrash of arms. He could sense her hunting in the backpack of clothes behind his seat. 'Some pink tie strangling the life out of him. Looking particularly smart.'

Andrew pulled into a row of traffic queuing at a round-about.

'I thought his windows were tinted?'

More scrambling around behind his seat, an elbow in the back for good measure. Jenny's reply was muffled: 'I've got good eyes. Anyway, he's definitely up to something.'

Andrew glanced in the mirror, spying a hint of flesh and dark purple bra strap before tugging his eyes away again, instantly feeling guilty. He really hadn't engineered this: it was her idea. The stupid ideas were always hers, except that they never failed – meaning they weren't stupid at all. Just . . . *chaotic*. Like this.

Another elbow walloped into his chair, sending his head thudding forward.

'Sorry!'

At the roundabout, everyone was giving way to everyone else in what was either a giant circle of friendship, or a state of inertia that could potentially go on forever.

More drumming on the steering wheel, another thump in the back of his seat. Andrew didn't dare check the mirror again.

The driver to Andrew's right broke the impasse, accelerating ahead with a cheery wave to all of the give-wayers, and starting a chain reaction where everything moved except for the line Andrew was in.

Not that he could focus on the road anyway as Jenny deftly slipped herself through the gap between the two front seats, landing with a plop in the passenger's side. She had completely changed her clothes: the chavvy jeans, trainer-boots and shirt lay discarded on the back seat, replaced by a pair of black trousers, flat black shoes and a white blouse, as if she was heading off to a secretarial job. She ran her fingers through her long untied black hair, yanking out a knot.

'That was fun,' she said.

'What would you have done if he'd got out of the car?'

'What was he going to do?'

'That's what I'm asking you.'

'Pfft.'

Well, that settled that argument.

'Where's the kit?' Jenny added, moving on without missing a beat.

'Glove box.'

Jenny popped it open and began hunting around before pulling out a tablet computer.

'You *actually* keep gloves in there,' she said disbelievingly, shoving a pair back inside and slamming the compartment closed.

'It is called a glove box.'

'That's just a name though, isn't it? Do you keep boots in your boot?'

'No.'

'Exactly.'

Andrew thought about arguing the point but he wasn't sure he'd ever won, or would win, an argument with the young woman who was supposed to be his assistant. There was something matter-of-fact about the way she spoke that ended all disagreements – not that they ever argued about anything serious. She appeared to respect him as a boss and never questioned his judgement, at the same time doing the things he needed her to. She certainly liked having the last word, though.

Andrew kept his eyes on the road, forcing himself not to grin. 'What was "You don't own the *world*" all about?'

'I couldn't think of anything better at the time. I was going to say he didn't own the road – but then I realised I'd look stupid because cars own the road more than pedestrians do. I should've probably thought it through a bit better. Perhaps put a scriptwriter on it, got a bit of Hollywood money into the project.'

Andrew could tell she was grinning, even though he didn't turn. As he finally got across the roundabout and continued ahead, the corner of his eye caught Jenny's fingers flashing over the tablet screen as she mumbled something inaudible under her breath.

'Right,' she said, rolling the R, 'he's just gone onto the M62. We're about half a mile behind but there are hold-ups where it joins the M6. If we keep going on this road and take a left at the next roundabout, we should be able to stay parallel and catch up.'

'You sure?'

Jenny ummed for a few moments. 'No – but if he turns off we can follow him anyway.'

Andrew glanced sideways at the tablet on Jenny's lap, which was displaying a map. In the year and a bit he'd been a private investigator, Andrew had looked at tracking devices at various conferences and technology fairs. All of the sales people had their own pitches about their devices being smaller and better than the others but it wasn't until he'd hired Jenny four months previously that he had really started using them. Jenny seemed to be a natural when it came to technology, like most people her age, he guessed. Although he got by and knew more than most, he was no match for her.

After turning left as he'd been told, Andrew relaxed, sticking to the national speed limit as the built-up areas of Manchester shrank into the distance in his rear-view mirror.

Unexpectedly, Jenny made a lunge sideways, reaching for her rucksack in the well behind Andrew's seat.

'Fancy a biscuit?' she asked.

'What have you got?'

Jenny slopped back into her seat, rucksack now on her lap. 'Aah, so you're one of *those* people . . .'

'What people?'

'One of *them*. See, if you ask people if they want a biscuit, the normal response is "yes" or "no" – you either do or you don't. If you're one of *them*, you're already thinking too far ahead.' She paused to put on a deeper voice which sounded nothing like Andrew's. '"What if it's a coconut ring? I don't like coconut. What if it's a custard cream? They give me the runs".' Back to her normal voice: 'By trying to over-analyse, you're denying yourself the opportunity of happiness. It's a really bad habit – something you should think about changing.'

Andrew paused, watching the road and listening to the strains of Lionel Richie's 'Dancing on the Ceiling' bubbling from the speakers. They really did play some shite on local radio.

'Did you get that from a book?' he asked.

Jenny squished the bag between her knees onto the floor. 'Almost – some lad I was seeing at uni was a philosophy student. He did his dissertation about biscuits. Got a first and everything. Anyway, the question still remains: do you want a biscuit?'

'Er . . .'

'Fine, I'll let you cheat – but if you become a deeply unhappy person because of it, don't say I didn't warn you.'

With a swish of her hair, the rucksack was open again. 'Right, I've got Viennese fingers, or chocolate Rich Teas?'

'What are you having?'

Jenny flung both arms into the air, almost bumping the packets into the roof. The tablet was balanced precariously on her knees. 'There you go again. That's what's called mirroring – you don't feel as if you can live your life for yourself, so you take your cues from others.'

'I only asked so that you didn't have to open both packets!'

Jenny grinned. 'I know – I'm winding you up. And don't even ask why I've got biscuits in my bag. I think I'm hypo-glycaemic, or whatever it's called. What's that one where you need sugar all the time? Diabetes? Either way, life would be a lot calmer if people carried chocolate Rich Teas around with them.'

She slid a nail across the top of the Viennese fingers packet and thrust a biscuit in Andrew's direction. He glanced briefly away from the road, clasped it between his teeth, and continued driving. He'd certainly had worse breakfasts.

Jenny bundled everything back into her bag and picked up the tablet again. For a few minutes they sat listening to something by Phil Collins before Andrew couldn't take it any longer and switched the radio off.

'I only listen for the traffic news,' he said. Jenny didn't reply, which only compounded the lie. Everyone secretly loved Phil Collins, but just couldn't admit it.

Buildings turned into hedges, the urban areas into green, before Jenny spoke again. 'He's slowed right down by the way. We're going to catch him in a minute or two.'

Andrew kept going, trusting Jenny's judgement. Quite why he had such faith in someone he'd only known for a few months he wasn't sure. There was something fascinating about her confidence that bordered on recklessness. It was the complete opposite to his own nature and sometimes Andrew found himself simply watching her. There was nothing romantic or sinister but he'd seen her talk people around to her own way of thinking without even trying. It was as if she did everything without getting out of first gear, as if life itself was something she could bend to her own will. Even though she was naturally pretty, he didn't think her appearance was part of it, she just had something about her that other people didn't – certainly something that *he* didn't. Andrew could blend into a crowd and go unseen: a normal guy with a normal face, sandy-gingery hair, not too fat, not too thin, not tall, not short . . . just *there*. It was the way he'd always been and, in many ways, made him perfect for poking his nose into other people's business. Unless they knew to look for him, people could walk straight past, gaze into his eyes, and continue as if there'd been nobody there.

Jenny was the antithesis. No one would forget her in a hurry – unless she was in unflattering clothes with a baseball cap covering half of her face. She was like a human chameleon, able to become whatever she needed to be.

'He's turned onto the M57,' Jenny said.

'Where does that go?'

'Huyton, Kirkby, Knowsley. You need to go right here.'

Andrew checked his mirror and flicked the indicator. 'When I tried following him last week, I was coming from the other way and lost him in Huyton.'

'What do you think he's getting up to there?'

'Hopefully, that's what we'll find out. Probably the usual.'

'You think he has a woman on the go?'

'I imagine that's what his wife is paying us to find out.'

Jenny paused and, for once, Andrew knew what she was going to say next. 'When I first started, you said that you didn't do adultery cases.'

'Strictly speaking, we don't know what it is. His wife said her husband kept sneaking away from the house and office and that she didn't know where he went. He could be creeping out to go to Alton Towers for all we know.'

Another pause.

'He's going the wrong way for that.'

'I know.'

'Still, that'd be a great reason to escape the house. Your wife thinks you're having an affair but really you're going on the rollercoasters in full suit and tie.' Jenny returned her attention to the tablet. 'You never did say why you don't do adultery cases . . .'

Fish, fish, fish.

Andrew sighed inwardly, a sort of non-sigh that wasn't for anyone's benefit, including his own. 'They're just very boring. Someone's sleeping with someone else. Take a picture, bug a room, bribe a hotel worker. Anyone can do that.'

Jenny didn't look up from the tablet but continued fishing. 'Good money, though . . .'

'I'm sure it is . . .'

Andrew didn't give her the answer for that particular piece of angling. She was intelligent enough to notice that the money coming in barely matched what he was paying her, combined with the rent on the office. Still, she was so used to getting her own way that he figured she could keep guessing about that particular enigma, at least for now. One day, she would no doubt talk him into telling her the truth about where his money came from, probably by making him think it was his idea to tell her all along.

'He's got a nice car,' Jenny went on.

'That's what I couldn't figure out when I tried following

him the last time. He just disappeared. One minute there was this brand-new grey thing in front of me, then he turned off the road and he was gone.'

'Stewart Deacon . . .' Jenny rolled the man's name around her mouth. 'Stew-art. How much do you think he's worth?'

'It's hard to know from his credit report and it's difficult to figure out who owns what in regards to his companies. His wife isn't named as a director of any of them, which should tell you one thing.'

Jenny made an umming sound, although it might have been a yawn. 'Not a bad business really. Buy houses dead cheap because no one wants them, pay someone to do them up, sell them on for more.'

'People have been doing that for years – it's picking houses in the right area. There's no point in buying a house in the middle of some sink estate – you could turn it into a palace but no one's going to want to live there.'

'True.'

Andrew kept driving, waiting until Jenny cut in again as they passed the sign for Huyton. 'Okay, you need to ease off,' she said.

A small rank of shops and thirty-mile-an-hour signs were signalling the end of the countryside and the beginnings of the town. Eight or nine cars ahead, Andrew could see the sleek grey Audi waiting at another set of traffic lights.

Green for go and the car turned right onto a housing estate, with Andrew telepathically encouraging the drivers ahead to put their sodding feet down and narrowly making the turn before the lights flickered back to red.

'This is where I lost him last week,' Andrew said.

He continued driving straight ahead, but the grey car was nowhere to be seen, even though there were no turn-offs.

'Pull over,' Jenny said, lifting the tablet. 'We're sort of on top of him.'

Andrew parked on the road and switched off the engine. Ahead, the road stretched away in a straight line, rows of houses flanking both sides with neat gardens, low walls and lines of satellite dishes. He twisted to get a better view through the back window, taking in the junction and the shops.

'He's behind us,' Jenny said, opening her door.

Andrew climbed out, rounding the car until he was on the pavement next to her. Jenny angled the tablet towards him and he blinked his way into the map, trying to figure out how the two-dimensional lines were a representation of where he actually was. The red dot which signalled their car was motionless, with a blue one showing the Audi half-overlapping.

Jenny began pointing towards the shops a moment before Andrew worked out where they were in relation to the map. She took a few steps forward, Andrew at her side.

Running around the shops was a smattering of cracked paving slabs masquerading as a car park. Andrew and Jenny walked to the main road, still watching the unmoving blue dot on the map as they realised they'd apparently gone past the Audi without seeing it. Andrew gazed back towards his own vehicle on the empty road – they must have passed the car they were following, even though they definitely hadn't.

In front, fluorescent bulbs from inside the row of shops blazed out onto the pavement, lighting up the overcast day. There was a Spar at the end, advertising six cans of shoddy lager for the price of four and two-for-one on ginger nuts. Jenny's old boyfriend with the first-class degree in philosophy would surely have something to say about that. Next to the Spar was a hairdresser's, with a sign declaring that you could be 'cut and blown' for a tenner: a bargain, with or without the cutting. After that was the customary pizza shop, betting hole and a florist. Nothing advertising car vanishing, which would have made their lives a little easier.

Jenny began walking back in the direction they'd come, tablet thrust in front of her.

'He's got to be here somewhere . . .' She stopped on the pavement at the end of the row of shops and turned in a full circle. 'His car is right here.'

Along the back of the shops, disjointed mounds of gravel had been piled to either side. Wide wheelie bins were shoved into alcoves, with overgrown trees drooping ominously and casting a deep shadow across the space. Andrew took in the scene, wondering what he was missing. He began walking along the alley, feet scrunching across the grit. It was only when he passed the back door of the florist that he realised what they hadn't been able to see. From the pavement, it looked like one long alley but it was an optical illusion because a garage door at the end was painted the same colour as the wall beyond. He doubted it was deliberate because both the wall and garage were so ramshackle, but it was certainly clever, even if it was inadvertent. Either way, it wasn't the sort of place you'd usually leave an almost new car. It was unlikely to be a portal to Alton Towers, either.

Andrew continued along the path, Jenny just behind him until they reached the garage.

'Is he in there?' Andrew asked.

'His car is.'

On the left-hand side of the garage, a concrete set of steps curled their way up to a flat above the Spar. Unless he was *in* the garage, which Andrew doubted, this was the only place Stewart Deacon could have gone.

Andrew turned to Jenny, who was putting the tablet into her backpack. 'Want to go up?' he asked.

'Paper, scissors, stone?'

'Fine.'

They each held out their left palms, tapping their right fists into them.

One, two, three: rock.

Shite.

Rock was a total waste of time, like choosing heads in a coin toss. Tails never fails and only a cock chooses rock. He should have just ordered her to do it and yet the moment she'd said 'paper, scissors, stone', he'd agreed without even thinking. Like a siren luring him onto the rocks – which was probably why he'd been subliminally pressured into going for rock in the first place. What did rock defeat anyway? Well, scissors – but who went for scissors? Only a psycho whose first thought was to come up with something sharp.

Andrew edged his way up the stairs, fearing the worst.

Who lived above a Spar? It was probably a crack den. Stewart Deacon had pretended to make his money through property, all the time dealing crack instead. It dawned on Andrew that he had no idea what a crack den looked like. Would he knock politely, walk in and find a bunch of old dears drinking tea, only to discover it was tea laced with crack?

At the top of the stairs was a scruffy once-cream door with '1A' scratched into the paint via a green-inked biro. Green ink? This had psycho written all over it.

The windows on either side had the curtains pulled, which was surely the type of thing you'd do if you were dealing crack.

Andrew glanced down towards Jenny, who shrugged in the way young people seemed to, as if language was devolving into a series of gestures. He knocked on the door gently and took a step backwards, waiting . . .

The door opened a sliver, a beady eye appearing in the darkened gap. Andrew barely had a moment to say anything before the door opened fully. Nobody spoke, so he stepped inside, gasping at the toxic scent of some sort of perfume combined with something else he wasn't sure about. Probably crack. The room was awash with crimson and pink but the lights were so dim, it was like wearing sunglasses indoors.

He turned to see a woman wearing a top cut so low that it almost touched her belly button. A valley of cleavage heaved forward threateningly as she turned and walked around him, her fragrance practically weaponised.

'You got an appointment, luv?'

Her accent was thick, northern and nasally, every word sounding as if it came with a threat to smash a brick over someone's head.

'No, I . . .'

'So d'ya know what yer after? Aurora's phoned in sick but Angel's come in instead. It's a fifty-quid house fee for half-hour.' She nodded towards a door. 'There's a shower in there if you need to sort yourself out. Money upfront and then the girls are through there.'

She nodded towards a second door but Andrew had already turned for the exit: Stewart Deacon would indeed have a bit of explaining to do.

3

Andrew's life had changed six months previously when he'd inadvertently ended up investigating a teenage girl's suicide. Before then, the private investigating had been something of a joke. Well, a lot of a joke. It was something to spend his money on, a reason to get up in the morning and leave his flat. After that case, something had clicked and he'd decided that if he was going to do this as a job, then he'd have to do it properly. He left the old office, ditched the rubbish chairs and jammed filing cabinets, and found himself somewhere decent to work. He kept the pot plant though – he wasn't a complete philistine.

The new office wasn't big but it was central for Manchester, a little off Minshull Street, close to the court and, even more crucially, a short walk to the numerous cafes, restaurants and pubs if Andrew ever wanted to go out for lunch. Which he didn't. The floor, walls and desks were all bright white and new, with a window that faced Piccadilly Gardens if he squinted a bit, and spinny executive-type chairs that actually supported his back.

All in all, it wasn't too bad.

Jenny sat behind her desk, fingers blurring across the keyboard in a frenzy of tip-tapping. She sometimes wore glasses when using the computer, making her look even more secretarial, though she was anything but.

'I found the website of that brothel,' she said, not looking up. 'It's called Dream Girls.'

Andrew glanced up from his monitor towards her. 'From what I saw, the only dream you'd be having in there was a nightmare.'

Jenny peered over her glasses at him but said nothing. Clearly there was a second type of dream he'd forgotten.

She continued without a breath. 'I've got photos of Stewart opening the garage door when he came out, the car exiting the garage, plus the tracking details. Obviously we don't have anything of the inside but I do have pictures of one of the girls leaving.' Jenny twisted her monitor around to show a woman shuffling her cleavage into place as she descended the concrete steps. 'Best I could get. Add that to the website with the address and it's pretty nailed on. Unless he was there fixing the plumbing, I'm not sure what else he could say. I wonder what his missus will think.'

In describing the situation, Jenny had underlined all of the reasons why Andrew generally turned down anything that tried to uncover someone's infidelity. Ultimately, the wife already knew what her husband was up to, else she wouldn't have got an investigator involved. Meanwhile, the husband could try to find a way to wriggle out of it if he really wanted. Perhaps Stewart was looking into buying the flat to renovate and the half-hour he spent inside was an exploratory mission looking for damp patches.

On the walls, Andrew thought to himself, suppressing a childish grin. How old was he?

'I'll go first thing tomorrow,' Andrew said. 'I can't face her today. If you can separate everything up for the bill—'

'Already done.'

Jenny stood, stepping around the corner of her desk and stretching a file out to Andrew. He took the cardboard wallet and opened the cover, skimming through the pages. It was the usual – mainly hours billed, as if he was a solicitor, but with a few expenses here and there. It would be easy enough to overcharge people – especially when you got a result – but Jenny knew Andrew's policy about doing things properly.

That was the other reason he did his best to turn down anything involving warring partners. It was bad enough having to tell someone their other half was getting up to no good behind their back, let alone adding: 'Oh, and by the way, you owe me some money. Cash or card?'

He'd taken the case really hoping there was more to it than a simple husband-after-a-bit-on-the-side but the work was beginning to become tedious again. After the suicide investigation, he thought he might be able to do some good by picking up cases that the police didn't have either the time or resources for. Instead, it was small-time pieces of due diligence, tracing people with debts, or varying amounts of surveillance. Nothing extraordinary or particularly interesting – especially considering Jenny was so good at taking the smaller things away from him. Paperwork: done. Typing, accounts: sorted. Reports: no problem. She didn't even complain, which in many ways made her the perfect employee – except that Andrew had never quite been able to figure out why she wanted to work with him. He had the sense she could go away and make a success of anything she tried, yet here she was, day after day, doing menial things, all for the promise that, now and then, she'd get to do silly things like dress up and jump in front of cars to plant trackers.

The laser printer in the corner hummed to life with a guff of energy, pleased to finally be doing something, before it started shooting sheets of paper into the out-tray.

Jenny crossed the room, palm outstretched as if she was about to shake hands with the printer. At the last moment, she clasped the pages and returned to her desk with a twinkle of a smile.

Andrew's thoughts were interrupted by a knock on the door. A tall silhouette was visible through the frosted glass, blocking the light from the corridor outside.

'Come in,' Andrew called, standing as a man dripped his way into the office. Jenny was instantly on her feet, full of smiles and 'hello's, taking the man's sodden coat and spreading it out over the radiator.

The man was similar to Andrew in build: not big, not small – but he was at least twenty years older, somewhere in his mid-fifties, with greying dark hair that was thinning at the front. He was wearing a suit but the trousers were drenched as if he'd been swimming with his clothes on. In many ways, going outside in Manchester without an umbrella was exactly like that. He was hooking a leather satchel over his shoulder.

'It's chucking it down out there,' the man said as Jenny fussed around him. 'If you know of anyone named Noah, make sure he's not building a boat.'

He smiled wearily, not expecting – or getting – a laugh.

It was a dad gag handed down through the ages, barely funny in the first place and certainly not now.

The man shook Andrew's hand, introducing himself as Richard Carr, before Jenny headed off to the corner and clicked on the kettle. Andrew had never asked her to do any of those sorts of things but she just did. She grabbed a mop from the other corner and began swishing away the thin trail of water from the door to Richard's chair.

'Sorry, sorry,' he said, brushing the remains of his hair away from his face. 'I couldn't find anywhere to park, then they're doing roadworks on my usual spot off Deansgate. I ended up walking for about a mile.'

As Jenny distracted him by asking about tea or coffee, Andrew took a moment to properly stare at the man. There were wisps of stubble around his mouth that he'd missed shaving and his hair looked a little longer than it was meant to be, as if he'd had the same style for thirty years but forgotten to get it cut recently. There was something familiar about him too. Andrew had definitely seen him before and the name rang a bell.

Jenny asked Richard for his milk and sugar requirements and then hurried away again. If social networks were crying out for one thing, it was surely an option to add your tea preference.

Name
Date of birth
Single/married/in a relationship/it's complicated
A splash of milk, no sugar, leave the teabag in
Richard squashed himself into the chair and peered up,

catching Andrew's gaze and holding it. 'You're Mr Hunter, I presume.'

'Yes.'

'I looked on your website and it said you search for missing people . . . ?'

'That's right.'

'I've got a . . . complicated one for you.' Richard glanced towards the floor and swallowed. 'My son disappeared on his eighteenth birthday nine months ago.'

As Richard looked up again, the penny dropped for Andrew. 'Your son's Nicholas Carr.'

Richard nodded. 'I take it you saw everything in the papers at the time. It was a big deal . . .' He tailed off. '. . . not so much now.'

Andrew tried to force his brain to remember the details. They were in his mind somewhere, probably buried under irrelevant information such as who played Bones in the original 'Star Trek'. If only he could get rid of all the junk and keep everything important for his life and job, he'd be a much better person. There had been posters around the city, broadcasts on the news, front pages of newspapers. Everything always moved on though – somebody went missing, they were a big story for a day or two, and then they either reappeared or they didn't. Nobody ever went back to check.

Richard paused as Jenny returned with the tea, placing it on the desk in front of him. He twisted the cup around on the saucer with a ceramic squeak, making it neat before taking a sip. 'According to the police, Nicholas is dead. It's been nine months, so there's every chance he is. They found three fingers from his right hand in Alkrington Wood a few days after he disappeared. They checked cameras, spoke to his friends – all that type of stuff – but we've heard nothing from him since. At first they thought his body was buried with the rest of his fingers in Alkrington but they dug a whole patch of it up and didn't find anything.'

The cloud that had been fogging Andrew's memories finally started to evaporate. 'You're a councillor, aren't you?'

The man nodded without looking up. 'District council. It's been awkward these past few months. You're supposed to be at these votes and rallies but, well . . .'

Richard tailed off again, Adam's apple bobbing as he reached for his tea. Jenny placed a box of tissues in front of him and he glanced towards her, eyes hanging on for a fraction of a second too long. There wasn't anything particularly out of the ordinary in it; many men, and women for that matter, found themselves noticing her, but Andrew always felt uncomfortable, like a father dropping off his daughter at her first school disco.

Whatever anyone thought, he hadn't hired her based on looks. After choosing his new office and deciding to act more professionally, Andrew realised he needed an assistant. He'd gone through an agency to advertise the position and they'd sent half-a-dozen graduates his way.

Andrew's own degree was in criminology, a social science more based on the reasons for crime as opposed to crime-solving itself. Of the graduates he'd approved for interview, three of them had qualifications in computer-based science, one in electronics, one in psychology and one, bizarrely, in radio journalism. He wasn't as interested in the pieces of paper they held as the individuals themselves.

Jenny was an information technology graduate but barely talked about that in her interview. If anything, the reason he'd hired her was because she didn't have desperation seeping from her every pore. She hadn't said it out loud but her body language had screamed it: 'Give me a job, or not – see if I care. I'll get by.' It had ended with her almost interviewing him, making suggestions about how the office could be better organised and asking how long he'd been doing the job. He felt guilty for hiring her over the other candidates: people who actually wanted the job and thought about their answers in the interview. Instead he'd chosen a young woman who'd shrugged her way through it. He'd been right though – she was perfect.

Andrew waited until Richard had put down his teacup. 'If the police are still involved, I can't insert myself into their investigation.'

Richard waved his hand. 'There is no investigation. They held the inquest, which declared an open verdict – but that's no closure for me and my wife. For them, it's over but we have to go on wondering. If he's dead, where's the body? If he's alive, where is he and why hasn't he come home? How did three of his fingers end up in those woods?'

Andrew squirmed in his seat. 'I'll be completely honest here, Mr Carr—'

'Richard.'

'Sorry, Richard. I'm not exactly sure what you think I can do that a police investigation couldn't.'

Richard ran his hands through his hair and breathed out loudly. Behind him, Jenny tapped gently away at her keyboard. 'I suppose somebody doing something is better than a bunch of people doing nothing.'

He reached into his satchel and handed over a small photograph. A teenager, perhaps sixteen or seventeen, was lying on a patch of grass giving the thumbs-up to the camera. He had dark blond hair similar in colour to Andrew's, tousled in a just-got-out-of-bed look that so many young people seemed to have. Were people really that attractive first thing in the morning? From Andrew's experience, it was all yawns and trying to remember which day it was.

'That's Nicholas around eighteen months ago,' Richard said, counting on his fingers. 'That was taken eight or nine months before he disappeared.'

'Was he living at home?'

'Yes – my wife and I have a place in Prestwich. He lived with us while he went to college. He was talking about university and had a girlfriend. There was no reason for him to go off, let alone for anyone to do anything to him. He was just a normal kid.'

'Did the police ever come up with a motive or a theory?'

Another shrug. 'Not that they ever told us. They didn't seem to have a clue.'

Andrew glanced over Richard's shoulder, catching Jenny's eye as she peered over her glasses towards him, probably reading his mind. She was seemingly naturally gifted at everything else, so telepathy wouldn't be a push. Jenny turned back to her monitor without a word.

'We'll need a few initial pieces of information from you,' Andrew said. 'Nicholas's full name, his date of birth, national insurance number, details of any bank accounts. If he had a mobile phone and you know the number, that would be good. Ditto for personal email addresses and any social media accounts, that sort of thing. If you don't know it, then fair enough – but anything you can give us will be helpful.' He nodded towards the other desk. 'Jenny will take your details and if there's anything you don't have on you, you can either phone in when you get home, or drop us an email. Everything that comes in and out of here is encrypted at our end, so don't worry about security. Will you be in tomorrow afternoon?'

Richard nodded. 'I'm retired, so I can always be in.'

He leant forward, extending his hand but Andrew hesitated before shaking it. 'I know it's awkward but . . .'

'Oh, don't worry about money,' Richard replied. 'I know it'll cost – but you can't put a price on your son, can you? We just want some closure. It sounds dreadful, I know, but if he's dead we'd rather know – otherwise my wife and I are going to spend our days staring at the front door and hoping.' He paused to swallow. 'Do you have children?'

Andrew shook his head.

Richard smiled weakly. 'Then take my word for it: there's nothing worse than watching your child walk out of the front door and never coming back.'

WEDNESDAY

4

Nine thirty-five in the morning was a very specific time. Violet Deacon could have told Andrew to come around at half past like a normal person. It was an accepted fact of life that people worked in even blocks of time. Preferably, things happened on the hour. If that was impossible, then half past. At a push, quarter past or quarter to. It was the done thing, but apparently not for Violet Deacon. Still, her husband was driving thirty miles out of his way to visit prostitutes, so Andrew should probably give her some slack.

He parked outside her house at precisely nine thirty-four, hoping she'd forgive him the extra minute. He would have preferred to give her the report at his office but she'd insisted she couldn't leave the house. The road was wide and straight, a boy racer's dream, with bare autumn-racked trees swaying gently on either side in perfect rows. It was the type of tranquillity that could only exist thanks to busybody residents' groups with tape measures and clipboards. Still, good for them – if it was left up to the council, they'd plonk down a bunch of mismatched red-brick abominations as higgledy piggledy as possible in the name of 'community housing'.

Andrew got out of the car and looked both ways along the street: it was the kind of place you'd retire to. Peaceful and still, except for the TV engineer at the far end who was grappling with a tangle of cable, while simultaneously keeping a fag on the go. Smokers: the ultimate multi-taskers. Although it was probably good they could do more than one thing at a time considering they'd die of lung cancer ten years before everyone else. Best cram it all in as soon as possible.

The Deacons' house was a sprawling mass of bricks and glass, three storeys high, with a double garage and a driveway with paving slabs so perfectly even that it could have been laid by a mathematician, albeit one with big shoulders. Bay windows too – you couldn't be upper middle class if you didn't have curvy glass at the front of the house. A hosepipe slithered its way along the manicured lawn, with banks of pristine tufty jade grass surrounded by empty flower beds waiting for winter to come and go.

Andrew double-checked the address against the appalling scrawl of biro written on his hand and then made his way up the drive, satchel slung over his shoulder. It looked more professional to carry a bag, even if it did contain only a laptop he wouldn't need, a charger for his old phone, the file for Violet, a notepad and a pen which may or may not actually work. It wasn't what was in the bag that was important – it was the promise of what *might* be in the bag. For all his potential clients knew, it could be full of important surveillance gear, or technology so advanced it would blow their minds.

The doorbell made a deep bing-bong as Andrew checked his watch: exactly nine thirty-five. Moments later, the door creaked open, revealing the lightbulb-shaped Violet Deacon – bulbous on the bottom, small head at the top. Her dyed brown hair was clamped to the top of her head in a loose bun, while she had poured herself into a pair of leggings that did no favours either for her or the straining cotton.

Andrew stood to the side as she poked her head out of the front door and looked both ways. 'You didn't see anyone out there, did you?' she asked.

'Only some cable guy down the street.'

She nodded shortly, stepping aside to let him in. 'Bunch of nosy sods round here. That Mrs McIntyre across the road is always sticking her beak in other people's business. You can see her every day sitting in her window, spying on everyone going past, hoping she'll get a bit of gossip to report at their Friday coffee mornings. It's like they're winding down to death one coffee at a time. Old bags.'

Violet was in her early forties but looked older, a permanent yawning weariness etched on her face. Andrew didn't reply, allowing her to lead him along a photograph-laden hallway. He spotted Stewart and Violet in most of them, along with a boy in varying stages of adolescence. Here we are in Paris: snap. Here we are somewhere with elephants: snap. Skyscrapers, beach, sunshine, trees, next to a pool, holding up cocktails to the camera – all of the usual holiday pictures were there. They were one double thumbs-up away from a photo bingo full house when Andrew reached the kitchen.

A chunky unit sat in the centre of the room. Rows of pots and pans hung above, with the sides flanked by cabinets and counter tops. Everything was made of a glimmering black marble-type material, heavy with sharp edges and comfortably enough to crack open the head of a child who'd already been told to stop running. There was a health and safety officer somewhere with corks and polystyrene just waiting to come in and make the place safe. As well as the hallway door they'd entered through, there was another leading towards the garden and a third slightly ajar that led into another part of the house.

Violet plonked herself on a stool on the other side of the unit, making a vague gesture towards the seat on the opposite side. 'So, you found out what he's getting up to, then?'

Andrew reached into his bag, thumbing aside the laptop and plucking out the file. 'First, I should make sure that you definitely want to hear this.'

He eyed her closely, looking for any sense of alarm or worry. Instead, she scratched her ear. 'Go on.'

Andrew opened the cover of the file and slid it across the counter, tapping his finger on the top sheet. 'I'm afraid it's bad news, Mrs Deacon. We tracked your husband's car to this establishment. All of the details are in there; timings, photographs. We don't have anything of the actual . . . act . . . but there should be more than enough evidence.'

He sat back, waiting for either a torrent of denials and disbelief, or a tsunami of anger. Instead, he got neither.

'So it's just some brothel out Huyton way, then?'

She sounded almost disappointed.

Andrew was about to reply when the third door

squeaked open, revealing a scowling teenager, all hands in pockets and slouchy, as if he was missing a vertebra or five. In a flash, his hands were raised, a finger jabbing accusingly at Andrew. 'Are you the prick who's trying to drive my dad away?'

With a creak of the stool, Andrew was on his feet, taking a half-step away as the young man continued towards him. Violet leapt up, rounding the unit with a series of sidesteps, like a drunken crab. 'Jack, what have I told you about listening into other people's conversations?'

He ignored her, trying to manoeuvre around his mother's frame, finger still raised. He had deliberately greasy dark hair, smeared to the side as if he had been standing sideways in a wind tunnel, plus jeans hanging low around his backside and a long-sleeved top with a band logo that Andrew vaguely recognised.

'You bender. What's any of this got to do with you, eh? Sticking your nose into other people's business—'

He was interrupted by a crisp, clean slap across the face that cracked around the room, like a backfiring car. This time, it was Violet jabbing the finger. 'You have no right to be listening in to my private conversations. I don't care if it is half-term – we're not going over this again. Now go upstairs and get out of my sight. I don't want to see you again today.'

The pair stared at each other, gesticulating fingers at the ready, as if they were fencers ready for a swordfight.

Jack caved first, peering around his mother one final time to sneer at Andrew before turning on his heels and heading into the hallway. Seconds later, the front door banged closed, making it feel as if the entire house was in danger of collapse.

Violet stayed standing for a few moments, before smoothing down her top and sighing her way back to her stool.

She didn't look up from the counter: 'Do you have kids?'

Andrew retook his seat. 'No.'

'Don't. Honestly, fifteen-year-olds are the worst. Well, not compared to thirteen-year-olds, but you know what I mean. Well, you don't but . . .'

Andrew got it.

Violet yanked a flexible tap towards her and filled a glass with water, downing half of it in one and wiping her mouth with her sleeve. 'It's really not his fault; he's had to put up with this his entire life. I would have left Stewart years ago but decided to keep things together for Jack, at least until he leaves school.' She paused, holding a hand up to indicate the house. 'It starts getting messy when you have to divide things up too. I do a lot of the paper-work for the businesses – the clever stuff.' She slid the file back and leafed through to the second sheet with a stifled yawn, before continuing as if she hadn't stopped. 'Sometimes you settle for second-best because third- or fourth-best is even worse and first-best doesn't exist.'

Andrew wasn't sure if he should say anything, so he let Violet read. She flicked through the top few sheets before clapping the file closed, muffling another yawn with her hand.

'Jack's at an awkward age,' she added. 'He has been for a few years. His father's behaviour doesn't help, then I make sure I have my say too and he's stuck listening to us fight. Poor kid.'

Another pause.

'What was the place like?' she asked.

'Which place?'

She made bunny ears with her fingers. 'The massage parlour.'

Andrew scratched his face, a little embarrassed. 'All red and pink and it stank.'

Violet nodded. 'To be honest with you, I really don't mind the sleeping around. If he wants to do what he does with a bunch of Eastern European girls then it saves me a job. I just wish he was more discreet about it. It's no example to be setting to his son.' She swallowed. '*Our* son.'

Andrew usually knew when to keep quiet, and this was one of those occasions. Sometimes letting a client rant was the best thing for it. If anyone had reason to, it was Violet Deacon.

She had another sip of water before continuing. 'I found condoms in his car door the other week, then there are the text messages he gets. He dives for his phone saying it's someone from work before he's even looked at it, then spends the rest of the evening grinning to himself. Prostitutes I can deal with; I just don't want him falling in love. Not yet, anyway.'

Andrew thought about asking but felt better of it.

Violet peered up from the counter and met his eyes with a steely gaze of determination. 'Oh, I know what you're thinking – how weird this all is, why I'm letting it go and so on. I'd be thinking the same. Don't worry, I'll be leaving him one day, just not yet. Like I said, I do the books for his companies. I know where the bodies are buried.' She finished her water. 'Not literally, of course, but I know plenty to bring him down. I'm just biding my time.' She patted the folder. 'This is everything I need for now. I might come back to you for help again in future – you never know when a good investigator might come in handy. One day, there'll be divorce proceedings and the more of this, the better.'

She blinked, sighed and stood, offering her hand. 'Sorry about Jack. I'll have a word when he comes back. I didn't know he was there, if I did—'

Violet stopped as a whooshing boom of fury erupted from somewhere towards the front of the house, as if an articulated lorry had steamed past far too quickly. They looked at each other for a moment before Andrew turned, dashing through the hallway towards the front door. Through the dimpled glass at the front of the house, he could already see the ominous glow but the actual sight was still a shock as Andrew pulled open the front door. At the bottom of the driveway, his dark blue Toyota was parked where he'd left it, bright orange flames blazing through the gaps around the bonnet, eating into the cold morning.

5

The fire officer stood with a single hand on his hip: short and stout like a teapot. He eyed Andrew suspiciously, the words 'insurance scam' clearly at the front of his mind.

'So, to be clear,' he growled with a gruff hint of a Scottish accent, 'you were in the house, you heard a "noise"' – more bunny ears – 'then you and Mrs, er, Deacon came out of the house where you saw your car on fire.'

'Right.'

'And if you could repeat for me, in your own words, what you did then.'

What was it with police- and fire-types with their 'in your own words'? Who else's was he going to use?

Andrew gazed up towards the overcast clouds. He'd already been through this three times with various officers, police and fire, and now the main officer/marshal/whatever he was, whose name Andrew had heard and instantly forgotten, was having his go. At the far end of the road, the cable van was still parked, three workers crowded around drinking tea and gossiping. If Britain ran on one thing, it was tea. Two things and it was gossip coupled with tea. The entire economy would come grinding to a halt if either was somehow outlawed.

So much for keeping his head down – this was supposed to be a quick in and out, deliver the report, don't hang around and certainly don't wait long enough for Stewart Deacon to get home. So far, Mr Deacon was still to appear but the clock was ticking.

'There was a hose on the garden,' Andrew said, trying not to sound too exasperated with the whole thing. 'I ran out of the house, grabbed it and put out the fire. Then I called you – that's pretty much all there is to it.'

The fire marshal's pose became a full-on sugar bowl, both hands on hips, peeking over his shoulder towards Andrew's smouldering car, which was being loaded onto a flatbed lorry with a groaning heave of machinery and a beep-beep-beep in case the people five streets over didn't know what had happened. Parked in front were two fire engines and a police car. Nice and surreptitious. The case had become a true disaster.

The sugar bowl became a teapot again, foot tapping on the floor. If the marshal's accent grew more Scottish – and therefore incomprehensible – with suspicion, then Andrew was clearly prime suspect for torching his own car.

Andrew leant forward, straining to hear, even though the man was standing in front of him. 'As best we can tell, *someone* poured some sort of accelerant – petrol, diesel, lighter fluid, that sort of thing – over your bonnet and then threw a match over it. If you were going to blow up a car, then there are better ways. It's too early to say how much, if any, damage has been done to the actual vehicle, but as a minimum, it'll need a new paint job.'

Behind him, the crane groaned with the strain of the car, before lowering it onto the back of the truck with a thump.

The marshal stopped to watch, before his hoarse growl started again. 'We'll take it away, look into things and come back to you. Did someone take your details?'

Andrew pointed towards one of the other officers. 'Yes, your guy—'

'Good, then someone will be in contact. One of our lot will sort you out with a number you can give to your insurance company. You probably know the drill.' He raised a single eyebrow conspiratorially, a gesture Andrew didn't respond to. The marshal continued tapping his toe. 'Private investigator, eh? I guess you've pissed a few people off in your time?'

Andrew opened his mouth to reply but the man didn't hang around, spinning and wrapping his thick coat tighter around himself before whistling towards one of his colleagues.

The moment he had told them he was a private investigator, their attitudes had changed – and not even subtly. Raised eyebrows, knowing glances and elbow nudges were just the start. In many ways, he didn't even blame them. If the roles were reversed, he'd be thinking the same too. 'Oh aye, some private cop's got too big for his boots and someone's tried to bring him down a peg or three.' That's why people like him were supposed to work in the shadows.

Violet hovered close by, peering up and down the road, no doubt wondering what the neighbours were going to think. She also kept trying to make eye contact with Andrew, telling him without words that it wasn't necessarily her son who had dashed out of the house in a strop and set fire to his car.

Poor Jack. Andrew didn't know if the lad had thrown the match but he did know he'd have been annoyed too if some bloke had come into his house, apparently trying to break up his parents, when he'd been a teenager.

As the marshal marched away, Violet took her opportunity, stepping quickly towards Andrew and lowering her voice. The breeze almost carried her words away but Andrew just about pieced together her stage whisper.

'He's never done anything like that before,' she said. 'Honestly, if it *is* him, I'll make sure he pays you back. We'll sort something – just don't get the police involved. He's only fifteen. Imagine how that's going to look on a college or job application.'

Across the road, a figure had appeared at the window. The elusive Mrs McIntyre, no doubt. Andrew watched her watching him. She was an older woman with a perfect bob of permed grey hair, crossed knees, and a recliner which faced the street. Mrs McIntyre continued looking both ways until she realised she herself was being spied upon. For a fraction of a second her eyes locked onto Andrew's, before she turned away again, gazing down the road towards the cable TV van.

Andrew didn't know how to reply. Omitting something from a police statement was as bad as lying, and this would affect him the worst because it was his car to which someone had set fire.

At the bottom of the driveway, one of the police officers realised Andrew had been ditched by the fire investigators and turned on his heels. He was some tall bloke in uniform with a posture that suggested he'd spent his formative years strapped to a board.

'Please . . .' Violet hissed, before snapping back into a fake smile as the officer approached.

He nodded Andrew off to the side of the driveway, removing his notebook from his pocket and taking a deep breath. 'So, Mr Hunter, I'm afraid it's mainly bad news. We've been up and down the street talking to neighbours but it appears nobody saw anything.'

It was typical that Mrs bloody McIntyre wasn't having a nose when it might have been useful.

'Anyway,' the officer added, 'we'll take a proper statement but I may as well ask the obvious: is there anyone you know of who could have a grudge against you?'

Andrew glanced over the officer's shoulder towards Violet Deacon. Her husband and son would be a good place to start.

'I don't think so,' he said.

The officer nodded, making himself even taller. 'We've got a few issues with staffing today but I can either make an appointment to come and visit you for a formal statement, or you can drop into whichever station is convenient for you.'

Andrew could imagine the reception he'd get down the local nick: a few hours being dicked about in a waiting room with vague promises that someone would see him soon. That was better than having someone poking around his apartment or office, though.

'I'll come to you,' he said.

The flatbed lorry grumbled to life, before being revved

mercilessly. You didn't need to be a mechanic to know there was something a bit dodgy with the engine – although an actual mechanic would likely come up with something slightly more precise than 'yeah, it's a bit wonky, pal'. Well, depending on the quality of garage.

The officer handed Andrew a business card, offered a 'don't-hold-your-breath' look and then ambled back down the drive.

Instinctively, Andrew fumbled in his pocket for the keys to his car, ready to head back to the office, before realising the obvious.

As if he hadn't had a bad enough morning, he was going to have to take a bus.

6

Andrew reached his office a little after lunchtime. As he bundled through the door, Jenny peered up from the desk, over her glasses, with the hint of a frown coupled with a smile. 'You look like you slept in a bush.'

'It's windy out.' Andrew dropped his jacket over the back of his chair. 'You won't believe the morning I've had. First, Violet Deacon doesn't mind that her husband's sleeping with prostitutes, then her shit of a son tried to set fire to my car.'

Jenny removed her glasses, the frown overtaking the smile. 'Really?'

'Well, I assume it's her son. He stormed out because he said I was trying to break up his parents, then a few minutes later, my car was on fire. Don't even get me started on the buses. First, this old couple got on and started unloading a sodding picnic – sandwiches, tea in a thermos, cut-up pieces of apple. You name it and she dragged it out of her coolbox. Who takes a coolbox on a bus? Then I had a bunch of lads on the back seat behind me going on about their various girlfriends. It's like a different language nowadays. I thought they were in a brass band, then it dawned on me what they meant by tromboning.' Jenny grinned as Andrew hit his stride. 'Oh, don't think it won't happen to you. One minute you're listening to the right music and having normal conversations, the next it's like the dialect you know is medieval English – and *you're* the one who's somehow fallen behind. They kept calling each other "Bruv".'

Jenny bit her bottom lip, no doubt thinking he sounded like her dad, or another generic old person. She said nothing out loud, the dimple in her cheek offering its own retort.

She was out of the office-type receptionist clothes, wearing some sort of pinafore dress, like a throwback to the days of long, hot summers. Her long black hair hung around her shoulders.

'Anyway,' she said, 'the phones have been quiet around here. Someone popped in earlier asking if we could test his wife's toothbrush to find out if his son really is his son but I told him we didn't do that sort of thing.'

Jenny's mobile phone began buzzing, accompanied by some poppish song Andrew didn't know. She held it up, as if apologising for the ringtone pointing out what an old git he was. Andrew turned on his computer and spun his seat away from her, pretending not to listen into her half of the conversation.

'. . . All right, but I'm at work, I told you not to call . . .'

'. . . I don't know, sort yourself out . . .'

'. . . I don't care what you think. If you want to go, then go. You don't need me there . . .'

'. . . How many times do we have to go through this? We're not going out . . .'

'. . . So what if I stayed over? Look, I'm not having this conversation now and I'm not having it later. Just grow up . . .'

There was silence for a few moments. Andrew wasn't startled by the fact Jenny was having an argument with someone – everyone did that, at work or not – but he was surprised at the lack of edge in her voice. When she'd been putting it on the previous day to argue with Stewart Deacon, standing in front of his car, there was real venom in her voice. This time, there was a simplicity: this is what's happening, live with it.

After a few moments, Jenny spoke again, this time addressing Andrew. 'Sorry about that.'

He turned to face her. 'About what?'

'That was this lad I know. He thinks we're boyfriend-girlfriend, or whatever. I suppose we sort of are. I dunno what his problem is. I've told him not to call when I'm at work but he's a complete dickhead.'

Andrew opened his hands out. 'Don't worry about it. People's personal lives don't shut down just because it's Monday to Friday, between nine and five. If you need to deal with something, go for it.'

She shook her head. 'I dunno what it's like for you but lads are mental. You say hello, smile at them, ask them where they got their T-shirt and they think you're joined at the hip. No one's up for a quick bit of fun any longer. You get to that point where you're like, "all right, piss off, mate, I quite like my own bed, thank you very much".'

Andrew didn't want to query what 'quick bit of fun' actually meant. In his mind, the words 'young enough to be your daughter' rang around, even though it wasn't quite true. She spoke as if she had no comprehension of what was appropriate. Still, hearing about young people being young kept him from feeling too old.

'Sorry,' Jenny repeated. 'Anyway, I did the usual check on our client.'

That was the other thing Andrew insisted upon: if they took on a case that had any merit, they not only looked into the person they were supposed to be investigating, but they did a general check of the client too. The last thing any of them wanted was a nasty surprise along the line.

'Most of it, you'll already know,' she added, putting her glasses back on. 'Richard Carr worked as a risk account manager for an insurance company before retiring six years ago. I'm guessing he made a fair few quid from that and his credit report is healthy. He's married and lives out Prestwich way with his wife, Elaine.' She peered over her glasses at him, checking he was keeping up. 'Elaine's his second wife, by the way. He divorced his first wife, Carol, nineteen years ago and married Elaine eighteen years back – a week before Nicholas was born.'

Another glance over the glasses, the implication clear: there was every chance his wife-to-be was pregnant at the time Richard had been married to his first. Jenny swirled her hand in the air.

'Blah, blah, blah . . . elected as a councillor three years ago, a bit left on his mortgage but not much, decent pension. He's not mega-rich but not poor either.'

She shuffled through the papers on her desk, muttering to herself. 'I've printed out some of the news reports from the time—'

'Aah.'

Andrew interrupted her but Jenny grinned back, already a step ahead.

'I know, I know – you want a clean investigation without knowing too much of what might have gone before, but there are a few pieces of information I'm going to have to give you.'

Andrew returned her smile. It was true that he preferred to ignore as much of any previous investigation as he possibly could. Part of that was for practical reasons – he had no right to read police reports – but it was also impossible to know how much of a news report was true. He could seize upon an inconsistency in a piece of journalism, only to find out the reporter had got the wrong end of the stick. Or just made it up: you never knew with these journalist types. Either way, if possible, it was better to talk to people himself and make his own judgements.

Jenny picked up a piece of paper from her desk. 'As far as I can tell, Nicholas Carr disappeared on the night of his eighteenth birthday. Three fingers from his right hand were found by a dog-walker four days later in Alkrington Wood. Do you know the area?'

Andrew cringed, not wanting to say it out loud. 'Sort of.'

'How do you mean?'

'When I first started doing this, before hiring you, before my infidelity policy, I was doing a trail one night. This poor woman had come in beside herself. Her husband kept telling her he was working late at a call centre but he didn't seem to be bringing any extra money home.

She had these wee kiddies at home – three boys, two girls, all under ten. They'd basically stopped having any sort of relationship because he wasn't there and whenever she asked if there was anything wrong, he'd hit the roof. She came into my old office one morning and just cried. She said she could give me fifty quid if I could figure out what was going on.'

Jenny held his gaze, brown eyes wide, staring into his, dragging the information out. 'Fifty quid?' She didn't say it in a way to ridicule the woman, more because she knew what their hourly rates were. Fifty pounds wouldn't have gone very far.

'I didn't even take her money,' Andrew said. 'I told her I'd see what I could do and took her phone number.'

'You old softie.'

'Less of the old.'

Jenny's dimple reappeared.

'Anyway, it wasn't that much work. Her husband was hardly the brain of Britain, or the brain of anywhere, really. When he knocked off at the call centre, he drove out to this car park on the edge of Alkrington Wood. It's not the main one but between these two hedges you wouldn't normally look twice at and then down a dirt path. I left my car on the road and walked it, but there was a Land Rover with the back doors open, a dozen blokes and a couple of girls . . . well, you can probably guess.'

Jenny picked up a pencil and started to twiddle it between her fingers, tapping each end on the desk in the exact way Andrew's mother had repeatedly told him not to do many years ago for fear of 'breaking the lead'.

'Aah, the passion of it,' she said. 'Do you think when Shakespeare wrote *Romeo and Juliet*, he thought that the great romance and tragedy would one day be eclipsed in starry-eyed terms by a bunch of fat people dogging in a secluded car park?'

Young enough to be your daughter.

Andrew pretended she hadn't spoken. 'Either way, yes, I know where Alkrington Wood is.'

Jenny returned to her notes. 'There's nothing more specific about where the fingers were found and the woods are a whole bunch of hectares, whatever a hectare is. It's big, anyway. Details are *really* sketchy. I've gone through a few reports and they all say the fingers were found by the man's dog – nothing about digging or anything like that. They spent a few days excavating afterwards but the reports tail off after that. The person who found the fingers isn't named, either. I've read up on the rest of what was reported and made you a list of the people you might need to speak to. Do you want them emailed, or—'

'Hard copies are best.'

Jenny hopped up and passed across a file. 'Good, that's what I thought.'

Andrew began thumbing through the top few sheets but it was all there. It was scary how quickly she worked.

Jenny leant on her desk, motioning a cupped hand towards her mouth: 'Brew?'

Andrew shook his head but Jenny pottered to the corner anyway and filled the kettle before clicking it on.

She perched on the edge of her desk, ankles crossed, head tilted slightly to the side. 'What I don't get is what

Richard Carr is hoping to achieve. The police found his son's fingers and looked for the body. He'll just be buried somewhere in the woods, won't he? Or his body will be washed up on a beach somewhere? There's plenty of things we'll be able to look into, it's not like we're ripping them off, but the police have already done this. What's he hoping we can do?'

Andrew didn't reply for a few moments because, to him, the answer was obvious. 'Do you have any brothers or sisters?'

'No.'

'Cousins?'

A shrug.

'Okay, what about your parents?'

Another shrug. 'They live abroad.'

'Do you get on with them?'

Shrug number three. 'I suppose.'

This wasn't the response Andrew had expected.

He took a breath. 'Okay, you know I don't have children, right.'

'That's why you've not gone grey yet.'

Andrew couldn't resist a smile. 'And neither do you.'

'Nope.'

'But imagine we did. Imagine there was somebody who was literally a part of you – and then one day they weren't there any longer. You'd want to know what happened to them, wouldn't you?'

Jenny gazed at him, eyes narrowing, before she did a very strange thing.

She lied.

Perhaps it wasn't the mistruth that was strange, it was the fact Andrew spotted it. Jenny was always so convincing, so perfect, that it was a natural assumption she was telling the truth. Certainly if she'd ever lied to him before then he hadn't spotted it.

'I get it,' she said, her eyes darting sideways, clearly telling him that she didn't.

Andrew was so taken aback that he stopped speaking, forgetting what his point was.

'Okay, bad example,' he said after the pause. 'Who's the most important person in your life?'

Jenny stared at him blankly. 'I dunno. I suppose I see you more than anyone else.'

Andrew stopped again. That was news to him, even though it sort of made sense in terms of the time they were at work – but no one else would have answered like that. They might have mentioned a boyfriend or girlfriend, husband or wife. Perhaps even a parent or sibling.

He returned to his original argument, having confused himself more than her. 'Sorry, right, er, let's say you did have a child – a part of yourself – you'd do everything you could to discover what happened to them. The police tell you they're dead but you don't have a body, so you keep believing. A year from now, five years, ten years: you still keep thinking they might return. It's the natural way to be. It's about closure.'

Jenny nodded slowly but Andrew still wasn't certain she got it. Perhaps it was an age thing; she was so naturally confident that sometimes he forgot how young she was.

Andrew stood, accidentally sending his chair spinning

across the room just as the kettle clicked off. 'You busy?' he asked.

'Not really. I've got a bit of typing to do but it won't take long.'

'Fancy going for a ride?'

'I thought you didn't have a car?'

Andrew had already been reaching for his coat and the car keys. 'Oh yes. Shite.'

Jenny pushed herself up from her desk and picked up her jacket. 'Never mind, we can take mine.'

7

Andrew squished himself into the passenger seat of Jenny's Volkswagen Beetle. He felt like he was in a circus act, as if he was going to fall out when they reached their destination, only to be followed by three dozen more clowns as the wheels fell off. The seat was so close to the ground that he was struggling to see over the dashboard. His knees were pressed into the glove box, while the neck rest was doing such a fabulous job of digging into his spine that it was like getting a tantric massage from a sumo wrestler with bratwurst fingers. Not that Andrew knew what that felt like, of course.

'Seatbelt,' Jenny scolded as she pulled away, no hint of a joke in her voice.

'I was just reaching for it! Bloody hell, it's like a baked bean tin in here with less room.'

'It's not my fault someone set fire to your car. Besides, there are buses if you need to get around.'

Andrew shuddered. First job when we get back to the office, sort out a hire car.

Jenny crept her way into a stream of traffic heading north, away from the city, talking to herself quietly as she acknowledged the various signs and lane instructions. The inside of the car was completely clear of clutter: no ornaments, no air-fresheners, no soft chimpanzees from a day-trip to Monkey World – nothing except for an ice scraper and a cloth, both neatly tucked into the door pocket. She really was unnatural. Where were the screwed-up McDonald's wrappers? The scratched CDs? The bent-in-half atlas with a footprint on the front cover? That thing that blocked off the cigarette lighter rattling around the back seat which was always the first item to get lost? Hers was actually *in* the socket.

'Do you know where we're going?' Andrew asked.

'Obviously.'

'It's just that you don't have a map, or your tablet?'

'So?'

'How do you know where you're going?'

Her eyes didn't leave the road. 'Up Bury New Road, past the parks, over the motorway, right, left, second right, keep going for half a mile, then left, right, left. What's difficult to remember about that?'

Andrew had lost her at the first left.

He sat back as best he could, even though the uncomfortable chair made it feel like he was being mauled from behind by a gorilla with wandering hands. This was what it must have been like to work at the BBC in the 1970s.

From what he could make out, Jenny was sticking rigidly to the speed limits. He'd been in a car with her many times before, but never with her driving, and the adherence to the law was something he wasn't sure he expected from her. It wasn't as if he'd ever seen her break the rules but there was a defiant, rebellious streak to the way she spoke that wasn't matched by the way she drove.

Trundle, trundle, trundle.

Richard and Elaine Carr's house was much like Stewart and Violet Deacon's: big without being extravagant, on a sleepy street away from the main road. It was somewhere between Prestwich and Bury, a little outside of the city of Manchester itself but part of the Greater Manchester county.

All the houses were pretty four- and five-bedroom places, with wide driveways and trimmed expanses of lawn at the front. On a patch of green separating two houses a few down from the Carrs', three young boys were kicking a football around, using a tree and rucksack as a goal. Their improvised commentaries drifted on the wind, added to – and perhaps improved – by the squawk of a blackbird somewhere nearby.

Andrew and Jenny made their way up the driveway, each looking around and taking in the scene. For Andrew, he'd seen much of the same that morning: clean brick-work, paving slabs, a lawn, tidy hedges. Apart from the cosmetic differences, the Carrs and the Deacons seemed to be largely similar.

Richard Carr was already standing on the front step before they'd reached the door. He squinted past them at Jenny's Beetle at the front of the house.

'I had an *accident* in my car,' Andrew said in answer to the question which hadn't been asked.

Richard hurried them inside with various offerings of thanks. Out of the rain, his hair looked thicker than it had the previous day. He seemed thinner and a little frailer now he was dressed down. He'd obviously discovered the middle-aged man clothes shop too, the location of which was only revealed to you once you'd had children. His brown slacks were topped off with a purple and yellow monstrosity that was masquerading as a woolly jumper.

He led Andrew and Jenny into a living room that screamed 'beige'. From the light brown carpets to the greyey-browny nothingness of the three-piece suite, with matching lampshades, it was as if someone had pointed to a page in the IKEA catalogue and said 'that one'.

Elaine Carr was pretty much what Andrew would have guessed: mid-fifties like her husband but with a hint of the looks she'd once had. Her greying hair had been coiffured up into a backcombed bob and she was wearing a below-the-knee skirt with a knitted cardigan.

She stood and shook hands with Andrew and Jenny, introducing herself and offering to make them all some tea. Before she could leave the room, Jenny blocked the door in a not-blocking-the-door-half-in-half-out-look-at-me-smile way.

'I'll make it, if you want,' she said. 'Let you two have a good chat with Andrew.' She pointed towards the back of the house. 'Through there, is it? I'm sure I'll find everything.' A nod towards Richard. 'Milk with one sugar, wasn't it?'

He tilted his head slightly. Jenny had spoken so quickly that it seemed like he needed a moment to catch up. 'Right, er, well remembered. Elaine has it the same way, don't you, dear?'

After a nod from Elaine, Jenny skipped away, all smiles, swinging hair and single dimple, as if what had just happened was perfectly normal. In many ways, with Jenny, it was.

Andrew sat in the armchair as the Carrs took the sofa. Richard reached out for his wife's hand, giving it a squeeze before they returned to their own corners.

After taking the notepad and pen from his satchel, Andrew offered a sympathetic smile. 'Thank you for the information you sent through yesterday. If possible, I'd like to go more or less back to the beginning. I realise you've been over this, probably many times, but I always prefer dealing with primary information.'

Two nods.

'Can you talk me through the circumstances leading up to when Nicholas disappeared?'

Elaine pressed back into the sofa, clearly willing her husband to do the talking. Richard took the cue: 'There's not an awful lot to tell you that I didn't send over yesterday. Nicholas was a very normal teenager. He was at college and his reports seemed to be good. He'd been talking about going to university when he finished and had stepped that up over new year.'

'What about friends?'

'We wrote down the names of the ones we know but you know what it's like being young. You know all sorts of people; some of them are close friends, others are just people you say hello to. Then you've got the issue that most teenagers do all they can to keep their best friends away from their parents. I know the police went into the college to interview everyone. It's even more awkward now, of course, because Nicholas was in his final year so people are spread all over. One of his older friends is at a university in Europe: France or Germany or something. I've passed on all we know.'

Andrew glanced down at the notes Richard had emailed the previous evening. 'How much do you know about "Lara"?'

The two Carrs exchanged a quick glance but it was Richard who answered again. 'Not loads but a bit. She's an orphan – his girlfriend and, of anyone, they spent the most time together. We've not really seen her since he disappeared. I think she's at university somewhere around here.'

'Did she ever stay over?'

'Once or twice. You can't say "no" nowadays.'

'Generally, were there any other problems at around that time?'

Richard Carr shook his head. 'Only the usual things with teenagers. One minute they'd be shouting the house down because there was no Marmite in the cupboard, then it'd be all sweetness and light five minutes later. He was just normal.'

That may well have been true but Andrew suspected that was what a lot of parents thought about their children until something happened. When it came out they'd been acting as a rent boy for the local MP, no one would be able to believe it. There would definitely be something there, though probably not the rent-boy thing.

Andrew opened his mouth to speak again when Jenny breezed into the room, expertly balancing a tea tray on the tips of her fingers like a waitress in a posh restaurant. She placed four sets of cups and saucers on the table, with a pot in the centre, a small jug of milk, and a separate egg cup of sugar next to each of the Carrs' drinks.

Elaine Carr stared up at her. 'Where did you find those?'

Jenny sat on the spare armchair, twiddling a strand of her hair. 'That cupboard over the sink, right at the back behind the butter dish. Sorry, I hope you don't mind. I was looking for the teacups and they were just there.'

Elaine snorted slightly. 'No, dearie, I didn't mean it like that. I spent *ages* looking for them the other week. I thought Richard had thrown them out.' She leant forward and poured tea into the four cups, emptying the egg cup of sugar into her own and stirring twice clockwise, twice anti-clockwise like a James Bond villain. Muhahahahaha, Mr Bond. Just watch how I stir my tea.

Andrew picked up his own and took a sip, mainly to be polite, before returning to his notepad.

'Can we talk about the actual night Nicholas went missing?'

Richard was tugging at his jumper. 'What's to say? We weren't there.'

'But tell me what you understand happened.'

'He went to some sort of gig, or perhaps just the pub with his friends and Lara. They all say he and Lara left the pub at around nine, he walked her home, and hasn't been seen since. She said he'd set off to walk back here. It's perhaps a mile or two but he'd regularly walk to the city centre, so it wasn't that rare.' Richard leant forward, taking out a padded envelope from underneath the coffee table and handing it over. 'That's everything we emailed you yesterday, plus a few other odds and ends. I found his mobile number after all. When he went missing, we called it over and over but there was no reply. What's that thing they do . . .'

He swirled his arm in the air, searching the word until Andrew gave it to him: 'A trace.'

'Yes, they did that trace thing but they said the card thing, simple something—'

'A SIM card.'

'Right, they said that had been removed, or it had been turned off. We found a few old bank statements around too, plus he's had mail in the past few months. Mainly things from the bank and college. We kept it all just in case and it's in that envelope.'

Richard sat back with his tea, taking a sip and then gulping again. He'd just handed over his son's life in a pack; no wonder he was a little upset.

'Is there anything else you can think of?' Andrew asked.

Richard shook his head, his blank expression matched by his wife's. 'I wish I could.'

8

Andrew gazed around Nicholas's bedroom as Jenny approached the window and nudged aside the lace netting to peer outside.

Richard Carr waited in the doorway, bobbing from one foot to the other. 'The police went through everything, obviously. They took away Nicholas's laptop but returned it covered in that dust stuff. Other than that, everything is pretty much how he left it.' He paused. 'I never used to come in here. I remember what it was like when my parents came into my room. I hated it.'

He blew out uncomfortably, unsure what else to add. Andrew smiled weakly again; it was the best he could do. 'If you leave us here, we'll see if there's anything that could help and come downstairs when we're done.'

Richard waited for a few moments before nodding, turning and closing the door quietly.

Andrew joined Jenny by the window, gazing out to where the boys were still playing football on the green.

'I hated it when my parents came in my room too,' he said.

Jenny turned with a smirk: 'Is that where you stashed your massive porn supply?'

'No.'

'You kept it somewhere else?'

'No, I . . .' Andrew stopped himself, not taking the bait. 'It's just your own haven, isn't it? When you're that age, you need somewhere you can lock yourself away and moan about the rest of the world.'

Jenny breezed across the room towards the bed. 'I used to get pocket money if my room was tidy. My mum would come in every Friday and make sure there was nothing on the floor and that everything was packed away where it was meant to be.'

'How long did that go on for?'

Frown lines appeared on Jenny's forehead as she stuck out her bottom lip. 'Until I was sixteen, seventeen. Something like that.'

'That's quite, erm . . . strict.'

Dimple, get-out-of-jail smile: 'Yeah, but it's not as if she was *really* inspecting what I kept in my room. She'd have a quick rummage, make sure there was nothing lying around the floor and then I'd get my money. It's not as if she went poking around underneath my bed. I used to have this soft elephant thing that had been in my room forever. I don't remember being given it, it was one of those things that end up being around. I pulled all of the stuffing out of its arse for the perfect hiding place.'

Andrew wondered if he should follow it up by asking precisely what it was Jenny was keeping in her elephant's backside but he wasn't sure he wanted to know.

'Did you find anything poking around the kitchen?' he asked.

Jenny shook her head. 'Lots of cleaning stuff. The cupboard under the sink is like that aisle in the supermarket where no one ever goes with all the detergents and stuff. Mix it all together and you could probably whip up some crystal meth. The whole room was spotless, shiny handles, sparkling worktops – like an advert for Mr Muscle.'

Perfect: it wasn't as if Andrew had expected her to find Nicholas's body tucked into the freezer but you could tell a lot about people from their kitchen.

'Draining board?' he asked.

'Clear.'

'Dishwasher?'

'They don't have one.'

At least one of the Carrs preferred things to be cleaned away in that case – which explained a little about Nicholas's room. Richard told them that his son's room had been gone through by the police but you wouldn't know it to look at it. The bed was made with neat corners and tucked edges in a way that hardly anyone would be able to sleep in. There were two plump pillows without the hollow in the centre from a dozing head, and underneath the bed, a neat row of shoes was lined up, heels facing outwards.

If the bed had been completely remade, then what else had been moved?

Jenny began taking photographs of the various corners as Andrew watched her work.

'Do you think teenage lads are usually this tidy?' he asked.

'The ones I knew barely even changed their underwear, let alone lined up their shoes.'

As Jenny opened the wardrobes and began flicking through the rows of shirts and tops, Andrew focused on the shelves running above the bed. There were a dozen or so real crime paperbacks next to rows of computer game cases. Andrew opened the first few, noticing the correct disc in each box, with the pristine instruction booklet tucked neatly into the clips.

Andrew turned to see Jenny sat cross-legged in the wardrobe, picking through a shoebox. 'See anything?'

'Not really. Some Top Trumps cards, an old mobile phone without a battery. There are a few boxes in here too from items he must've bought at some point. There's one for a PlayStation, with the receipt inside.'

Perhaps the neatness ran in the family after all.

Andrew sat on the floor and started tugging the shoes out from under the bed. He lifted up the overhanging covers and ducked underneath, pulling out a wide plastic tub from the far end, with a bonus mouthful of dust.

As he spluttered his way through scanning the contents, Andrew stopped to take in the room again. The walls were clean and unmarked by pieces of Blu Tack or other pins to hold up posters. The windowsill and the rest of the surfaces were all clear and polished to within millimetres of their existence.

'Jen . . .'

'What?'

'Have you found anything . . . well, normal, I suppose? Ornaments? Trophies? Medals or certificates?'

'No.'

'Photos of mates?'

'Nope, but everyone keeps that stuff on their phones nowadays.'

'Come and have a look.'

Jenny emerged from the wardrobe and scuttled across the carpeted floor until she was sitting next to Andrew and the plastic tub. It was about a metre long with low sides and packed with an assortment of objects.

'This was under his bed,' Andrew continued. 'It's like his parents – probably his mum – couldn't bear looking at the room with all of the clutter around, so she put it in a box and shoved it out of the way.'

Jenny began poking through the items, tugging out a film and holding it up. '"Killer Vampires versus Toxic Zombies"? Sounds good.' She moved on to the next one. '"Attack of the Nightmare Mannequins" – I think I've seen that.'

'Really?'

'Probably on Channel Five or something. Look at this.' She held another movie case in the air: 'Night of the Killer Chainsaw Bitches'.

Jenny flipped the case around and began reading, putting on a deep-toned continuity announcer's voice: 'What do you get when you cross a chainsaw factory with a bachelorette party and an alien invasion? "Killer Chainsaw Bitches"! This is the movie your parents warned you about. BANNED in forty-four countries around the world, OUTLAWED in nineteen US states, SLATED by the British Parliament, SLAMMED by the US Senate, this is the uncut version of "Killer Chainsaw Bitches" with twelve new minutes of never-seen-before gore, gore, gore! Warning: if you have a heart condition, do NOT watch this movie.'

71

She looked up at Andrew, verdict scathing: 'Sounds shite.'

Andrew couldn't disagree.

Jenny continued flicking through the items, taking out a framed photograph. Nicholas looked exactly the same as he had in the picture Richard had given them in the first place but the girl he was with was a walking advert for emo chic: long black hair, a month's supply of eye-liner, some sort of black corset with a matching tutu and long stripy socks up to her thighs.

'Lara?' Jenny said.

Andrew shrugged. 'I guess so.'

'She's quite pretty under all of that.'

Jenny pushed the photo back into the tub and continued rummaging.

Andrew could sort of understand it; the room was now a shrine to their ideal of a perfect son. Everything was tidy and his taste in dodgy B-movies, his goth girlfriend and everything else was shunted to one side as if it didn't exist. If he somehow did come knocking on their front door one day, all of his things would still be here.

Jenny plucked out a hardback book with binding held together with sticky tape. The cover was cyan fake leather, with a faded gold imprint on the front. She started flicking through the pages, sucking on her bottom lip.

'What is it?' Andrew asked.

'I'm not sure. Some sort of spell book.'

Jenny passed it across and Andrew started to look through the pages. The paper was heavy, almost parchment, with a faint aroma that reminded Andrew of trees and leaves, although he wasn't sure why. He tried to read it but the contents were largely incomprehensible: a history of magic, mentioning various witch trials, interspersed with apparent recipes for potions and various chants. There were two pages about the healing potential of bones, plus lists of useful herbs and plants. Aside from the quality of the actual book, the passages seemed a little juvenile.

Andrew glanced up to see that Jenny was flipping through a second, similar book.

'What do you reckon?' he asked.

'Dunno. It's all the rage nowadays, isn't it? Vampires, zombies, witches, wizards . . . probably more of a girl thing than a boy thing, though, plus this seems a bit more real than you might expect. It's not all teenage girls fawning over boys, it's actually "real" magic. Well, if that exists.' Jenny turned the book around for Andrew to see. 'Look, it's some sort of recovery spell to reignite your karma, whatever that means. There was a hex in here too for getting back at your enemies.'

Andrew pulled out an A4 pad which looked and felt a lot thicker than a simple few pages of paper. Stapled throughout were pages printed from the Internet with various spells, hexes, curses and symbols. The words were largely Latin-sounding, with instructions above and below about how dangerous the words could be if you misused them. To Andrew, it was all nonsense – but you could apply that to any creed or religion. If you decided you believed in something and chose to live according to that, then it became your own truth.

'Was he into magic?' Andrew asked.

Jenny held up the photo of Nicholas and Lara again, pointing at the upside-down metal cross hanging around Lara's neck. 'Or she was?'

'Perhaps they both were?'

Jenny shrugged, sliding the book back into the tub and crossing to sit at the computer desk. 'Am I okay to go through his laptop?'

'If you can get in. It sounds like the police already had a good go.'

'They couldn't find porn on a top shelf.'

Andrew wriggled uncomfortably on the floor. His back wasn't what it used to be, though that applied to most of his body parts. He wondered what the exact age was where you crossed over from being naturally young, fit and athletic to being a creaky old sod with joints that objected to anything other than the tamest of workouts. It was definitely somewhere around thirty.

Jenny tap-tap-tapped her way around the keyboard, la-la-laaing under her breath. 'No password,' she interrupted herself to say, before continuing with ferocious speed.

Andrew pulled out the magic books and the photo of Nicholas with Lara from the tub and placed them on the bed. He had a rummage through the rest of the items: swimming certificates, ticket stubs from gigs and movies, a few more photographs – nothing out of the ordinary. Andrew pushed the tub back under the bed and rearranged the shoes just as Jenny was spinning around in her chair.

'It'd take ages to do a deep search on his hard drive, but

he's not bothered trying to hide the things he's downloaded. There are a few pirated films, some music, a bit of porn. What you'd expect from a teenage lad, I'd suppose.'

'Can you get into his email?'

'He doesn't have any mail client programs on here, but it would have been on his phone anyway. He's probably got a webmail account. I checked to see if there were any auto-logon details in his browser's history but there aren't. This isn't the way people work nowadays.'

'Shall we ask to take the laptop?'

Jenny held out her hands. 'Up to you. I can keep going through it but I'd be surprised if there was much there.'

Andrew knew that if she thought it was a waste of time, then it would be.

'What do you think in general?' he asked. 'You're only a few years older than Nicholas.'

Jenny puffed out her cheeks and began twiddling her hair. 'Yeah, but I liked all the school stuff. I read textbooks. My room was nothing like this.'

'What about mates?'

'I didn't have a boyfriend at school because it didn't interest me. I left all the other girls to fuss around. I hung out with a few people here and there but I'm not that needy.' She paused, chewing on the skin inside her cheek, head at an angle. 'I suppose I don't really hang around with people that often.'

'What do you do after work?'

'Dunno really . . . stuff. Watch TV, read, go walking around the city. There's always something going on. I don't really plan ahead that much.' She flicked her hair backwards and spun in the seat back to the laptop. 'Anyway, if you're asking what I think about the room, then it looks normal enough. He's got a weird taste in films but so have lots of people. You're probably right that his mum hid everything under the bed because she didn't want to look at it. Times are changing, though. If people want things to be known, it's all over social networks, or half-a-dozen other places. Searching people's rooms will only get you so far. When I get back to the office, I'll track down the pages of Nicholas, his mates and Lara. That's where we'll find the real dirt.' She stopped again as the laptop screen went black. 'If there is any, of course. I didn't mean—'

'I know what you meant.'

Andrew carried the magic books and photograph downstairs. Richard and Elaine were in the living room, watching a television programme about auctions. As soon as Andrew entered the room, Richard lunged for the remote control, muting the show and looking up expectantly, as if Andrew and Jenny would have already found a vital clue.

Andrew thrust the books up into the air. 'Can we take these? Obviously we'll return them.'

The couple replied in unison: 'Of course.'

Andrew indicated the book on top. 'Did these belong to Nicholas?'

Richard answered: 'We guess.' He glanced sideways at his wife, giving away the fact it was her who had packed them away under the bed. 'Kids go through phases, don't they? One month it's all football, then it's computers, or whatever.'

'Did the police keep anything?'

Richard shook his head. 'They returned it all a few weeks ago. I suppose that was the catalyst for me coming to you. That was the point where we knew they'd given up.'

Andrew bounced from one foot to the other, balancing the books between his hands, with Jenny apparently reading his mind and slipping her car key into his pocket. 'I'm going to take these outside,' he said. 'If you could show us the rest of the house afterwards, that'd be appreciated.'

A couple of minutes later, Elaine led Andrew and Jenny into the back garden. The day had brightened up but it was hard to tell as tall, swaying conifers bathed the lawn in a dark horror movie-esque shade. If 'Night of the Killer Chainsaw Bitches' was going to have a sequel, then its location manager would struggle to find a better spot than this.

Andrew peered upwards but everything except for the tops of the neighbours' houses was blocked, leaving a darkened, mud-soaked amphitheatre underfoot. The temperature was a degree or two lower as well, with Jenny wrapping her arms around herself and Andrew trying not to shiver.

Jenny headed straight for the shed midway along the garden, its dark wood almost camouflaged in the murk. There was a twinkle in her eye as she turned. 'I used to have a den in my dad's shed.'

Perhaps surprisingly, Elaine returned the smile. 'Me too when I was a girl. Me and my friends used to keep piles of blankets in there and we'd sit around chatting and complaining about boys.'

She took a key from her pocket and popped open the padlock, pulling the door aside and holding it open. 'It's fine for you to look around but Nicholas never spent much time here. He preferred to go out with his friends.'

Andrew followed Jenny inside, feeling the noxious odour of creosote surging through his nostrils. The ultimate medicine for nasal congestion: sod those nose sprays, get sniffing fence paint – although that probably wasn't official medical advice.

Tools and plants lined the walls, with the wooden floor creaking through age and neglect. In the corner, a deflated football sagged pitifully, wedged between a mud-caked rake and an overturned wheelbarrow. Jenny walked in a circle, running her fingers along the grain of the windowsill.

Andrew turned to see Elaine staring towards the ball in the corner. 'Are you okay?'

Her voice cracked. 'I don't come out here very often. I remember when he was young enough to kick that ball around the garden.'

Andrew opened his mouth to reply but Jenny got in there first. 'It's normal for you to keep believing. A year from now, five years, ten years: you still believe he might return. Hopefully we'll be able to help you find some closure.'

She smiled meekly, not her usual smirk, but with her lips thinner and clamped together. Elaine bowed her head graciously but Andrew couldn't take his eyes from Jenny, trying to remember if those were the exact words he'd said to her only hours earlier.

9

Andrew and Jenny said their goodbyes and set off down the driveway. Jenny rounded her car and was touching the handle when she nodded towards the house next door. Andrew turned to see a squat middle-aged woman wearing a knee-length skirt with legs so skinny, they didn't seem large enough to hold her up. An oversized red jumper hung to her thighs as she bobbed around the corner of the hedge, flicking her head to the side, like a robin with Tourette's.

'I'll wait,' Jenny said, opening the door to the car and getting in without needing to be told. Sometimes she was the right person to stick her nose in, other times she'd rub people the wrong way. Instinctively they both knew the strange woman in the ridiculous jumper wanted to talk to him.

Andrew glanced towards the Carrs' house, before sidling across the pavement, hands in pockets.

The woman had a sharp squawk to her voice. 'You from the council?'

'No.'

She huffed in annoyance. 'Bugger. I've been complaining about those hedges blocking my light for months. I thought you might be 'ere to chop 'em down.'

'Sorry.'

'Soddin' useless, that council lot. You phone 'em up and it's press one for this, press two for that. By the time you finally get through to someone, you've forgotten what you phoned 'em for. Two years ago, that's when I first asked them about looking into the height of the trees. Then again a year ago, then every other month since.'

Andrew nodded at the Carrs' house. 'Have you ever asked them about trimming the bushes?'

The woman waved him forward, lowering her voice. 'Did you hear about what happened to their son?'

'Go on.'

She started to reply and then stopped herself. 'Who did you say you were?'

Andrew dug into his pocket for a business card. At one point in history, it would have been a sign of importance: 'Ooh, he must have something about him if he can carry his phone number around on a card.' Now anyone could knock a hundred cards up at the nearest train station. It was the only way Andrew could remember his own number and email address though.

The woman took it, turning it over in her hand suspiciously. 'Private investigator, eh?'

'That's me.'

'What sort of things do you investigate?'

Andrew looked both ways and tapped his nose conspiratorially: 'This and that.'

She opened her mouth, letting out a breathy 'ahh' and nodding slowly as she pocketed the card. 'I'm Gloria,' she whispered. 'So you're looking into what happened to *you-know-who* . . . ?'

Andrew lowered his voice, playing along. 'Did you know him?'

Gloria's reply was an endless stream of babble, one word running into the next. 'Oh, it's awful isn't it? That's why I've not been over to talk about the hedges. You can't, can you? They've been through enough as it is – don't need me banging on about their bushes. One minute he's there, next minute he's gone. Whatever next? Are you going to find his body? His poor parents deserve that, at least. I was having tea with Mrs Tanning from number fifty the other week and we were saying how dreadful it all must be.'

It took Andrew a few moments to take everything in. She'd somehow gabbled a stream of consciousness without answering the question.

'What was Nicholas like?'

'Oh, he was lovely – helped me in with my shopping once or twice when he was younger. He was ever so polite, a right little gentleman. Wouldn't say boo to a goose.'

Andrew wondered if anyone had ever said boo to a goose. Almost certainly not.

He looked both ways again, lowering his voice even further. Throw in a false moustache and an attaché case and he'd be all set for 'Carry On Spying'. 'Was there anything, *you know*, out of the ordinary?'

It took less than a second for Gloria to drop the concerned neighbour façade. Her nose began twitching as if the bullshit she was spreading was real. 'Well, it all changed about two years ago when he went off to college. Before then, he'd say hello and give me a little wave. Even just a nod. After he started seeing that girl, well . . .'

Andrew was beginning to understand why Richard Carr wanted some privacy.

Gloria leant forward, licking her lips. 'Between you and me, he changed overnight. Overnight, I tell you. No more waves or nods. You'd see them on the doorstep at night, whispering in each other's ears, giggling and so on. Then they'd be getting back all hours of the night. You should've seen how she dressed! I mean, I'm as liberal as the next person but she'd have skirts up to 'ere, those sock things down to 'ere . . .'

Andrew somehow prevented himself from wincing as Gloria tugged up her own skirt to indicate – unnecessarily – what she meant. The attractiveness of a flash of thigh was a subjective thing but when the thigh in question was riddled with bright blue veins and wobbled like an under-set jelly, it was something Andrew could've done without.

Not that Gloria noticed. 'Then they'd be arguing on the doorstep, ranting and raving—'

'What did they argue about?'

The interruption temporarily threw her off her stride. Gloria stopped mid-sentence, mouth hanging open, confused. 'Er . . . I dunno. They'd just be shouting. Who knows with kids today? Probably drugs. It's always drugs, isn't it? That's what they say on the telly. In my day, you'd have a sneaky fag on your lunch break but this lot nowadays, I've read there's this horse drug they're all into—'

'Special K?'

'No, love, that's the cereal, I've got that indoors. It's ketamine-something. I mean, I ask you, who wants to act like a horse? I suppose it'd get 'em eating their carrots but that's no reason to start doing horse drugs. Next thing you know, they'll be galloping around and jumping hedges.'

She giggled so hard at her own joke that a blob of snot flew out of her nose onto the red jumper. Andrew fake-laughed, one of the necessary skills if you spent your days humouring potential nutters. Because of their nature, around ninety per cent of what nutters came out with was completely barmy, it was the other ten per cent you had to keep an eye out for. Unfortunately, picking the ten per cent out from the rest of the nonsense was sometimes impossible. With Gloria, ninety per cent might have been underplaying it. Andrew was wondering quite how much of what she had to say was going to be useful considering she was at least a few jokers short of a deck of cards.

'Did you tell the police?' he asked.

'Oh, I told them everything, but they looked at me like *I* was the crazy one. Can you believe that? I told them to call around any time – ask me anything. They took my details and I never heard from them again. It's no wonder they couldn't find him.'

'I don't suppose you ever overheard anything to do with him disappearing?'

'Well, no . . .'

'And you never saw anything suspicious?'

'Only the postman.'

'What about the postman?'

'He just sort of hangs around, going up to everyone's house. I mean, I know it's his job and all that but it's a bit convenient, isn't it?'

Andrew realised his mistake. He thought by playing up the hush-hush thing, he'd appeal to Gloria's gossipy side. What he'd actually done was encourage the fruitcakey side to come to the fore.

He really wished he hadn't given her his card.

Just as he was losing hope, Gloria took a step back, sounding earnest again. '. . . still no one deserves to just disappear, do they? Those poor parents. It's awful the things that happen nowadays.'

For a moment, she angled forward as if she was going to hug him but then Gloria turned and headed up her driveway, head down in defeat. Andrew suddenly felt sorry for thinking badly of her.

He turned back towards the car but a flicker of movement further along the street caught his eye first. Andrew stood staring for a few moments before ducking back behind Gloria's hedge. He took his phone out and sent Jenny a text message.

'Drive away now – wait around corner. Explain soon'

He pressed send and, for a moment, nothing happened. Then he heard the flare of the Beetle's engine and the chuntering exhaust disappearing into the distance.

Andrew leant into the sharp evergreen boundary, listening and rerunning the flutter of movement through his mind. He counted to ten and then spun around the corner of the hedge, turning straight into the stooped teenage figure of Jack Deacon.

10

Jack slumped to the side, back still hunched as if he needed spinal surgery.

'Are you following me?' Andrew asked, trying to sound calm.

Jack's hair was as stiff, angled and sharp as it had been that morning. His jeans were still low and he was wearing a different black sweatshirt with a band's logo. At first he stepped backwards in alarm at being caught out but then his lips twisted into a snarl.

'I'm allowed to be here. It's a free country.'

'Bit of a coincidence that you happen to be here at the same time as I am.'

Jack's eyes narrowed, his sneer becoming a smile. 'How's the car?'

'The only reason I didn't give your name to the police was because of your mother.'

'Who says I did anything to it? I hope you've got proof if you're going to go around accusing people.'

'That fire could have caught on the wind and latched onto anything else. Or there could have been passers-by . . .'

Jack leant forward, shoulders down, spiky hair angled as if he'd glued a porcupine to the side of his head. 'Why are you telling me?'

'Did you set fire to my car, or didn't you?'

A small laugh. 'Wouldn't you like to know? Perhaps if you weren't trying to stitch my dad up, your things wouldn't spontaneously combust.'

'What do you think's going to happen when the police and fire report comes back to say – officially – that someone tipped lighter fluid over my bonnet and then tossed a match on it?'

'Seems like you know a lot about it. Maybe you did it yourself?'

Andrew thought about replying but there was little point. He'd already made his decision not to mention Jack to the police and getting into a public argument with the boy wasn't going to help anyone. Jack continued to stare at him, wanting an argument, but Andrew shook his head and walked past, reaching for his phone to find out where Jenny was.

'Oi!'

Andrew turned to see Jack pointing a finger at him in the same aggressive manner he had shown that morning. 'Do you reckon that Beetle needs a paint job? Perhaps a burnt brown colour?'

In a step, Andrew was back in front of the teenager, batting his finger away. 'If anything happens to my staff, their property, or anything else to do with me or my business, then I'll be straight onto the police about what you did to my car.'

'Yeah, right, mate. You keep telling yourself that. Meanwhile, I'm going to make sure my dad knows he's being spied on by a right bunch of nosy bastards. Some slutty girl and her sugar daddy. Is that what gets you off? Breaking up other people's families and then going home with someone half your age? You're just a filthy old man and you've picked on the wrong people.'

Andrew stood, staring at Jack for a few seconds. *This* was exactly why he tried not to get involved in family disputes. Money or no money, it wasn't worth it.

'Just leave me alone,' he replied, pathetically – the best he could do. What were the other options: threatening a fifteen-year-old? There was no proof, not yet anyway, about who had set fire to his car.

Andrew turned and walked away, the heckles of the teenager echoing along the street behind him.

11

At the office, Andrew was still brooding. He'd allowed Violet Deacon's doe-eyed defence of her son to influence him when he should have told the police that he suspected Jack was responsible for setting his vehicle on fire. It might not have done much good considering the lack of witnesses but it would have meant the police would have had a word, making Jack far less likely to be following him around.

Jenny sensed the mood, not saying too much on the journey back, other than to ask what the neighbour had to say.

As Andrew searched the Internet trying to find a suitable hire car, Jenny got to work. Within half an hour of them arriving back, the printer was buzzing with activity and then she perched herself on the edge of his desk, sheaf of papers in her hand.

'I've found Nicholas's old Facebook page, a tribute site set up by his college friends, and then various accounts on websites linked either to his apparent friends, or Lara.' She leafed through the front few pages, drawing red felt-tip circles around names. 'It's difficult to know for certain but there seem to be five lads he knew fairly well from college. "Kingy" is at Bristol University, Ricky's in Lincoln, the poor sod. I've been having problems tracking down someone named "Gibbon" and "Belly" is working on the Isle of Wight. The only one that seems to still be living in the area is this lad.'

Jenny pointed towards a grainy black-and-white acne-scarred face on one of the print-outs. 'This is Scott and he's an identity thief's dream. His profile is accessible by anyone, plus his phone number, email address, workplace and pretty much everything else is on there. If you're looking at talking to one of Nicholas's friends, he's your guy.'

She passed across more print-outs, which Andrew started to skip through. The first was Nicholas's own page, confirming he was 'in a relationship' with 'Lara Malvado'. It was the first time he'd seen her surname. Nicholas didn't seem to be particularly active but he'd been tagged in various photos, and friends had posted various jokes, pictures and articles in the way people did when they had nothing better to do.

Among the pictures was an old photo from primary school, with Nicholas standing bolt upright, hands behind his back in a black and navy uniform. Someone had typed 'U look like a write nob' underneath, which had a certain poetry to it, if grammatical-anatomical mash-ups were a person's thing.

The other photos appeared to have been taken in the year or so leading up to his disappearance: at a theme park, at the beach, with his friends at the park – and then many selfies, apparently taken by Lara with her phone at arm's length. Their faces were smooshed together, Nicholas's lips pursed into a half-smile, half-grimace in the way only grumpy teenagers could pull off properly. Start pulling faces like that as an adult and it'd look like you had something jammed up your arse.

Jenny was right about Lara: she was pretty underneath the eye-liner, dyed hair and beanie caps. Even with all of that, there was clearly an appeal to her. From the pictures, one other thing was very clear: she was definitely into Nicholas, perhaps more than he was into her. Nicholas had that stony-faced, give-nothing-away expression in all of the photos but she was constantly peering away from the camera towards him, or staring glassy-eyed towards the lens in a 'this-is-true-love' way that was also exclusive to teenagers. By the time you were thirty, true love was spending fifteen minutes with someone and not wanting to throttle them. Or not arguing over whose turn it was to put the bins out.

The final few papers were printed from the tribute page set up by Nicholas's friends. At first, the posts were along the lines of: 'Where u at? Why don't u come home?' but a few days later, they had degenerated into various rest-in-peace notices.

Jenny took the rest of the pages from him but handed back the bottom one. 'There's something interesting at the end.'

Andrew scanned down, frowning as he read the tribute: '"Rest in piece, bruv. Your wiv da angles in heavin now"?'

Jenny smiled. 'Below that.'

Scott's name was next to a slightly more legible remark: 'Rest in peace, Wizard man.'

Andrew peered up to Jenny. 'Wizard?'

'I know. I've gone through the other pages but no one else seems to have called him that. It can't be a widely used nickname, but it's not going to be an accident either.'

'What about Lara?'

'She just calls him "babe" or something like that. Aside from the pictures, they don't really interact with each other on there. I suppose they preferred actually spending time together. He didn't really use it. The only thing she's updated since Nicholas went missing is where she's living: at Salford University. I don't know what course she's on, though.'

'Anything else interesting?'

'Not really. Before that, everything she wrote for months on end was about her and Nicholas. Always "Nicholas" too – never "Nicky". Some of his friends called him Nicky, but never her. There was never anything too extraordinary, just things like, "Had a great day out with Nicholas today", "Just watched a movie with Nicholas".'

'Anything about magic?'

'Not a peep. Aside from a bit of teenage angst, they're exactly what you'd expect. In fact, it'd be stranger if there wasn't that anxiety. I looked around for the surname Malvado. It seems Portuguese but it's hard to trace anything definitive.'

'The next-door neighbour said they used to argue on the doorstep.'

'That's not really the type of thing you'd tell all your friends about, though it's strange that Nicholas's parents never mentioned it.'

'Perhaps they didn't know? Gloria didn't say how late it

was when they were arguing. If you were a heavy sleeper, you might not realise. Either that or the neighbour was exaggerating?' Andrew checked his watch: time for Jenny to finish for the day. 'When you get in tomorrow, see if you can discover anything else from our usual sources about Lara. I'll see if I can get hold of Scott to find out what he thinks of Nicholas and his girlfriend.'

Jenny took back the final page and passed them across to her desk. 'Do you need a lift home?'

'No, I'll sort it. Thanks for your help.'

Jenny turned back to her desk before stopping on the spot, spinning round. 'Oh, it's Wednesday, isn't it?'

Andrew wouldn't meet her eye. He wished he'd never told her weeks ago what Wednesday night was. 'Is it?'

'Have you got your weekly *thing* tonight?'

'You can say what it is.'

Without peering up, Andrew could tell Jenny was grinning. 'It's all right. Have fun!'

12

Andrew scanned up and down the menu, knowing it off by heart but hoping something new had somehow slipped in between the usual items. There was that too runny, allegedly tomato, soup he'd tried once that tasted like the gloop found in the bottom of bins; or the floppy, oil-soaked garlic bread that had the consistency of slippers that had been through the washing machine. Perhaps love wasn't about spending fifteen minutes with someone and not wanting to throttle them, it was actually about allowing yourself to be taken to hellhole restaurants like this and not complaining about it.

Across the table, Sara gazed over the top of her menu towards him. She'd made an effort tonight: straightened blonde hair combed to the side and clamped in place, hanging provocatively around her shoulder. Then she'd done that eye make-up thing with the curly bits in the corner that made it look as if she was paying attention, even when she wasn't. Not to mention a low-cut dress that helped Andrew remember why he'd started seeing her. Physically, she was ridiculously out of his league.

Around the restaurant, couples chatted to each other; knives, forks and spoons scratched plates and bowls; waiters fussed in and out, sashaying and do-si-doing around each other while balancing a gravity-defying amount of items.

'. . . so I said to Cheryl that if Geoff keeps talking to her like that, then she's going to have to put an official complaint in. You should see him, hovering over that photocopier like he owns the place. He's not even the assistant manager. He's the stand-in assistant and there's no way he's going to get that job permanently . . .'

Back to the menu. If he somehow digested the garlic bread as a starter, that ruled out anything bready for a main. Mentally, Andrew crossed all the pizzas from the menu, focusing on the pasta. What was the name of that one with the tubes? He was pretty sure they did that with some fish concoction. What was the name of it?

'. . . I was like, "It's only you who can deal with it, Chez", but she was like, "He's always going on at me." Then I remembered that I'd ended up talking to the regional manager at last year's Christmas party. Jeremy-something. He was lashed off his face that night, too pissed to stand up. Someone reckoned he ended up sleeping in the toilets of the hotel reception . . .'

Penne, that was it. Andrew scanned along the menu: Penne con Pesce. That'd do. He glanced up, trying to catch a waiter's eye. The quicker they could order, the quicker they could eat, the quicker his bowels could start trying to evacuate. How this place was anyone's favourite restaurant, he had no idea. He'd had better meals at school.

'. . . I mean, you can't go around behaving like that when you're a regional manager. But anyway, somehow I ended up with his phone number. I don't know where it came from, or when he gave it to me, but there it was in my bag the next day: Jeremy Somethingoranother and his phone number. Course, I didn't think anything of it, Christ knows I had enough wine to drink that night but what do they expect when it's a free bar? . . .'

Where was a sodding waiter when you needed one? The restaurant was laid out in a circle, the bar in the centre, the kitchen next to the entrance, and tables rippling outwards in a tidy concentric pattern. In the centre, the barman tossed a metal cocktail shaker in the air, spinning and catching it in one neat movement as a group of women who looked suspiciously like they were on a midweek hen party gathered around, whooping and cheering.

'. . . If you don't want people getting drunk, then don't put on free wine. There was champagne at the start too and you know what I'm like when I start on champagne. Anyway, where was I?'

Andrew blinked as the hyenas at the bar continued cackling. 'Your friend Cheryl.'

'Right, yeah. So I was like, "Chez, don't worry about it, babes. I've got that Jeremy Whatisname's card and you can go straight to him. He outranks Geoff and you can put a complaint in directly." So we phoned that number and it turned out Jeremy Thingamabob doesn't even work there any longer. He got offered some management job at BP and is off in the Gulf, raking it in. I mean you wouldn't have known it to look at him when he was sleeping in the toilets last Christmas, but then I guess that's not the sort of thing you put on a CV . . .'

Finally a waiter! Andrew held his hand up and caught

the man's eye. He was a typical Italian restaurant-type, all greased-back black hair, too-tight trousers and tufts of dark chest hair sticking out of his white shirt. The man scuttled across, notepad at the ready.

'Are you ready to order, Sir?'

'Yes, I'll have the garlic bread to start, the penne con pesce for main and a pint of Peroni.'

And earplugs, definitely earplugs.

'And for you, Madam?'

Sara seemed slightly put-out at her story being cut off mid-flow. She glanced at the menu, then back up at the waiter, who had definitely just sneaked a peek down her cleavage.

'What's that thing with the shells?'

'Mussels?'

'Yeah, I'll have some of that to start, then a chicken Caesar for main and a large glass of red.'

The waiter finished writing with an elaborate swish, snapped their menus closed, had another peep down Sara's dress, and then disappeared off in the direction of the hen party.

'After that, Chez was all down in the dumps but I said to her I'd help sort it, and I'm a woman of my word, so that's what I did. When Geoff turned in, late as usual, I asked if I could have a word. In his office, like, so that everyone knew what was going on. He said it'd have to be later but I said it had to be now. By then, of course, everyone was listening in, so he couldn't say anything out of place . . .'

Andrew peered over Sara's shoulder towards the bar,

where one of the women was leaning across, skirt riding up, knickers on show, all the while being egged on by her friends as she tried to get a kiss from the now slightly more sheepish barman.

Classy.

He focused back on Sara, who didn't seem to have breathed in for over a minute. If she could turn her attention to swimming as opposed to talking, she'd be Olympic standard.

'. . . So I'm in Geoff's office, just me and him, and he's like, "So what's the problem, Sara?" And I'm like, "You know what the problem is, Geoff – it's the way you talk to people. The girls on the floor won't stand for it. Poor old Cheryl's talking about official complaints because she can't take it any longer. People are talking about unionising." Course, that tips him right over the edge, which is why I said it. By now, everyone's watching through the glass, expecting fireworks . . .'

Andrew wondered exactly what caring for a person really meant. He'd been in love once before and blown it. At the time he'd blamed it on other people, mainly his father-in-law, but recently he'd started to see that it was his own choices that had driven him and his former wife apart. He'd definitely cared about her, of course, but could people fall in love twice?

'. . . He's ranting and raving, saying joining a union invalidates our contracts and that he'll sack the lot of us, so I'm like, "Geoff, we all know you can't do that. You're the stand-in assistant manager. All I'm saying is that you need to watch the way you talk to people." Then he's like,

"Some of that lot need a good kick up the arse, their timekeeping's appalling" . . .'

It was a difficult scale for Andrew to figure out. Did he even like Sara? If she walked out of the restaurant and got hit by a bus, he would certainly feel bad – awful in fact. He'd go to the hospital with her and hope she got better. He'd spend time with her, reading and chatting, as long as she couldn't talk back, but was that what counted as a relationship? Caring if the other person was hit by a bus? What if she was hit by a car? He'd probably still care then. Motorbike? Definitely. Mobility scooter? Perhaps not. Equally, if she walked out of the restaurant, didn't get hit by a bus, but he never saw her again, he really wouldn't mind.

'. . . So I said, "*Their* timekeeping's appalling – what time did you get in today?" He looked like he was going to pop, all bulging eyes and pumping veins. He just shouted, "What did you say?!" I stayed calm and was like, "You know what I said – and you know it's true" . . .'

She'd be one of those people he might bump into in twenty years' time. They'd stop on the street, staring at each other, vaguely trying to remember each other's name, before going for a coffee, catching up on each other's lives, and then not seeing one another for another twenty years.

'. . . He just shouted, "My personal life is none of your concern!" He was so loud the windows were rattling, like an earthquake. I just stood my ground and said, "That's exactly what the girls say, Geoff. Sometimes things come up. They don't mean for things to happen but that's what it's like when you've got kids." Poor Cheryl's lad's got that mental thing, what's it called?'

She snapped her fingers annoyingly at Andrew.

'Alzheimer's. No, that's the old people thing, isn't it? No matter, anyway, he's got that mental thing, so I said to him, "You've got to understand what it's like for some people" . . .'

Andrew eyed the shape of Sara's face, the high cheekbones, plump lips and straight white teeth. He skimmed across the curve of her dress, knowing that he definitely didn't have the same feelings for her as he'd had for his ex-wife. He was certainly attracted to her, when she stopped sodding talking, but it wasn't enough. Hoping someone avoided being hit by a bus wasn't enough to spend significant amounts of time with them.

The waiter interrupted Andrew's thoughts as he returned. By the time he'd finished going through the drink-sipping routine with Sara, along with another peep down her top, Andrew had already downed a third of his beer. As soon as the waiter disappeared again, Sara picked up where she'd left off.

'After that, Geoff was all right but that's what I said to Chez. Sometimes you've got to talk about these things. Anyway, as soon as I got out of there my phone went and it's only my mother on the phone, isn't it? I'm like, "Mum, it's half ten in the morning, I'm at work" but she's had a falling out with Dad again and he's stormed off to go fishing, so I'm trying to calm her down—'

'I don't think I can do this any longer.'

Sara paused mid-sentence, flicking her shoulder so that her lacquered hair dropped behind it. 'The beer? If you want some wine, we can call him back. The red's good.'

'I mean us. I'm sorry, it's not you, I just don't think things are working out.'

Sara stared at him, eyes widening until the red veins started to show. She took a sip of the wine and then placed the glass back on the table very delicately.

'You're dumping me?'

'Well, no . . . not like that, I just think—'

'*You're* dumping *me*?'

'Well—'

'Seriously?'

'I'd prefer it if—'

'You're lucky I'm still with you. All my friends say they don't know what I'm doing but I defend you. I say, "No, he's not just a stuck-up dickface with a nice apartment".'

Dickface?

'I say, "Honestly, he's really thoughtful and always remembers the important things, like my birthday and so on".'

'I'm not trying to—'

'And even though you always complain about meeting my friends and you don't like coming to the places I like; even though you didn't come to Leanne's wedding because you were "working"' – more bloody bunny ears – 'even though you hired that young piece of skirt to perv over—'

'That's not why I hired her.'

'You keep telling yourself that. Of all the people you could have hired, it just happens to be some pretty young girl with pointy tits and—'

'Please don't talk about her like that.'

Andrew wondered whether it was his own calm tone or

the fact that he'd defended Jenny that finally tipped Sara over the edge. Likely a bit of both. She stood, leaning over the table, Wonderbra-enhanced cleavage swinging freely as she wafted a talon-like nail in Andrew's direction, her voice so loud that the hen party had fallen silent. Andrew risked a quick peep around Sara's breasts to see the women staring in his direction on the edges of their stools, ready for the night's entertainment.

'Oh, I get it. It's about *her*, isn't it?'

'Jenny?'

'Keira.'

Andrew sighed. Of course it was. Who else was it going to be about?

Sara was in full flow. 'You do know you broke up with her eight years ago? Eight sodding years?!'

'I know.'

'So how are you still hung up on her? It's been eight years! Be an adult and grow up.'

Sara hoiked her bag up from the floor, turning towards the exit and then spinning back as if she'd forgotten something. In a flash, she had the wine glass in her hand, lunging forward and tipping the contents over Andrew's head. The liquid sloshed through his hair, dripping over his nose and running across his eyes. He gasped in surprise, trying not to blink in any of the vinegary concoction. Even the wine was shite in this place.

'You're not dumping me, because I'm dumping you,' Sara said, almost calmly. 'Have a nice life.'

With an elaborate swish and a rousing cheer from the hen party, she strutted her way towards the exit, dignity as intact as it was going to get. Andrew used the napkin to mop as much of the wine away from his face as he could just as the waiter emerged from the kitchen, bounding towards the table with two plates in his hand.

'I've got mussels and garlic bread . . .'

THURSDAY

13

Andrew drove up and down the road in his rented car, trying to find a parking space where the charge wasn't more than the car's daily hire rate. Sodding central Manchester and those NCP bandits. He eventually found a spot on the edge of a housing estate out towards Longsight and then walked back along Oxford Road until he was surrounded by university buildings and student types. Being before ten in the morning, there weren't many out; he guessed this area didn't warm up until they got out of bed some time around two-ish. Well, that was what it had been like when he was at university anyway. Since he'd met Keira here, the area had changed dramatically: out with the dingy students' union and tiny bolt-hole pubs, in with the wine bars, 'student services' buildings, music venues, fancy aquatics centre and all sorts of other smart glass-fronted buildings that only 'under-funded' universities could afford.

The side streets and cut-throughs were still the same as in his day, so Andrew weaved his way along the paved areas until he found the all-new red-brick set of private halls two streets over from the main road. In the summer, the stretch of lawn at the front would be covered with young people kicking balls around, drinking their way through crates of whatever was on special down the offy and, occasionally, revising. In the gloomy beginnings of a November morning, it was a giant mud pit, almost filthy enough to host a music festival.

A sign at the front listed the buildings next to rows of numbers, with arrows pointing off in all directions. Andrew checked the note on his phone about where Scott lived and then tried to figure out exactly what that meant in practical terms. It was a good job the people living here were studying for a degree, given that you'd need something that advanced to decipher what the sign was trying to say.

Eventually, Andrew gave up, asking a passing lad with an oversized backpack if he knew the location of the flat. He even got a sensible reply.

Two minutes later, he was making his way along a darkened corridor, using the light on his phone to check the numbers on the various doors before finally finding Scott's. He had to knock twice before a yawning teenager opened the door, towel around his waist, pasty white chest on display.

As Andrew was invited in, it dawned on him that, to the casual observer, a man in his mid-thirties being invited into a student's apartment by a half-naked young man might seem a little *off*. Still, it wouldn't be the worst thing that had happened to him in the previous twenty-four hours, given his disastrous break-up.

Scott led him into a cluttered living room, full of football posters, scattered lads' mags, pizza boxes and various computer games. He muttered something about being right back and then disappeared through a door.

The smell of tobacco clung to the furniture, despite the open window allowing cool air to chill the room. On the windowsill, a saucer was overflowing with cigarette ends, flecks of ash peppering the carpet underneath. An air-freshener was sticking out of the electrical socket, with a small transparent bulb of yellow liquid being squirted into the air, doing a half-arsed job of masking the fags.

In the corner was a jumbled stack of textbooks, mingled with newspapers, more magazines and the odd novel. Andrew checked for anything spell-related but there was nothing similar to what he'd found in Nicholas's room.

A few minutes later, Scott emerged back into the room, rubbing his wet brown hair with a towel. Luckily, he was now wearing jeans, with a T-shirt and hoody. His accent was as local as it came. 'Sorry about that, pal, lost track of the time.'

He flopped onto the sofa, squishing himself into the corner, before digging a remote control out from underneath him and putting it on a table that had more coffee rings than clean wood.

'So you're a private investigator?'

Andrew sat opposite him. 'Right.'

'And you're looking into what happened to Nicholas?'

'Exactly. I gather you were one of his better friends?'

A shrug. 'I s'pose. I only knew him from college.'

'How long did you know him for?'

Scott began counting on his fingers, muttering under his breath. 'About a year and half before he . . . went away.'

'What sort of things were you into?'

107

Scott glanced nervously towards the window. 'Mind if I have a fag?'

'It's your flat.'

He dug into the pockets of his hoody and pulled out a crumpled packet of cigarettes, lifting one out and clamping it between his lips as he rooted in his jeans pocket for the lighter. Andrew spun to face him as Scott crossed to the window, sparking the cigarette and standing next to the fresh air. He took a deep drag, eyeing Andrew with suspicion.

'I'm not police, if that's what you're worried about,' Andrew said.

'Why would it worry me?'

'I don't know – I was eighteen, nineteen once. Sometimes you get up to things . . .'

The right side of Scott's lips curled into a smile. 'Aye, well, it's only really the usual. Bit of weed, some underage booze. He wasn't into fags at all. We went to a few gigs, had a day at Blackpool the other summer, drank cider in the park, played a bit of footy – what do you want to hear?'

An errant remnant of cigarette ash missed the saucer and landed on top of the air-freshener.

'What sort of thing would you want to keep from his parents?'

'He wasn't some crack-head if that's what you're thinking, he was just a normal lad.'

'I know, but there's lots of things normal lads do that they wouldn't want their parents to know about. That's what makes them normal, isn't it?'

A puff of smoke disappeared into the air and the half-smile returned. 'Fair point. I s'pose they didn't know about the weed but it was never a big thing. He wasn't a dealer or anything.'

'Anything else?'

'Not really. He liked a bit of porn but don't we all? He was looking forward to turning eighteen.'

'Why?'

'So he could drink legally. We always had pubs we could get into but the better places, the cheaper ones, they usually asked for ID. They had this big splurge on testing bars for serving underagers when we were at college and suddenly you couldn't get in anywhere.'

'Did you go out much?'

Scott sucked the cigarette in between his teeth, brushing his hands on his trousers before plucking it out again. A spiral of smoke disappeared towards the window. 'Not really. Too expensive, ain't it? We'd usually get a bottle of something and go to the park if it was sunny, or nick off down the canal and sit under one of the bridges. Either that, or we'd go round Kingy's house when his parents were out. That's when he wasn't with Lara, of course.'

Andrew made an effort to search through the pages inside the envelope, as if he didn't know who Lara was.

'She was his girlfriend, yes?'

'If you can call it that. They'd argue all the time: break up, get back together, fight, make up. You never knew if they were together or apart. One minute, he'd be saying he was done with her, the next they were all over each other again. At first we'd take it seriously but then we realised it was just what they did.'

'Who usually did the breaking up?'

'Oh, it was always Nicky – she was a right psycho. She'd threaten to cut her wrists if he didn't get back with her, then she'd dote on him the whole time they were together.'

'What did she do?'

'She'd get him food and booze, stuff like that. Promise him . . . *things*.'

'Why did he get back together with her if they were always arguing?'

Scott finished the cigarette and mashed the remains into the mound of butts in the saucer. 'Why d'ya think?'

Aah . . . seventeen-year-old lads only thought with one thing.

Andrew moved on. 'Were you out with him the night he disappeared?'

Scott took out a second cigarette and lit it. 'We all were – Kingy, Gibbon, Ricky, Belly, Lara and a couple of other girls. Nicky was the youngest, so we were all eighteen by then. It was our first proper night out where we couldn't be turned away for being underage.'

Andrew began writing on the back of the envelope: this was the information he'd actually come for. 'Where did you go?'

'Do you know Night And Day in the centre?'

'On Oldham Street?'

'Yeah, it's this smart little place that has bands. They don't let dickheads in, which makes it better than half the places in town. We'd gone out early because one of Kingy's mates plays trumpet in a band. They have this lead singer too, you should see her . . .' Scott held the cigarette in his mouth, using both hands to signal that she might have had a second job smuggling melons. '. . . anyway, they were on at half seven, so we'd been out since about six.'

'You'd had a bit to drink then?'

Scott switched the cigarette from one hand to the other, nodding. 'Aye, sort of. Nicky had been complaining about feeling a bit dodgy since we went out. Something to do with his stomach. Lara was all over him, fussing around, going on about how he should be drinking water.'

'What happened?'

A sheepish grin: 'Well, I was completely wankered. I just remember Nicky coming over and saying he was going to nick off because he was feeling rough. At the time, I thought it was because he'd been drinking, it was only later I realised it was because of his stomach. He said goodbye to everyone and then he and Lara left. The rest of us stayed out and it was only a couple of days later when the Old Bill came round that I realised he'd not got home.'

'What time did he leave?'

'Nine-ish? I only remember because the second band were about to come on. I couldn't work out why they'd walked. It was a really weird day – it wasn't raining but there were flashes of dry lightning around. You don't see much like that in February. Everyone kept going on about it when we left later on but I could barely see a thing by then. If someone had said there were frogs raining down, I would've believed them.'

The second cigarette disappeared into the pile and Scott joined Andrew on the sofa again. Andrew was about to ask something else when he noticed Scott's bottom lip bobbing. The student squeezed the top of his nose with his thumb and forefinger, speaking his way through a sob. 'Sorry . . .'

'It's okay.'

Scott reached for a box of tissues on the coffee table and turned away, blowing his nose. He spoke without turning back to Andrew. 'Look, he wasn't a great mate if I'm honest. Once he started seeing Lara, he spent most of his time with her. When they broke up, we'd hang around but I was better friends with Kingy. If things hadn't happened and we'd gone away to different unis, I doubt we'd be in contact . . .' He paused to blow his nose again, half-turning back towards Andrew. '. . . but it's still strange when someone you know just isn't there any longer. Sometimes I wonder what might have happened if I'd left early, or if we'd gone to a different pub – or gone out later, or earlier. Or if we'd all left together and got a taxi. You run it all through your head and wonder if you could've done something differently. I was so sodding pissed, so useless, that I barely even remember saying goodbye. If I'd known I wasn't going to see him again, I'd have told him that I thought he was a decent guy.'

Andrew let Scott compose himself for a few moments. He didn't know him well enough to say anything that wouldn't sound hollow. Missing people cases were worse than murders in so many ways, because they didn't come with answers. People could understand killings, even senseless ones. What was hard to figure out was when somebody walked out of a door and never came back.

Scott blew his nose one more time and then threw

the tissue into a bin on the other side of the table. 'Sorry, man . . .'

'You don't have to apologise.'

'I wish there was something I could tell you. The police talked to us all at the time, took our statements, and then went away. I think we all thought he'd just wander into college one day wondering what all of the fuss was about.'

'How did people take it?'

'They didn't really. No one talked about it. I think everyone was scared that it could happen to them.'

'What about Lara?'

'I didn't really see her too much after that. We were on different courses and I only knew her through Nicky. I think she was off for a few weeks or a month. I honestly don't know.'

Andrew took a breath, judging the moment. 'What was the Wizard nickname all about?'

Scott turned to face him, blinking rapidly, the corners of his eyes an irritated pink. 'How'd you hear about that?'

'I saw it somewhere.'

Scott shook his head softly. 'It was a sort of wind-up thing.'

'I don't get it. Was he into magic?'

'Sort of. He never used to talk about it but he had this thing on his wrist. It was like a tattoo but not a proper one. The sort of thing you'd draw yourself with a compass. I think Lara might have done it.'

Andrew dug into the envelope for a blank sheet of paper, handing it across with his pen. 'Can you draw it?'

Scott was biting his lips, missing the cigarettes as he

rested on the table. He drew a wobbly circle with an upside-down triangle in the middle. 'Sorry, mate, that's supposed to be an actual circle,' he said.

'Did you ask him why he had it?'

'At first he said it was something to do with Lara but then he refused to talk about it. Someone said it was a mark of the devil, so we had a bit of a laugh, which is why I called him the Wizard.'

'So the magic was Lara's thing?'

'I s'pose. He never really talked about it to us but she'd make these little straw dolls, plus she'd always be doodling those pointy star things—'

'Pentagrams?'

'Aye, with the five points. She'd talk about how plants could be powerful and all that. We thought she was a bit of a hippie-nutjob but Nicky always had a strop on if we joked about that in front of him, so we let it go. Girls can get away with that kind of shite, can't they? You don't see many lads carrying around straw dolls.'

'Did you tell the police all of that?'

'Yeah, but they never came back. As far as I know, she went off to uni. If I'm honest, there was always something not quite right about her.'

14

Jenny's voice trickled from the tinny speaker somewhere above Andrew's head. 'You could've called me before setting off.'

Andrew accidentally hit the hire car's indicator as he aimed for the windscreen wipers. The drizzle had started moments after he'd left Scott's flat, blanketing the city in a smoggy, overcast haze. Somehow he'd hooked up his phone to the vehicle's Bluetooth, even though he was struggling with almost every other function.

'I was trying to multi-task,' he said.

'How's that going?'

'I'm talking and driving, so not too badly. How have you got on with Nicholas's other friends?'

Andrew could hear Jenny tapping on her keyboard. 'I left a few messages and sent some emails. A couple have come back to me without much to say: decent guy, relatively quiet, Lara doted on him but they argued a lot, blah, blah, blah.'

'That's more or less what Scott said.'

'I used the information from his parents and called in a few favours. His mobile number hasn't been used since the night he went missing. He sent a text message to his mum at a couple of minutes to nine to say he was on his way home but nothing after that. I got a list of his calls and texts but it's the usual stuff, mainly to Lara. As for his bank accounts, they've not been touched, though they were pretty much empty anyway.'

Andrew had his own contacts at various phone companies and banks which he'd shared with Jenny but she'd gone beyond that to make her own. Whether it was a flirty giggle on the phone, or a good way with words, he didn't know, but she consistently got her hands on the information they needed.

'What about Lara?' he asked.

'Next to nothing. There's almost no personal information on her Facebook profile, except her name. I've cross-referenced a few of her friends' profiles with hers and got a little more but not much. She's a smart girl: all As to Cs in her exams, plus I've found out which halls she's staying in at Salford. I've got a phone number for the block but no mobile number. Somebody should be able to knock on her door though. Shall I try to get hold of her?'

'Text me the number for her block. I'll see if she can talk to us tomorrow.'

'Do you think she'll be a problem?'

'I suppose we'll find out.'

'If there's a chance we could find out what happened to her boyfriend nine months ago, wouldn't she want to help?'

'Let's hope so.'

Andrew squelched his way up the back steps of the community housing block of flats. It was only two storeys but the tough granite made his legs ache as if he'd been running – which he hadn't done in years. The stairs opened onto a rickety balcony, with a waist-high metal fence stretching to the far end of the row. The once-magnolia walls of the flats were now a grey mix of grime and filth as the dripping guttering drummed an ear-shattering chorus. Andrew stepped around a puddle, trying not to touch the flaking paint of the fence for fear of sending the rusting metalwork tumbling to the ground. How this entire block hadn't been condemned as a health hazard, Andrew didn't know.

He stared over the balcony towards the identical row of flats stretching away at a right angle from where he was standing. There was a green separating the blocks, with a pile of tyres in the centre, a leftover burnt-out reminder that Bonfire Night and the associated bell-endery hadn't long passed. If ever there was a night for dickheads, the fifth of November was it. Still, if Darwin's theory of natural selection was true, then the people who launched fire-works into their own faces were probably destined not to procreate anyway.

Andrew weaved his way along the balcony, dodging in between the areas where rain was flooding through the holes in the roof until he reached a flat near the end. He rang the bell and knocked hard, pulling his coat tighter around himself and cursing the weather under his breath.

He counted the locks as they were rattled backwards from inside. One bolt at the top, one in the middle, a chunky chain and a final one near the bottom. The door was inched open to reveal a stubby old woman in a flowery dress that might have once been a duvet cover. She had a huge, clearly dyed, afro-style perm that looked like an oversized frizzy lollipop. Her wrinkled, gnarled face broke into a grin. 'Well, look who it is.'

Andrew stepped forward, arms out, his foot sinking into the sopping welcome mat. 'Hi, Aunt Gem.'

Gem was barely five foot tall to start with, and her hunched frame didn't quite reach Andrew's chest. She bear-hugged him around the midriff, squeezing with far more gusto than someone in their seventies should manage. Andrew tried not to wince but as soon as she pulled away, she was pinching his stomach.

'Look at you wasting away. I've got some lamb shanks in the freezer.' She scuttled down the hallway, leaving Andrew by the door, calling over her shoulder. 'Don't forget to lock up and take your shoes off.'

Andrew did as he was told, wriggling out of his boots and placing them next to his aunt's fluffy slippers.

So much for not stopping.

The hallway was dark, embers of bright light creeping into the corners from the far door through which Gem had disappeared. Andrew blinked rapidly, trying to adjust to the dimness as he slid the bolts into place. He wasn't sure how a woman in her seventies consistently reached the bottom one, given he almost threw his back out straining for it.

Her creaky voice reverberated through the tight space from the room beyond. 'Did you put the chain on?'

'I'm doing it.'

Click-clunk.

'What about the bolts?'

'I've done those too.'

'Even the bottom one?'

'Yes!'

Andrew padded through the hallway in his socks, emerging into a cream kitchen that would have been in vogue around the time he was born. Aunt Gem was bent over a chest freezer, top half-buried inside it.

'I've not got time to stop,' Andrew protested.

'Nonsense, you're wasting away. How'd you ever expect to find yourself a young lady if you're not eating properly?'

There was a scrape of ice as his aunt leant further forward, both feet coming off the floor as she almost toppled into the freezer. Andrew lunged ahead, placing a hand on the back of her dress and pulling her out. She emerged with the lamb in a polythene freezer bag.

'I'm perfectly healthy,' he said.

'Rubbish. I've got a freezer full of these. That ginger lad over the way came knocking on everyone's doors saying he knows a farmer with a herd of lambs that had to be put down because they were ill. He said the meat was going cheap, so I took half-a-dozen off him.'

'They're probably stolen.'

Aunt Gem dropped the freezer lid into place, jumping back as a mist of ice seeped out. 'Nonsense. He's a good lad, whatever his name is. Does all sorts around here. Reg's television was on the blink the other week and he got him a brand-new one. One of those flat things.'

'That was probably nicked, too.'

She bustled around Andrew towards the cooker, twiddling the knobs until a low hum started. 'You sit yourself down and it'll be about forty-five minutes. Do you want some veg?'

Andrew placed a hand on her shoulder. 'Gem, I'm only here for a few minutes. I came to take Rory for a walk.'

Her wrinkly hands hovered over the stove before a frenzied bout of knob-twiddling made the low hum go away again. 'Oh.'

'I can come back another day if you want to go out somewhere? Or I'll take you shopping again?'

She crossed back to the freezer, with an over-the-top limp, her entire body suddenly more frail than it had seemed twenty seconds earlier. 'No, no, don't you worry about me. I'm only your dear old aunt stuck away in a tiny little flat.'

'Gem—'

'I remember when you were a little child and your mum was poorly. Who was it who took you in for that week, wiping your nose, cleaning your backside . . . ?'

The week Andrew's mother was poorly had apparently happened when he was around six months old, something he couldn't remember but had never been allowed to forget.

'I've offered so many times to help find you somewhere better than this.'

The freezer popped open again, sending an icy cloud into the air.

'Ha! I grew up here. Why would I want to leave?'

'Well, the offer's always there. Anyway, I'm really busy with work. I just popped around for Rory. We can do something later in the week if you want?'

The lamb shank landed with a thump in the bottom of the freezer, followed by a louder clump as his aunt dropped the lid.

'Oh, I wouldn't want to be an *inconvenience*. God forbid the woman who wiped your backside as a baby should want to cook you dinner.'

'I'll come around for tea tomorrow if you want—'

'I'm at bingo on Fridays.'

'Saturday then—'

'Reg is having a party on Saturday. One of the meals on wheels women is his niece, so *she's* putting on something nice for us all.'

'Sunday?'

'I don't know what I'm doing Sunday.' She brushed past Andrew towards the living room. 'Rory, where are you? Someone's here to see you.'

Aunt Gem's living room looked as if someone had cleared out a seaside tat shop and dumped everything in her flat. The walls were lined with plates, snow globes, still sealed rainbow-coloured lollies, coins, postcards, sticks of rock, miniature houses, statues, tea-cups and an almost infinite amount of useless crap in neat rows. All mementoes of places someone she knew had visited. Gem herself had barely left the estate on which she was born, with a bus ride to the city centre considered a day out.

She tottered around an armchair that had more claw marks than fabric. In the corner, a brown and white pug with large brown dinner-plate eyes pottered his way out of a pile of blankets and started sniffing around Andrew's socks.

'I wouldn't smell them, pal.'

Aunt Gem dropped herself into the armchair, before levering herself back up instantly with an annoyed tut. 'Someone's going to have to lock up after you.'

Andrew bent down to give Rory a pat as the dog chugged his way into the kitchen, already out of breath, like a mini barrel on legs.

'Don't get him all excited,' Aunt Gem chided.

'I'm just taking him for a walk.'

'Yes, but he's a delicate little thing who doesn't like having his feelings hurt. Go at his pace, not at yours.'

'You say that every time.'

'That's because he gets back here all sleepy and the poor little fella ends up dozing all evening. He wouldn't wake up for the Corrie theme tune last time and you know how much he likes that.'

Andrew walked through to the hallway and started putting his boots back on. As it went, getting in and out in under ten minutes was quite good going.

'Where are you taking him?' Aunt Gem asked.

'Out to the woods for a wander.'

She crouched low to the floor, holding her hand out for the pug to lap at. 'You hear that, Rory? Your uncle Andrew's taking you out to the woods.'

Rory the pug didn't seem too enamoured, turning in a circle with the elegance of an oil tanker and only marginally greater speed.

Andrew plucked the dog lead from the hook on the

wall. 'I'll bring him back in a couple of hours.' He bent down and pecked his aunt on the head. 'And don't let me forget about that lamb shank lunch.'

Rory trotted across the packed, mulched leaves of Alkrington Wood with his tongue hanging out. Plumes of his breath twirled into the air as he bobbed left-right-left-right-left-right-left.

A few years previously, Aunt Gem had found him at the bottom of the stairs outside her flat, eye socket smashed, blood dripping from his nose and a long slash along his side from where a bunch of local shits had used him for a game of football. She'd phoned Andrew frantically, had him drive her to the vets, promised to pay whatever it cost, and then spent the next three months studiously nursing him back to health.

Now the soppy little sod was the centre of her life, except that she wasn't agile enough to take him for anything more than a gentle trundle across the green once in a while. Andrew was killing two birds with one stone by taking Rory for a walk while simultaneously not having to explore the woods by himself as if he was some sort of perverted flasher. Not to mention the fact that it was impossible to overestimate how much goodwill the chubby brown and white softie could get him. If Andrew was actually in the market for trying to find a new girlfriend, the first thing he'd have done was go out with Rory for a day and he'd have had friendly female dog-owners falling over themselves to fawn over the pug. And, hopefully, Andrew himself.

Rory's stubby legs and underbelly were already covered in filth, leaving Andrew wondering how the car rental company was going to feel about the tangy wet-dog smell upon the vehicle's return.

Aside from the dogging incident, Andrew had never been to Alkrington Wood before but he followed the path, coat zipped tightly like a straitjacket. The rain had stopped as he'd left Aunt Gem's but that meant the stinging cold had settled. Winter was on its way but if it could sod right off for an hour or two, it'd be highly appreciated.

Two thirty-something women in matching purple coats and red woollen beanies waved a hello, although their grins were definitely directed more towards Rory than Andrew.

As the patches of wet leaves got thicker, the trees became denser, with the direction of the path harder to figure out. The giveaway was each time Andrew's feet went through the top of the brown and green covering directly into a puddle. By the fifth occasion, both of his feet were drenched and he was trying to stop himself from shivering.

Rory continued bumbling along without a care, occasionally glancing backwards towards Andrew, silently asking why he kept stopping to look at his feet.

'All right, pal, I'm right behind you.'

Andrew continued over the next ridge, where a grey-haired man with an olive-green waxed coat twice the size of him was whistling like a demented teapot.

'Poppy, come back over here. Poppy!'

A dirt-soaked Labrador emerged from a copse of bushes, tongue lolling to the side. Rory sidled across to Andrew and hid behind his legs. He didn't like other dogs.

The man turned to Andrew, lop-sided grin on his face. 'I don't know about yours but my Poppy loves it when it rains.'

'Rory just likes being out.'

The man crouched and pulled a lead from out of his pocket, connecting it to the Labrador's collar.

'Lovely out here, isn't it?' Andrew said.

'Beautiful.'

'Still, not quite the same since those fingers were found . . .'

The man's face darkened slightly as he straightened himself. Instinctively, he nodded towards a bank to his right, exactly as Andrew had hoped. 'Aye, those police-types had it taped off for months. All that digging and what did they find? Sod all and then they sodded off. Every time you walked past, you got the dirty looks, as if you should have known there were three fingers buried up there.'

'Always the way, isn't it? Spend all their time worrying about people going five miles an hour over the speed limit instead of catching real criminals.'

The man began to walk away with Poppy at his side but he nodded in ferocious agreement. If in doubt, bang on about the police catching 'real' criminals and someone would always agree with you.

When they were out of sight, Rory poked his head through Andrew's legs, made sure the coast was clear and then began plopping along again. Andrew headed towards the direction in which the walker had nodded, calling over his shoulder towards the pug. 'This way, buddy.'

The ridge was steeper than it looked, thick clumps of leaves slipping from underneath Andrew's feet as he tried to climb. Rory sauntered a few steps behind, waiting until Andrew had slipped his way up the slope before deciding it was safe for himself. As Andrew reached the peak, he turned back to ensure Rory was with him. Aunt Gem was going to be beside herself. The little dog was definitely more brown than white now, streaks of mud running all around his body, his stumpy tail wagging back and forth furiously.

Over the crest and it was clear where the police had been digging. They'd done their best to replace the dirt they'd lifted but the land was uneven and boggy. The leaves were a lot thinner, with much of the mud visible for the first time since Andrew had moved deeper into the woods. Instead of the condensed woodland of lower down, the plants were far more widely spaced higher up, which Rory took full advantage of, galloping down the slope until he began to roll, completely covering himself in filth.

Andrew followed, feet sinking into the soft soil, squidgy thick mud oozing over the top of his boots. He hadn't brought any others out with him, so there was a good chance the car rental company was going to hammer his credit card for cleaning costs. It'd probably still be less than parking in the city centre.

At the bottom of the decline, Rory was waiting faithfully. The moment Andrew arrived next to him, he shook himself viciously from side to side, sending a spray of muddied water in all directions.

Andrew peered down at himself, flecks of dirt drenching

his jeans, with thicker gloops of muck covering his lower legs. Great.

He took a step towards the upwards slope, feet sinking again. As he lunged forward, trying to haul himself out, he stopped, realising where he was. This wasn't just the area where Nicholas's fingers had been found, there was something different about the spot. Andrew wrenched his feet from the mud and turned as best he could. The natural curve of the land had created a basin shape that was almost round. Plotted almost equidistantly around the edge were three bare trees, which, if he drew a line from one to the other, would create what was more or less an equilateral triangle within the circle.

Just like the improvised tattoo that Nicholas had on his wrist.

FRIDAY

15

Jenny sniffed the air and then took a deep breath. 'I can't quite figure out what it smells of.'

Andrew shifted the car down into second gear and took the turn into the parking area for the Salford University halls. 'It's that new car smell thing they put in rented cars.'

Jenny shook her head. 'It's more like a wet dog.'

Andrew kept quiet, parking in the 'residents only' bay, unfolding an A4 sheet of paper with the words 'contractors at work' from his pocket and leaving it on the dashboard. 'I spoke to Lara last night via a communal phone for her block of flats. She wasn't happy but when I mentioned Nicholas's parents had asked me to look into things, she agreed to have a chat. She gave me her mobile number but she's in lectures from ten to twelve.'

Jenny opened the passenger's door. 'So why are we here at half ten?'

'Because it's not just her we need to talk to.'

Manchester and Salford were each cities in their own right, separated by the River Irwell and sitting next to each other like slightly envious siblings, arguing over which was the *real* city. Manchester had two universities of its own and, with Salford's student population a mile and a half away, around 100,000 young people were added to the general population during the academic year.

Andrew clambered out of the car, trying to get his bearings. Ahead, a large area of parkland curved down towards the river as it hooped its way between the cities. Individual dorms were scattered in the distance: three-storey sand-coloured landscape blights with peeling green awnings over the doorways. Like a holiday camp that had gone bust twenty years previously that had squatters. A large noticeboard towered over the car park, every spare centimetre taken up by posters advertising gigs, karaoke nights, various pub events as well as photocopied pictures of someone's hairy arse with 'Vote Dave P for President' imprinted across.

Andrew followed the signs for the block number in which Lara was apparently living, making sure Jenny was close by just in case anyone asked who he was. She could easily pass for a student; he would either be seen as one of those creepy older people who ended up trying to fit in among the younger students, or a pervy old man trying to groom undergraduates outside their dorms.

Lara's block was identical to the others: flaking cream paint on the outside, military green overhang next to the door. The front door was clamped shut, so Jenny pressed the buzzer for a random flat. Moments later the door clicked open in what was clearly an entry system only marginally more compromised than Britain's border control.

'Which flat is she in?' Jenny asked.

'Eight.'

'Right at the top.'

Jenny led the way up the stairs but there were no signs

of life. More posters were stuck to the walls and banisters. 'The ultimate end-of-term party: fishbowls for a fiver', 'Back to Skool fever', 'Back together (again), back in concert (again): Steps – live at the Bee Hive'.

Seriously?

More print-outs urging people to vote Dave P for President. An A4 flyer with tags to rip off at the bottom, urging people to get in contact about a rat problem. That sounded particularly lovely.

On the top floor, Jenny scooted around the banister and rapped on the door for flat eight. For a few moments, nothing happened and then the door swung open violently, thumping into the inside wall. A thin young man, naked from the waist up with frizzy black hair, was eating a yoghurt with his fingers.

He eyed Jenny up and down. 'Y'all right?'

Who said love was dead?

Jenny took a half-step over the threshold, making yoghurt boy bounce backwards. 'Is Lara in?'

'I think she's at lectures.'

'No worries, we'll wait.'

Jenny edged forward, making space for Andrew, who pressed in behind her, closing the door with the flat of his hand. They were in a hallway with dim strip lighting across the top and four doors on either side.

'Which one's your loo?' Jenny asked.

Yoghurt boy scooped another blob from the pot with his finger and sucked on it, nodding towards the door at the end of the corridor on the left. Andrew could smell the previous night's alcohol and/or curry on his breath even from a few paces. Perhaps he was studying chemical weaponry?

Jenny arched her body so that she didn't have to touch his bare torso as she skirted around him, before hurrying to the end of the corridor and entering the toilet for a poke-around.

'What d'ya want Lara for?'

Andrew turned back to the student, who was swaying slightly, pupils large and unfocused. 'We're here for a chat. She knows we're coming. Is there somewhere we can wait?'

Yoghurt boy spun around, shoulder colliding with one of the door frames along the side. 'Kitchen.'

'What's your name, by the way?'

'Alex.'

The kitchen was directly opposite the bathroom, an expanse of cheap lino, various brown and orange stains, a fridge that buzzed like a vacuum cleaner, and a row of cereal boxes in the windowsill that looked like someone was collecting them. Pushed against the mustard-yellow wall was a rickety dining table, with a glowering young woman half-slouched over a laptop.

'For God's sake, Alex, will you put some clothes on?' she said. 'No one wants to look at your nipples.'

Alex dropped his yoghurt pot on top of an overflowing bin, crossed to the sink, plucked out a bowl, gave it a wipe with a tea towel, and then moved across to the windowsill. He opened a box of Rice Krispies and emptied a few sprinkles into the bowl, before adding to it with a cascade of Coco Pops.

He grinned towards the girl at the table as he yanked

open the fridge door and reached for a carton of milk. 'Ebony and ivory, innit? Paul McCartney, give peace a chance. All that shite.'

'It's just cereal, and I still don't want to see your nipples.'

'You love it, babe. It's our destiny.'

'It sodding isn't, now piss off. I'm trying to work.'

Alex stumbled towards the door, still smiling as he fumbled his way through. As it slammed itself shut, Andrew heard voices on the other side – Jenny back out of the bathroom. There was a girlish giggle and then footsteps retreating along the hallway.

Andrew offered a flimsy smile to the young woman at the table. 'Sorry, I'm Andrew. I'm waiting for Lara. I think she's in lectures.'

She leant back in her seat, more relaxed now that Alex had gone. She had thick-rimmed glasses, with wavy gingery-fair hair that was a similar colour to Andrew's. She was still in her pyjamas, thick felt-looking things with a teddy-bear pattern. Comfy.

With a dismissive wave, she pointed to the empty chair opposite her. 'I'm Alex – and before you say it, yes, we're both named Alex. That's why he keeps saying it's "destiny" for us to be together. The only destiny he's going to know is when my knee shatters his bollocks if he ever comes anywhere near me.'

She yawned widely and loudly as Andrew perched uncomfortably on the chair opposite. For some reason, the back arched inwards, meaning that there was no option other than to hunch forward.

Alex tapped the table with the palm of her hand. 'You're not one of the council's residency inspectors, are you?'

'Sorry.'

'I've been trying to get someone out to check for rats for ages. Everyone always passes you on to the next person and you end up going in circles.'

'Sounds grim.'

Alex pressed forward again, ready to vent. 'Oh, this lot don't help.' She pointed at the bin. 'I only emptied that yesterday but no one else ever does it. It's like living in anarchy. You can never keep track of who's in this building, let alone the flat. There are always people popping in: boyfriends, girlfriends, one-night conquests, and, occasionally, people interested in studying. The other Alex is always trying to get girls into his room.'

She crossed to the row of cupboards above the sink and took out a packet of jam rings, spinning it around to show the words 'ALEX (MAN)' written on it in felt-tip.

'He's pathetic. He could just keep them in his room but he knows it annoys me.'

She opened the fridge, taking out a packet of cheese and turning it to show the post-it note.

'ALEX'

In smaller letters underneath, in different handwriting, were the words:

'(NOT MAN)'

Alex returned the cheese to the fridge and then sat back down. 'He's such a prick. It doesn't matter if you put names on stuff anyway because things are always going missing. Then the bin's always overflowing and you can hear the rats. It's disgusting – there's six of us living here and it's only me who ever does anything. If it wasn't so cheap, and if I hadn't paid up front, I would've left already.'

'How long have you been here?'

'Since September – two and a bit months . . .' She stopped herself, eyes narrowing. 'You're not Lara's dad, or something, are you?'

Andrew took a business card from his pocket and handed it over. From what Richard Carr had told them, Lara was an orphan – something clearly not shared with her flatmates. 'Lara's ex-boyfriend went missing nine months ago,' Andrew said. 'I'm doing what I can to find out what happened to him.'

'Oh . . . right . . . so you don't really know her, then?'

'No. What's she like?'

Alex stared at Andrew for a few moments, trying to read him. With a puff of her lips, she apparently decided he was all right. 'She's a bit . . . *weird*.'

'How do you mean?'

'She doesn't *do* anything. She doesn't seem to have any friends, doesn't go out, doesn't get pissed. On our first night here, we all arranged a flat night out. There's this pub at the front by the car park. It's like hell on earth – sticky floors, full of chavs – but it's one fifty a pint so it's always rammed. We all set off there to try to get to know each other but Lara said she didn't fancy it. We didn't know about her boyfriend then but it's not as if *she* died, is it?'

Bit harsh.

'Does she ever go out with you?'

'You're lucky if she even talks to you. Someone on her course reckoned she applied to do medicine but then dropped out and started doing social care instead. How strange is that? Then she's always on the edge. Sophie in flat one moved in during the summer. They let you come early if you want. Three of them moved in but she was arguing over rooms on the first day. That'd be fair enough if one was bigger than the other, but they're all identical. Three look over the courtyard, three over the car park. Pick your view, get your bags inside, stop moaning. It rains all the time anyway.'

'Which room did she get?'

Alex nodded beyond the door. 'Next to the bathroom. Maybe she's got a weak bladder or something? All she had to do was say but Sophie reckoned they had a row about it. Not the best way to get in with your new housemates, is it?'

It was a similar story to the ones Nicholas's next-door neighbour and college friend had told: an angry teenage girl ready to pick arguments.

Andrew felt a strange need to defend the young woman he'd never met. Her boyfriend had walked her home one night and then disappeared, after all.

'She can't be all bad?'

Alex closed the lid of her laptop. 'I suppose she's quiet. In the first week we moved in, when it was just three of them, she'd play music all the time. That death metal shit where it sounds like a horse is having sex with a pig. They all ganged up on her basically, saying they'd get the housing management involved if she didn't keep it down. Everything's been fine after that. Well, except for the bins and the mess but that's not her fault.'

She crossed to the fridge and took out a loaf of fancy-looking bread – all multigrain-this and good-for-you-that. On the front was a clearly marked 'ALEX (NOT MAN)'. Alex counted the slices through the transparent packet. 'Some bastard's been nicking my bread again.' She dropped two pieces into a grimy toaster and pushed down the lever, then emptied the rest of the loaf onto the counter top. One by one, she licked each slice before putting it back into the bag. 'That'll teach them.'

Andrew suppressed a smile – student politics at its best. He'd been through all of this himself in shared accommodation.

'This might sound like a weird question,' he said, 'but has Lara ever shown any interest in magic or witchcraft?'

Alex screwed up her face, the assortment of freckles becoming one large splodge. 'Why'd you ask?'

'I'm following something up.'

The student let out a low hum before replying. 'There's a communal living room on the ground floor with a TV. Most times, the lads use it for FIFA tournaments, or whatever. It's like living with five-year-olds. Sometimes, someone will put a movie on. Usually it's "Zombie Porn Stars From the Planet Mars" or something else that no one with half a brain cell is interested in, but a couple of weeks after term started, one of the girls downstairs wanted to do a Harry Potter night. Someone got a few boxes of wine in, so we were sitting down there chatting when Lara appeared in the doorway. She was going mental, screaming about how magic was real and that we should turn it off.'

'What happened?'

'Nothing really. There were about a dozen of us in there, so we turned it off, waited until she'd gone upstairs, and then turned it back on again. Everyone thought she'd been doing mushrooms or something.'

Andrew didn't have time to ask anything else as the front door thumped into the hallway wall. Footsteps padded along the corridor and then Lara appeared in the kitchen door, dressed entirely in black: platform shoes, ripped tights, a short skirt and a long-sleeved sweatshirt. She had dark eyes, darker hair and ethereal white skin, as if she'd just stepped out of an old-fashioned film.

Lara glowered towards the table, face a mix of uninterest and annoyance. 'You Andrew?'

'Yes.'

She nodded backwards. 'Let's get this over with.'

16

Directly opposite the kitchen was the door to the bathroom, with a patch of blank wall between that and the door to Lara's bedroom. As Lara unlocked the door, Jenny emerged from Alex (Man)'s room, sidling along the corridor and winking at Andrew in a 'we'll-compare-notes-later' way.

Lara's room was cramped with a desk running the length of one wall and a single bed built into the space opposite. A window was across from the door, with a crack in the centre of the curtain allowing a trickle of light into the room, seeping into the dark shadows. Jenny stopped in front of Andrew, with barely enough room for the three of them to stand as Lara pulled a chair out from under the desk and sat on it.

Her tone was short. 'Who are you?'

Jenny held out her hand. 'I'm Andrew's assistant, Jenny.'

Lara didn't shake it. 'What do you both want?'

Jenny sat softly on the bed, leaving Andrew standing awkwardly. 'Can I turn a light on? Or open the curtains?'

Through the gloom, he could just about make out Lara's panda eyes glaring at him. She reached backwards and tugged the curtains aside, allowing the outside light to flare into the room. Andrew squinted around the space as he perched on the edge of the desk, the sharp corner

141

digging into his thigh. At the end of the bed, a wardrobe was built into the wall, stray arms of clothing poking out from the sides as a black curtain hung limply across the front. Instead of posters or pictures around the walls, there was a violet rainbow of drapes and throws pinned to the corners and allowed to hang, like an Arabian brothel.

Or at least the ones Andrew had seen in the movies.

Lara had shrunk into a collection of bony arms and legs, her elbows pointing out, knees angled in.

'Well?' she demanded.

'It's pretty much as I said on the phone last night,' Andrew replied. 'Nicholas's parents have asked me to see if I can find out what happened to their son.'

'What can you do that the police can't?'

'I won't know that until I've started talking to people and looking into things.'

'Why did he hire you?'

'I'm not sure.'

'There must be a reason he came to you instead of someone else?'

'You'd have to ask him.'

'How much are you getting paid?'

'I don't think that's the type of thing I should discuss.'

Lara flicked her long hair behind her shoulder, showing off a row of shiny black fingernails. 'Who have you spoken to so far?'

'A few people.'

'What are you hoping to find out?'

'Exactly what I said. I'm trying to figure out what happened to Nicholas.'

'You know he's dead, don't you?' Lara peered from Andrew to Jenny, face stony and serious. 'They found his fingers in the woods. The rest of him will be there somewhere too.'

Andrew bit his lip, waiting to see if she'd add anything. Instead, Lara stared at her feet.

'How do you know he's dead?' Andrew asked.

'Everyone *knows* he's dead.'

'Who's "everyone"?'

'It was in the papers, on the news. We held a service at college. Everyone's moved on.'

'His parents haven't.'

Lara sucked in her cheeks, making herself seem even thinner. For a few moments she was quiet and it felt colder, as if she was pulling the air from the room. When she replied, her voice was slightly softer and quieter. 'Everyone thinks I'm a suicide waiting to happen.'

Andrew was thinking of something sensible to say but Jenny got in first. 'Are you?'

She didn't sound provocative, more interested. Lara turned to stare at her, face creased into a frown. 'Of course I'm bloody not. Why would you even ask?'

On some occasions, Jenny was the perfect person for Andrew to have by his side. She'd most likely got something useful from the male Alex to share later but she seemed lost here.

Andrew cut in before the young women antagonised each other too much. 'How long had you been seeing Nicholas for?'

Lara dragged her eyes across Jenny before turning back to Andrew. 'It would've been two years this month.'

That meant she'd been seeing him for a year and three months when Nicholas went missing, but the fact she knew it was two years was of more interest. He clearly wasn't a lost memory, whatever she was trying to make them think.

'Can you tell us about the night he went missing?'

Lara drew her knees into her chest, sitting on the chair with her feet off the floor. 'Don't you already know?'

'It'd be better to hear your version.'

'*Version?*'

'Sorry, a poor choice of words. I just meant that you were there, the last person to see him. You know what happened better than anyone.'

Lara half-turned to stare out of the window. The overcast light danced across her face, making her skin seem even paler, hair even blacker. The eye-shadow had cracked around the top of her eyelids, with natural creamy skin eating into the darkness.

'I've told so many people so many times . . . we were at the Night And Day for Nicholas's eighteenth. He'd been saying his stomach hurt, so we left at about nine. We walked to the bottom of the road for a taxi but there were none around. I said we should wait but Nicholas thought he could walk off whatever was wrong with him so we kept on going to my house. We walked that way all the time.'

'Where did you live at the time?'

'Cheetham Hill way, straight up the main road.'

'But now you live in halls?'

Lara shrugged. 'So what?'

It was a question too far. Andrew was supposed to be talking about Nicholas, not sticking his nose into her living arrangements. It was a bit odd, though, given that commuting to university from a few miles away wouldn't have been that awkward. Perhaps she wanted the student 'experience' of halls?

He moved on as if it hadn't happened. 'So Nicholas said goodnight to you at Cheetham Hill, then set off to continue on towards Prestwich. That's, what, two or three miles?'

'If you already know, why ask?'

'What was the weather like?'

Lara finally let her knees go, putting her feet flat on the floor again. 'What?'

Andrew repeated his question, knowing she didn't understand why he was asking. The truth was people *always* remembered the weather. If something happened in their lives, good or bad, they'd associate it with how hot or cold it was, whether they were wet or dry, and so on. She should have been able to answer immediately and, once she'd pouted her way through trying to figure out why he was asking, she did.

'It was a bit strange – thunder and lightning but no rain.'

At least that matched what Scott had said.

'After he left you, did you ever get any emails, text messages, calls, anything like that?'

'Nothing.'

'And when did you find out he was missing?'

'I was the one who reported him. When I realised he wasn't answering my calls and none of his friends had seen him, I called the police. They said it had to be twenty-four hours and all that.'

Jenny was shuffling restlessly on the bed, probably feeling left out.

Andrew spoke quickly, just in case she was thinking about saying anything. 'I've heard you and Nicky used to argue . . .'

If the daggers Lara glared were real, Andrew would have been pinned to the wall. 'His name was Nicholas.'

'But the two of you used to argue . . . ?'

'Who told you that?'

'A few people.'

Lara slapped her hand on the desk, top lip flaring. 'It's that Scott, isn't it? Or Kingy? So what if we fell out once or twice? All couples do. What's wrong with that?'

'Nothing.'

'Exactly.'

'Did anything ever get further out of hand?'

Lara hunched forward aggressively, flicking a finger at Andrew. People seemed to like doing that. 'Are you asking if he ever hit me? Because he didn't and if anyone's told you that, then they're lying.'

Andrew was also wondering if *she'd* ever hit Nicholas but there was little point in antagonising her further. Not that it took much to annoy her.

Lara started tugging at her hair, pulling it straighter. 'What do you think happened?'

'I don't know.'

'But you must have some thoughts?'

'I think Nicholas disappeared and somehow lost three

fingers. I think the police believe he's dead but don't have the time or resources to find out for sure. I think his mum and dad would like some closure about what happened so they can carry on with their lives.'

Andrew saw the hostility drain out of her as her shoulders slumped. Her voice was a whisper. 'I really did love him.'

'I heard that too.'

Lara glanced up, teary blobs in the corners of her eyes. She huffed in a breath, seemingly relieved to know that people had said that about her.

Andrew pushed himself up from the desk, ready to leave. He sensed that if he was going to get anything more from her, then it would have to be another time. A jagged pain rippled through his legs from the desk corner that had been pressing into him.

'What did the police say to you?' he asked.

'Not much. They spoke to me a few times, usually asking the same questions, then they went away.'

Lara and Jenny stood in unison, each trying to occupy the same space of floor. Jenny flopped back onto the bed with a giggle, reaching up towards Lara's sleeve in one seamless movement.

'Oh, this is lovely material.'

Before Lara could pull away, Jenny slipped the other woman's sleeve up. Lara slapped her away, angrily yanking her top back down but the damage had already been done. Etched onto her wrist was a raw-looking red circle with a triangle inside.

17

Andrew drummed his fingers on the top of the steering wheel, a bad habit that annoyed even him. The traffic was backing up from the city centre towards Salford, with the lunchtime crowd hurrying into various sandwich shops and fast-food places for a middle-of-the-day spot of indigestion. It wasn't raining but the sullen wash of grey above had that thinking-about-it look.

'You really shouldn't have done that,' Andrew said.

Jenny was biting her nails in the passenger seat. 'You can't say you weren't interested.'

'I *was* interested but that doesn't mean you should just yank her sleeve up.'

'Pfft.'

They were going to have to have a conversation about Jenny's use of that exhalation to end conversations. Not today though.

She buzzed the window down and launched a chewed nail out into the ether. 'It looked like one of those ones you do with a compass at school,' Jenny continued. 'There was no ink in it, but her skin had been scraped away. It didn't look recent.'

'Scott said the one on Nicholas's wrist looked like that. Why would you do that to yourself?'

'Someone I used to go to school with used a pair of

scissors to scratch the name "Keith" into her arm. He dumped her three weeks later.'

'I guess nothing says "I love you" quite like slicing your own flesh open.'

'I prefer chocolate – or biscuits. But you're probably right, matching homemade tattoos could be romantic. Not *those* tattoos but something else.'

Andrew fiddled with the heaters of the rented car, trying to figure out how to make warm air come out. It was colder than usual today, with the city cowering under the onslaught. Jenny batted his hands away, pressing a sequence of buttons until a hushed surge of warm air began spilling from the vents.

Cars edged forward as pedestrians scuttled between, arms thrust out with cardboard-wrapped hot drinks. Somewhere behind, there were raised voices and honked horns.

Andrew continued drumming his fingers. 'Did you catch that Lara said she was the one who reported Nicholas missing, not the parents?'

'I thought that was a bit weird. Wouldn't they have noticed he didn't go home?'

'Probably – but he might have stopped out a lot. I was just surprised they didn't tell us that.'

'Her story about the night he went missing was the same as everyone else's, wasn't it?'

Andrew squished his lips together, thinking. 'Did it sound rehearsed to you?'

'How do you mean?'

'I don't know. It's just that they all say exactly the

same. There are nearly always inconsistencies. Someone says they left at nine, someone else at half nine. Someone thinks it's warm, someone else that it's cold. People's memories aren't perfect but here, they all back each other up.'

'Perhaps it's because they've been asked about it so much? In some ways it *is* rehearsed.'

'You're probably right. But why not get a taxi if the weather was so strange? I think I remember the night myself – I was watching the storm rumble around the city, thinking I wouldn't want to be out in it.'

Jenny was biting her nails again but stopped to reply. 'You're forgetting what it's like to be eighteen. If they'd been out since late afternoon, chances are they were either running out of money, or already out. Plus she said there were no taxis at the end of the road.'

'They could have called for a lift.'

'You don't want to do that when you're young. You want to explore, to walk. They might've sneaked off to some park somewhere for a bit of fun. What were you like at eighteen?'

Still a virgin.

Andrew moved on quickly. 'She's been through a lot, too. I keep forgetting that. Because his parents came to us, it feels easier to see things from their side, but she'll be hurting too.'

'Of course, if it *was* anything to do with her, reporting him missing would be the thing to do to get attention away from yourself. Except for Lara, no one saw him after he left the pub.'

The traffic surged ahead all at once as whatever had been holding them up apparently disappeared. Jenny was fiddling with the radio, settling on something that sounded like a cat being strangled.

Andrew glanced sideways at her as the window fizzed down and another fingernail disappeared.

'Do you remember the first thing I told you when I hired you?'

'That the toilet was the first door on the left?'

'Okay, the second thing: that you didn't have to do those stupid honeytrap things. I was never going to ask you to go out and trap cheating blokes.'

'I remember.'

'I'd never expect you to have to do the flirty, girly thing, like with Alex at the flat.'

Jenny wrapped a strand of hair around her finger. 'It's fine.'

Conscience clear, Andrew moved on. 'So, how did you get on with the other Alex?'

'Oh, he tried it on, at least for the first minute or two. I said I wanted to chat about Lara and he started stroking my arm, then got dressed in front of me—'

'Oh . . . sorry.'

'I've seen it all before. Anyway, he told me about some incident with Lara getting upset at a Harry Potter movie, telling them all that magic was real.'

'I heard that too.'

'That's it really. It was hard to get him to talk about anything apart from the other Alex who lives there. They've got a massive love-hate thing going on. She keeps accusing him of stealing and moving her stuff, he says she's doing it herself to try to get his attention. It's like some bizarre mating call – they should just do it and get it over with.'

Andrew pulled onto the street where his office was located, ready to accelerate towards the much-prized parking space. Jenny spotted it moments before him, pointing unnecessarily. Andrew pressed the footbrake, stopping in the middle of the lane, not bothering to check if there was a car behind.

His office's front door was double-glazed, white plastic with rippled glass at the top. The type of thing used by tens of thousands of houses around the country.

What now set it apart were the markings on the bottom panel: a crudely drawn circle with an upside-down triangle inside.

18

The symbol had been drawn in scuffed dark charcoal, the circle slightly oval-shaped, with a fatter bottom half. The triangle had slightly wavy lines, as if it had taken two or three attempts to get the markings close to straight.

On a wet day, it would have already been washed away.

Neither Andrew nor Jenny had been to the office that morning, so it could have been drawn at any time since they left the previous evening.

'Are you going to be okay by yourself here?' Andrew asked.

Jenny nudged him with her shoulder, dimple on show. 'Why wouldn't I be?'

Andrew watched her unlock the office, hovering by her shoulder in case there was something nasty waiting inside. She looked both ways, sniffed the air and then crouched to pick up the United Utilities bill. That was foul enough in itself, but definitely not enough to worry Jenny. She tucked it into her belt, tapped the alarm code into the wall, and then turned, beaming. 'All done.'

'You're definitely going to be all right?'

'Of course.'

Andrew pulled the front door closed, taking in the symbol one more time. He took a photograph of it on his phone and then scuffed the markings away with his palm, leaving a smudgy, dusky smear across the white. If someone was trying to intimidate him, they were going the right way about it. Jenny was definitely calmer about things than he was.

He crossed the street, accidentally sending a loose stone fizzing across the concrete and clattering into a wall with a solid *thwick*. Andrew stood outside a set of glass double doors, tapping gently on the front until the woman at the back of the wide reception area noticed him. She smiled and pressed a button on the desk, making the doors open.

'Can't let any old reprobate in,' she said with a smile as Andrew stepped inside.

The building opposite Andrew's office housed a collection of agencies on different floors. The receptionist had dark blonde hair that was wrenched into a ponytail. Even though she was looking directly at Andrew, her fingernails click-clacked expertly across her keyboard.

'Morning, Tina.'

'Afternoon actually.'

'Sorry, yes—'

'Oh don't worry, hon. If it wasn't for my giant planner, I'd forget what day of the week it was.'

Tina nodded at an enormous grid pinned to the wall behind her. Above it was a list of floors and occupying companies.

'Have you been on all day?'

'Since eight but I'm off tomorrow for a long weekend. Other half's been banging on about getting away for a few days but you can't guarantee the weather, can you?'

Andrew nodded back towards his office's front door,

clearly visible through the glass front. 'Did you see the circle on my door earlier?'

Tina's fingers continued flying across the keys but her eyes didn't leave Andrew. 'Some triangle thing? Is that a new logo you're trying out?'

'Not exactly.'

'Oh, just the local shites, is it? Remember the other month when they spray-painted the c-word on our doors? Course, the police don't do anything – didn't even come out.'

'Did you notice if it was there first thing?'

The tip-tapping halted, Tina's fingers poised over the keys as she sucked on her bottom lip. 'I think so. I assumed you'd had it done last night.'

'Did you see anyone out there?'

'No, hon. I'd have called you or the police if anyone was messing around. What's going on?'

Andrew turned to leave. 'I wish I knew.'

A group of kids bounced down the stairs of Affleck's, falling onto the pavement in a squirrelled collection of giggles as Andrew hurried past, hands in pockets. They massed underneath the '. . . And on the sixth day, God created Manchester' sign, arguing over who had whose fags.

The building was full of tiny stalls selling vintage and customised clothes, old-fashioned sweets, vinyl records, band T-shirts and any number of other things youths might want to buy in the name of looking exactly like everyone else. The girl at the front eyed Andrew suspiciously:

Converse trainers, torn tights, mini-skirt, a black sweat-shirt with a cannabis leaf on the front, long black hair and a trowel-load of make-up.

'What you looking at, paedo?'

Andrew ignored her. For a second, he'd thought it was Lara but the girl was younger, struggling to look eighteen even under the make-up. Weren't they supposed to be at school?

Her boyfriend was wearing shorts – in November – with spiky orange hair making him look a little like a carrot. 'Paedo alert.'

The howls of laughter caught the breeze as Andrew bounded along, embarrassed. A woman was crossing the road with a pushchair. She glanced nervously over her shoulder towards him, rushing ahead to make sure the kiddy-fiddler didn't get anywhere near her child.

Andrew continued across the junction, heading into the warren of alleys and ginnels that made up Manchester's Northern Quarter. The area was chock full of independent shops, cafes, pubs and galleries: an artistic flair brought to the huge city, let down only by the giant wheelie bins left on the cobbled cut-throughs, masking the area's homeless community.

A couple were standing outside a tattooist's shop, peering at the images in the window, smiling and speaking too loudly.

'. . . you should definitely get the dragon on your back . . .'

She bloody shouldn't, unless he was using some sort of euphemism.

Andrew zigzagged his way through the area until he reached what was essentially a garage. The rollback door had been hoiked up, revealing an emporium of books and papers stacked floor to ceiling. A grubby awning hung over the pavement, covering paperback-filled boxes with 'Two for £1' scribbled in felt-tip on the front. On the side of the wall, 'Scrumpy's Antiquarian Bookshop Est: 1980' had been engraved in the stone.

Trying not to kick anything over, Andrew edged around a table piled high with issues of *Enthusiastic Camper* magazine, which sounded niche to say the least. From the rear of the stall, the barely audible sounds of a man's voice crackled from a radio.

Andrew made his way to the back of the shop, where he found a bundle of hair sitting behind a heavy wooden table. The surface was covered with more magazines and books, towering precariously towards the ceiling, one good gust of wind away from burying the man. Hidden behind the books was an old-fashioned cash register with a pull-down lever on the side.

'Afternoon, Scrumpy.'

The man's face was barely visible through an overgrown white beard that stretched to his chest and a floppy fringe hanging around his eyes. He was wearing a blue velvet dressing gown, which flapped open as his knees crossed, exposing a pair of hair-covered legs that wouldn't have been out of place on an aged chimpanzee.

Scrumpy slipped a pair of glasses from the end of his nose, face breaking into a smile. 'Andrew, m'dear boy, it's been months since I last saw you.'

He pronounced the 'th' of 'months' like the letter 'f'. His accent couldn't have been more West Country if he'd been sitting on a hay bale with straw between his teeth and a jug of brown sludgy cider in his hand.

'How's business?' Andrew asked.

'Shite. You?'

'Not too bad.' Andrew nodded towards the radio on the shelf behind. 'What about the cricket?'

'Getting our arses battered in Sri Lanka. We're ninety-odd for six.'

Andrew wasn't entirely sure what that meant but cricket was always a good way in. He took his phone out of his pocket and brought up the photograph of the symbol on his office door. He handed it across. 'Any idea what that means?'

'You not got the Internet?'

'I figured it was better talking to someone who knew what they were on about.'

Scrumpy bounced back in his chair, uncrossing his knees and howling with laughter. 'Right you are.' He hopped up, squeezing his ample arse around the side of his desk and setting the stack of books wobbling. Andrew pressed into a nook, allowing the shop owner to pass and then following him along the aisle towards the front. Scrumpy pulled out a small set of steps from underneath a bookcase and then edged slowly towards the top. Andrew wasn't sure if the creaks were coming from the rotting wood, or Scrumpy's ancient joints. Probably both.

''Ere y'are.'

Scrumpy dropped a thick hardback down into Andrew's

waiting arms, sending a puff of dust into the air. As Andrew gasped for breath, Scrumpy groaned his way down the steps and nudged them under the counter with his knee.

Back at the desk, he shunted the pile of magazines aside with the dexterity of a seasoned professional, not even making the ones at the top wobble. Andrew put the book down on the newly cleared spot, sending a second dust cloud into the atmosphere.

Scrumpy grunted a word that sounded suspiciously like: 'Arse.'

'Sorry?'

He nodded towards the radio. 'Seven down now. Useless lot.' With a heft of the cover, Scrumpy began hunting through the pages, talking as he did so. 'Have you heard of the lizard people?'

'No.'

'Some nutters reckon we're ruled by something they call the illuminati: giant lizard people in human form. Recently, your symbol's been associated with them, but . . .' Scrumpy stepped back from the book, pointing at the open page. '. . . traditionally it's associated with the occult.'

Andrew peered down at the page of the book, which showed a collection of symbols: pentagrams, upside-down crosses, and other odds and ends. The one that interested him was the triangle in a circle, exactly like the tattoos on Nicholas and Lara's wrists and the charcoal markings on his door.

Scrumpy plumped back into his seat. 'Those are all

symbols of evil through the ages. Most of them are associated with witchcraft or sorcery: burnings, spells, curses, that sort of thing. Dangerous business to mix yourself up in.'

Andrew peered up at him. 'Honestly?'

Scrumpy howled with laughter again. 'Is it buggery. All mumbo-jumbo, made-up bollocks. It's all the films nowadays, of course. In my day if you told a girl you wanted to drink her blood and suck on her neck, they'd lock you up. Now they think you're the new Casanova.'

Andrew started flicking through the pages. It was like the one he'd taken from Nicholas's house but longer and far more in-depth.

'Do you get much demand for this kind of thing?'

'Not really – mainly confused teenagers. They see all these witch- and vampire-types on the telly and think they'd like to know more about magic. They don't realise it's just a bunch of symbols, words, and nonsense. The minute they see a bit of Latin, they realise it ain't all pixies, fairies and shagging each other. You get a couple of the old loons coming in too, but it's all on the Internet nowadays, like everything.'

'Any idea where I can find out more about your old loons?'

'You tried the yella pages?'

'*Almost e*verything's on the Internet nowadays.'

Scrumpy grinned upwards, stroking his beard and sending flecks of dried skin tumbling onto his lap. He reached under his desk and wrestled out a large leather-bound volume which he plopped on top of the magic book. The wood of the desk creaked, the magazine tower wobbling but not toppling. He started flitting through the pages, muttering under his breath. Andrew pressed forward, trying to read the contents upside down. Each page was filled with names, addresses and numbers, the spidery calligraphy almost impossible to understand even if it was the right way up.

'Blimey, there are some old names in 'ere.' Scrumpy paused, jabbing a thumb at an entry towards the top of the page. His knuckles had sprouts of wiry hair erupting in all directions. 'This bloke used to buy pornos off me. Course, they called it artistic back then.' Another name: 'He were into model-train collecting – used to get me hunting down obscure books and magazines. This lad 'ere liked road signs. Mental.'

He continued rummaging through the pages, reminiscing about what could only be described as a 'colourful' cast of customers. Who would have thought there was a magazine dedicated to barbed wire?

Scrumpy ran his eye along a row of the page, hairy finger tapping enthusiastically. ''Ere's yer man.' Andrew leant in to look but the shop owner clamped the pages closed. 'My old handwriting's bloody awful. So are my eyes. Such a shame it's hard to make out.'

Andrew dug into his pockets with a knowing sigh. He plucked a twenty-pound note from his wallet and placed it on the table. 'Will that help?'

Scrumpy's mass of facial hair crept upwards into a smile. 'Maybe a little.'

Another twenty-pound note.

'Aye, that'll probably do it.' He didn't bother reopening the book. 'You want to talk to someone named Kristian Verity. He's been coming in for years, seeing if I can get him stuff from the book fairs. eBay can only get you so far and I go out to Europe for various trade shows. He's always in the market for rare magic books – and not ones that teach you card tricks, if you get my drift.'

'How often does he come in?'

'Once or twice a year for ages, since he was a teenager.'

'How old is he now?'

'Mid-thirties? Forties? I dunno. He always pays cash so I haven't got anything else for you.'

Andrew stood to leave but Scrumpy wasn't finished.

'Oi! You didn't get his name from me – *comprendez*?'

Andrew held back a smile at Scrumpy's raw accent. 'Gotcha.'

19

Andrew tugged up the collar on his jacket and checked his watch. Somehow, it was already after five. The day had disappeared in a silvery gloom, punctuated by goth girls. He called the office, knowing Jenny would still be there.

Her answer was upbeat and chirpy. 'Hello.'

'Why haven't you gone home yet?'

'I'm busy.'

'So be busy on Monday . . .' He paused for a moment, walking and thinking. That's what you call multi-tasking. 'Have you got anything on tomorrow?'

'Dunno. I'll probably get roped into going out and doing something.'

'Do you want some extra money?'

'Maybe.'

'I've got a name I could do with you looking into. If I text it over, can you do your thing?'

'Definitely. It'll save me pretending to be interested in what other people want to do.'

'You'd rather be at work?'

'Wouldn't you?'

Andrew wasn't sure. There were a lot of things he'd rather be doing than working but none of them popped into his mind. 'Okay, well, it's up to you. I'll probably be in too.'

'Great.'

'But go home now. I'm walking back – I'll be ten minutes.'

'Fine.'

Jenny's apparent relationship was something he never pushed to know about. Andrew wasn't sure she'd ever told him her boyfriend's name, only making vague references to 'him' or, occasionally, 'my boyfriend'. He didn't bother to ask if this was the same lad she'd mentioned a couple of days before. What was clear was that, whoever he was, she didn't seem that into him, always complaining about the time she had to spend with him, rather than wanting to hurry off to enjoy something. He also didn't know anything that she actually liked doing. Some people would talk about bands they liked, gigs they'd been to, what they'd seen at the cinema, television programmes they watched, pubs and restaurants they'd visited, hobbies they had. Never Jenny.

The teenagers had disappeared from the front of Affleck's by the time Andrew passed by again, replaced by an enormous man squeezed into leather-studded lederhosen, with a matching cap. He nodded politely at Andrew and grunted a 'y'all right?' for good measure. It really was quite the area.

Late-running office workers skirted around the already packed tram stops, spilling onto the pavements and causing a bottleneck of annoyed shoppers laden with bags trying to squeeze their way through. It was depressingly dark, an all too familiar chilled wind blasting its way through the streets.

At the bottom of Piccadilly Gardens, there was an L-shape of outdoor food stalls that looked as if they might take off at any moment. People were queuing for Caribbean food, fivers in hand, oblivious that the only similarity between here and the West Indies was when a hurricane blew in from the tropics, wiping out all of the power and dumping an ocean-load of water on the islands.

The jerk chicken still smelled good though.

Andrew kept his head down, walking until the crowds thinned and he was close to the office. He turned the corner to see the lights were out, with Jenny either sitting in the dark, or heading home. Hopefully the latter, although he wouldn't be surprised by the former. He walked along the street, keeping tight to the wall before spotting a silhouette of a man leaning against the doorframe of the office. The nearby orange street light was close to useless, casting a pathetic tangerine hue directly underneath but nothing that could pierce the shadows.

The figure checked his watch and then looked both ways as Andrew slowed his pace, trying to figure out who it was before he got too close. It was the white glow from the man's watch that finally revealed his features: the hair thinning at the front and a little long at the back.

Andrew upped his pace again, taking the man by surprise as he thrust out a right hand. 'Mr Carr, you're lucky to have caught me.'

The man stepped back slightly, before shaking hands. 'It's Richard. I was in the city and wondered if you might be in. I was only going to give it another five minutes.'

The dark didn't suit Richard Carr. He looked like a

lumbering cinema version of Frankenstein's Monster, wide white eyes catching what little light there was.

'Can I help you?' Andrew asked.

'I was wondering how things were going . . .'

Andrew was used to this. With the police, people would give them time – they knew what they were doing after all. If you worked privately, you were somehow expected to get faster results with fewer resources. Tactfully telling someone he'd discovered sod-all was something Andrew was good at.

'Well, it's only been a few days, plus, as I said at the time, we do have a few things on. I prefer to start a case from scratch where I can, rather than rely on old reports and the like, so that takes time.'

He rocked back on his heels, waiting for the awkward question about the bill, but it never came. Instead, Richard exhaled loudly, using a finger and thumb to dab at his eyes. 'It's Elaine. I think she thought things might happen quickly now you were on the scene.'

'I'm sorry. It doesn't really work like that.'

'I know, I did say – but it's so hard to move on.'

Andrew rested a hand on the man's shoulder. 'All I can tell you is that I'm doing my best.'

A sorry-sounding sniff: 'I know you are.'

After retrieving his laptop from the office, Andrew walked back across the city towards his apartment. Beetham Tower was the tallest building in the north of England: a cathedral of glass and steel soaring into the night sky, red and green lights blinking high above as a warning to the jumbo jets that they were dangerously off course.

The wind was wrapping around the tower, tooting like a steam train. The reception area was quiet, with the security officer allegedly there at all times nowhere to be seen. Andrew caught the lift up to his floor near the top and let himself into his apartment, stopping momentarily inside the door to gaze through the floor-to-ceiling window across the marvel of the city.

Far below, streetlights and cars were alight, jagged collections of roads and queuing traffic, coupled with the barely visible ant-like dots of people. It might not be London or New York but there was a certain beauty to the mismatched assortment of buildings stretching into the distance. London had its architecture, history and towers; New York had its straight lines, bright lights and soaring skyscrapers. Manchester had a bit of everything: shades of industry long gone, waterways upon which locals claimed the western world was built, and people from every social class imaginable.

Andrew closed the door and moved into the apartment without turning on the lights, his heavy shoes rattling on the wooden floor. The view was extraordinary during the daytime, sweeping vistas of green far beyond the city lights, but there was something special about it at night. He'd never told anyone how much he'd paid for the flat but the estate agent's eyes had almost popped out when Andrew said he would pay the full amount outright.

He put the laptop down on the coffee table, thought about working, and then quickly discounted it. Whoever Kristian Verity was, he could wait until morning, and Jenny would do a better job of finding out who he was anyway. Andrew thought about watching television but wasn't in the mood. The mini gym in the corner sat in his eye line, unused, but he didn't fancy that either, nor the actual residents' gym on the lower floor.

What did people usually do when they weren't working?

Acting instinctively, he moved through to the bedroom, which he'd left exactly as it had been when he bought it. A double bed was pushed against the wall furthest from the window, with a built-in wardrobe that ran the length of the room. Aside from a lamp, the rest of the floor was clear of clutter, moonlight glinting from the varnished wood finish.

Andrew slid open the mirrored wardrobe doors, pulled out the first shirt he found, grabbed a jacket and then headed back towards the lift.

A couple of hours later and Manchester's nightlife had warmed up from non-existent to something that wasn't quite lukewarm. Andrew almost always went to the same place, a cross between a pub and a wine bar on a street parallel to Deansgate in the centre of the city. The high ceiling was held up by huge rounded pillars, providing spots for patrons to lean against, or alternatively walk into if they'd had too much to drink. Placed at intervals around the walls were crescents of seats, with 'reserved' cards planted around. Either the rich and famous of Manchester were about to take a wrong turn, or a hen party would be in later. Andrew knew where his money lay.

The bar was bent into a dogleg, flutes and glasses

hanging around the entire length, just waiting for someone to send one flying and set off a chain reaction. Andrew was sitting on a stool at the far end with a view of the entire room. Somewhere in the centre, a man with a porn-star moustache was flashing his crooked yellow teeth at a girl half his age. She was wearing a sprayed-on white mini-skirt, cradling a matching handbag, with heels on which only a skilled stilt-walker would attempt to get around. She flicked her viciously blow-dried black hair backwards, offered two short words in response and then tottered towards the bar with her mate. In the background, strains of Michael Bolton gurgled through the speakers.

It wasn't usually this bad.

Andrew turned back to his drink, Jack Daniel's and Coke – actual Coke, none of this Zero or Diet nonsense. He held the glass to his mouth, struggling to smell the alcohol but taking a swig anyway.

In the centre of the bar, the barman instantly had the two women laughing, much to the annoyance of the man with the dodgy moustache, who was angrily supping his pint of cloudy ale while staring at them.

From nowhere, there was an unexpected shuffling and somebody was sitting next to Andrew, appearing from either thin air, or the women's toilets.

Andrew turned to see a flash of blonde hair and pale skin. A woman, a little younger than him, had slipped herself onto the adjacent stool and was staring towards the barman serving the other girls. Andrew rarely saw women like her in this place and there was no one else within five metres of them.

'Wanna buy me a drink?'

Her voice was low and husky, like a 1930s movie star but with a slight northern twang that dispelled the image.

Andrew had a second, more careful glance sideways but definitely didn't know her. As well as the slightly wavy blonde hair and pale skin, she had intense blue eyes and a cute rounded chin that perfectly fitted her face. She wasn't stunning but she was certainly attractive – out of his league before he even got to the clingy red dress.

'What do you want?'

'Apple martini.'

The barman was leaning on one of the pump handles, trying his best smile on the girls: all white teeth, designer stubble and sparkly earring. He glanced sideways, catching Andrew's raised finger and whispering an apology to the girls, which drew a fluttering of giggles. He swaggered across, undoing a button on his shirt to allow more dark chest hair to spurt from the top. Behind him, the girl with the white skirt heaved her breasts up until they were almost popping out of her top. Wasn't this how chickens mated? All puffed-out chests and posturing?

The barman twirled a glass around in his hand, eyeing the blonde woman but talking to Andrew. 'What can I get you, squire?'

Squire? Andrew hated him already.

'Another Jack and Coke, plus an apple martini.'

The man flipped the glass from one hand to the other and caught it in mid-air, before pointing a finger in Andrew's direction and making a double clicking noise with his tongue. 'Good choice.'

If anyone deserved the nickname 'dickface' . . .

The barman sauntered back towards the centre of the bar with a mixture of sidesteps and spins, as if someone had set him on fire but without all the screaming.

The blonde woman tutted in annoyance. 'There are not enough words in the English language to describe the contempt I have for that man.'

Andrew sniggered. 'It's normally better in here.'

'Do you come in often?'

'Every now and then.'

She held out her hand, long slender fingers with perfectly manicured nails. 'Courtney.'

He shook it, forcing himself not to shiver as her cool fingers brushed his. 'Andrew.'

'Pleased to meet you.'

Andrew had just enough time to mutter a 'you too' before the barman returned with their drinks. Getting change from a tenner was going to be unlikely. The barman moved back to the girls in the centre of the bar, gurning like he'd just been electrocuted.

Courtney had a sip of her drink, leaving a pinkish-red lipstick mark on the glass. 'And what do you do, Andrew?'

'I watch people for a living.' Stupid answer. 'Not like that,' he added hastily.

She giggled, cradling the stem of the glass between her thumb and forefinger, twiddling it gently until the liquid began to ripple. 'Is that why you come to bars by yourself?'

'Sometimes.'

'Go on then, tell me something about the people here.'

Andrew sipped his drink. The alcohol was stronger this

time, drifting through his nostrils and giving him an ever-so-slightly dizzy feeling before he'd even tasted it. He scanned the largely empty room. Porn-star man was still in the middle, leaning against a pillar, empty pint glass in hand. In the corner, close to the door, a young woman had her knees draped across her boyfriend's lap and her tongue down his throat, while a bouncer watched on from the doorway. Three student-types were eating piled-high burgers in one of the booths; drained, frothy pint glasses massed in the centre, with at least four for each of them. One dropped a pickle on his lap without realising.

Then he saw his couple.

Andrew nodded towards the pair in the centre of three booths on the far side of the room. 'See them?'

'Yep.'

'She's far more into him than he is into her.'

'How do you know?'

The couple were on opposite sides of the table; she was wearing denim cut-offs over the top of dark tights with a low-cut top. He had a too-big shirt, jeans and a chunky silver chain around his neck.

'For a start, every time she says something, he replies with a much shorter response.'

'What does that show?'

'Watch.'

The man picked up his pint glass, took a large mouthful and then plonked it back on the table, staring sideways towards Sky Sports News on the big-screen television. Moments later, his partner had a small sip of her wine, before putting the glass back down.

'Did you see how he picked his glass up from the left side of the table as he was looking but put it down on the right? When she picked hers up, she put it down on the same side as his. It's called mirroring.' Andrew had known all about it long before Jenny tried to pull him up on it in the car. 'Look at his phone too. It's on the table but right next to his hand. If it rings or he gets a text, he can grab it straight away. There's no way he wants her looking at it first. It's all subconscious.'

Andrew continued watching the couple. It was largely guesswork, albeit educated. He felt a tugging on his sleeve and turned to see Courtney pouting at him, eyes twinkling. 'What about me?'

He laughed nervously, trying to escape her stare. 'I'm not naïve.'

'Have you got a place?'

'I've got an apartment in Beetham Tower.'

'How high?'

'Near the top.'

'Impressive.' She paused for another, larger, sip of her martini. 'So what do you say?'

Andrew downed the rest of his drink in one, swilling the alcohol in his mouth and feeling the Coke stick to his teeth. When he swallowed, he felt slightly light-headed. 'How much?'

'One fifty an hour or five hundred the night.'

Behind him, the girls in the centre of the bar were cackling again. Andrew stood and plucked his jacket up. 'Let's go.'

20

Typically, the security guard at the bottom of the tower was back on duty. Andrew ignored the knowing look as Courtney clung onto his arm and they headed for the lifts.

Inside, the journey was slightly more exciting than it usually was and by the time it sizzled up to his floor, Andrew's top lip had practically been chewed off. Courtney smudged a lipstick mark away from his face with her finger, pressing her body into his and rubbing her knee into the inside of his thigh.

Ping!

She leant in, husky breaths dancing across Andrew's ear. 'We could just use the lift all night if you want?'

'Er . . .'

'Or you can show me your apartment?'

'Okay.'

It was easier to talk with single words.

She clasped Andrew's hand as he led her along the corridor, half-hoping the other residents would actually come out of their flats to see the sight but really hoping they didn't. He fumbled in his jacket pocket for the keys, dropping first his coat on the floor, then the keys. Courtney ran a claw along the small of his back, digging her nails in just enough to make Andrew's entire body shiver.

Inside and she strode past him, heels clip-clopping on the hard wooden floor as Andrew closed the door behind them. Courtney stood in front of the huge window, gazing down towards the city as she wiggled her hips slightly, shaking her way out of her jacket until she was wearing just her dress, shoes and whatever might be underneath.

Andrew's mouth suddenly felt dry. He tried to speak but his tongue was stuck to the top of his mouth. 'Mmmf gdrm drrrink.'

Courtney turned, one hand on her hip, looking anything but a little teapot. She tossed her hair back, thrusting her chest forward. 'Sorry?'

'Do you want a drink?'

'I'll have whatever you're having.'

Andrew dragged his eyes away from her, heading for the kitchen. The glow from the fridge provided a cooling respite, although barely calming Andrew's pounding heart.

This was not the type of thing he usually did.

He poured himself a glass of water from the filter jug, dampening his mouth before carrying two glasses through to the living room. Courtney was still standing close to the window watching the city breathe, but now she was naked except for a pair of heels, dress ruffled on the floor next to her.

She turned and took the glass, sipping the icy water. Her mischievous eyes didn't leave his, before she carefully placed the glass on the small side table.

The sentence purred from her lips. 'Is there anything you'd particularly like to do? I'm not really shockable.'

Andrew tried to hide unsuccessfully behind the glass

and water. That was the problem with transparent things. He took another sip and put down his glass as Courtney click-clacked across the floor towards him.

'Just, er, normal things, I suppose.'

Her lips curved into a perfect half-smile. 'You sure?' She stood in front of him, pressing her body into his, and then leant forward and whispered her own ideas in his ear. When she was finished, she took his hand and headed for the bedroom.

Andrew perched on the edge of his bed, staring out towards the city below. In the distance, a fluttering orange glow burned bright on one of the estates. Someone clearly wasn't interested in the fact that Bonfire Night had passed a few weeks ago and was determined to keep the spirit of Guy Fawkes alive. Either that or they wanted to set fire to things. Strobing blue lights glided around the streets close to the blaze: police and fire officers on a normal Friday-night call-out. Andrew wondered if those who had set the fire would be waiting for the authorities, stones and bottles at the ready. He thought about the fires he'd witnessed and the people whose lives had been changed by them.

The bed covers moved and then Courtney was sitting behind him, resting the front of her body against his back. He wanted her to stop but didn't have the heart to say anything.

The husky tone to her voice had gone and she sounded more northern again. 'You really shouldn't worry about it.'

Andrew didn't know how to reply. It had been one of the most embarrassing moments of his life. He wished he

could go back to the bar and say that he wasn't interested.

'I know . . .'

'It happens to everyone at some point.'

That was no comfort.

'I'm sorry for wasting your time.'

Courtney nuzzled the back of his neck, being the
person he wanted her to be. Not exactly what he'd paid for
but close enough. 'Oh honey, you didn't waste my time.'

'It's not you . . .'

She didn't reply, knowing full well it wasn't her who
had the problem. For a while, Courtney simply held him,
arms wrapped around his chest, breasts rubbing against his
back. They watched the flashing blue lights surround the
fire in the distance, shortly before another smoky orange
flash sparked to life a short distance away.

'I hope they're not rioting again.'

Courtney's muffled whisper was perhaps the first honest
thing she'd said all evening and Andrew couldn't disagree.
The news had been full of it for the past month, with
two 'respected businessmen' dead. Everyone knew that was
code for possible crime bosses and Andrew had even seen
his CID friend on the news, scowling at the camera and
pretending she didn't care. It felt as if the underbelly of
the city was changing. Andrew was glad he only had to
skirt around the edges of it all. Other people would be at
the centre, trying to hold things together.

More pulsing blue lights flowed out of the city towards
the fires. Slowly, the pale lights of pubs and apartments
began to switch off as the rest of the centre decided it was

time to go to sleep. Above, the moon tried to fight through the clouds, faint wisps of white seeping through the mist.

Andrew didn't know how long had passed since they'd come into the bedroom. He was enjoying the warmth of her body against his, as if it was natural and something Courtney really wanted to do, as opposed to a service she was providing.

Her whisper flitted across the back of his earlobe. 'What would you like to do?'

'You can go if you want.'

'I don't mind staying. You have a beautiful place here.'

Andrew sank lower on the bed, pressing backwards against her, knowing what he'd had to do to afford the place. 'Perhaps we can just talk?'

'Are you sure?'

'I think so.'

'Well then, honey, I'm all yours until morning. How about you start by telling me what her name is?'

SATURDAY

21

The charcoal flakes were still smudged across the office door as Andrew put his key into the lock, before realising it was open. Inside and up the stairs, Jenny was already there, singing to herself, drinking a cup of tea and typing on her keyboard, all at the same time.

She turned as he entered noisily, laptop clattering into the doorframe.

'What's up?'

Andrew made his way across the room, managing not to bash into anything else as he unhooked the computer satchel and took his jacket off. He was hoping Jenny had stopped staring at him but she was like a bird of prey eyeing its morning meal, those brown eyes searching for answers.

'Who says anything's wrong?'

'I do.'

She might not have known the right thing to say to Lara, but Jenny was a bloody psychic when it came to him. One that hadn't just learned how to cold read and really did know what he was thinking.

Andrew didn't need to reply because she already knew. Jenny spun back to her screen. 'Why don't you just look her up? She shouldn't be that hard to find.'

'What makes you think I don't know where she is?'

Jenny twisted back, fixing him with a stare over the top of her glasses that he couldn't escape. 'So why not get in contact again? It's obvious you want to.'

'Who says it's obvious?'

'I do.'

And there was no arguing with that . . .

Andrew had no idea why he'd ever told Jenny anything about Keira. She still didn't know the half of it but had dragged the information from him like a succubus feeding on its quarry.

'It's not that simple,' he said.

'How hard can it be? Find out where she is, give her a call, say hi and away you go.'

That was love-life advice from someone who never mentioned her boyfriend's actual name.

'I can't.'

'Why not?'

Andrew wasn't sure why he didn't end the conversation but he was wilting under Jenny's gaze. He finally managed to gulp a half-hearted response: 'It was me who broke it off with her.'

Jenny paused, the whites of her eyes illuminated by the overhead bulbs. She started chewing on the end of a pencil. 'Do you want to talk about it?'

She sounded genuine but Andrew finally yanked himself away from her stare. 'Maybe another time?'

Jenny rotated back to her monitor, chewed pencil back on the desk. She rummaged in a box of Jaffa Cakes and pulled one out, nibbling around the sides. 'Do you want to hear about Kristian Verity?'

'Okay.'

She continued snacking until there was only a dark chocolate disc remaining. 'It's a bit of a different name so he didn't take too much tracking down. He's got an appalling credit report, mainly because he's moved around so much. It seems he stops in one place for a year or so, then drops off the radar, then emerges somewhere else.'

'Anything else?'

'Odds and ends. I thought you'd probably want to go and talk to him before I told you too much.'

Andrew reached for his coat again. 'Thanks. You can go home now if you want? I'll pay you for the day.'

Jenny peeled the cake base away from the Jaffa Cake with her tongue and reached for the box. 'I'd rather come with you.'

'Let's go then.'

Andrew hadn't heard from the fire service when he could have his car back, or if it was going to be salvageable, but was gradually becoming used to the hire car.

He turned on the ignition, with the radio blurting to life right in the middle of a weather report promising that another cold front was on the way.

Jenny offered the Jaffa Cake box in his direction. 'Want one?'

'No thank you.'

'Good – more for me.'

Andrew set the sat nav for the most recent address for Kristian Verity: a place out Eccles way which sounded awful, even on paper. The doomsday weather report led into a news item about how many shoppers were expected to be in the city centre that weekend with the advent of the Christmas markets and then it was on to an old Bee Gees number.

Balls to that.

Off went the radio, leaving just the sounds of the purring engine and Jenny's Jaffa Cake-munching.

Andrew cleared his throat, focusing on the road, wondering if he should risk it before finally blurting it out. 'Can I ask you a question?'

Nom, nom, nom. Jenny ate her way around the circumference of a cake. 'If it's about whether Jaffa Cakes are a cake or a biscuit, then they're definitely cakes. If you leave biscuits out, they go soggy. If you leave cakes out, then they go hard. That's how you know the difference – everyone knows that.'

'I didn't want to ask you about cakes.'

She scooped the cakey part away and started picking at the small flecks of dark chocolate. 'Go on then.'

'You're twenty-three, so why aren't you out and about? It's five weeks to Christmas, there's all sorts going on in the centre.'

Jenny licked the circular piece of orange jelly clean – a wonderfully professional job of Jaffa Cake demolition. It really didn't get better than that. Top, top work.

'Pfft.'

'Is it that you particularly like work, or that you don't like other things?'

Jenny popped the remnants of the snack into her

mouth and shrugged. A picture might paint a thousand words but a shrug could dismiss a thousand questions.

'I don't even know your boyfriend's name,' Andrew added. 'We've been working together for months. You just call him "my boyfriend".'

'Do you want to know his name?'

'Not necessarily, that's not what I'm trying to say.'

'You're trying to say that I don't seem to get on well with other people.'

'Yes, well no . . . sort of. Sometimes you do, other times you don't. I'm never quite certain where you're going to fall on things.'

She delved into the box for another cake. 'When I was at school, fourteen, fifteen, something like that, I had this RE teacher. He was pretty much the only teacher I actually liked. I think it was because there were no right or wrong answers – he'd let you argue whatever point you wanted, as long as you could back it up.'

'And you always took the opposite view to the majority?'

She laughed. 'How did you guess? Anyway, he called me back after class one day. I thought he was going to try to kiss me or something, you know the type – stubble, spiky hair, loose shirt and tight trousers, like they've not realised they're supposed to be the authority figure. There's always one at every school and we had about four. I think two of them ended up being suspended for copping off with students. Anyway, he didn't want to do that at all. He sat on the edge of his desk and he goes, "Have you ever heard of Empathy Deficit Disorder?" I thought it was a chat-up line, then I realised he was being serious. He said that when I argued with other people, I never bothered to consider how it would make them feel. He wasn't pushy, or anything, he just said I should go away and think about that.'

'That's quite an intense thing to say to a fifteen-year-old.'

Still, Jenny wasn't like many – or any – young girls her age, so Andrew doubted she had been a regular fifteen-year-old.

Another shrug. The box of Jaffa Cakes disappeared into her rucksack and out came a can of fizzy Vimto. 'Yeah, but he wouldn't have said it if he didn't think I'd understand. He was right, though. When I was walking home, I realised that I really didn't care what other people said or thought about me and I certainly didn't care what they were feeling.' Slurp of Vimto, satisfied sigh. 'I went back to him the next day and said he was right, but I didn't understand why it was an issue. He said that was the point. Most people have something within them that makes them feel sympathy.'

Slurrrrrrrrrrp.

Andrew went cold, wishing he'd never asked. This wasn't what he'd expected.

Jenny offered the can towards him. 'Vimto?'

'No.'

'He told me that adults call it all sorts of things: bipolar, psychopathic, sociopathic. I'm not even sure Empathy Deficit Disorder is a real thing.' She paused. 'Sorry . . .'

Andrew realised he must have been squirming uncomfortably in the seat. His speed had dropped to ten miles an hour below the speed limit and there was a BMW clinging to his bumper. Still, being a bumper-hogging bastard was a symptom of owning a BMW, so that wasn't unexpected.

'You, er, don't need to apologise,' he said.

Andrew risked a sideways glance but Jenny was staring directly ahead, the hint of a grin on her face.

'I'm not a psycho, if that's what you're thinking. I just need to teach myself things and I can only do that by watching other people. Like just now, I sensed that you were uncomfortable, so I said sorry, even though I don't really know why I should. People say sorry to each other all the time, so that's an easy one to pick up. You see strangers on the street stepping in front of each other, accidentally clipping one another, going for the same door, and it's all "sorry, sorry, sorry".'

'So are you bothered that I felt uncomfortable?'

Jenny didn't reply, didn't sip from her drink, didn't move. Ahead, brake lights flared. Andrew stopped in the queue of traffic, leaving them at a thorny impasse. The BMW must at least have had good brakes because it didn't slam into him. The driver was on his phone, another apparent requisite of owning that particular brand of German machinery. If he rammed cyclists, he'd have the holy trinity of how to drive a BMW nailed down.

'I think so,' Jenny eventually said. 'When you keep wondering whether you're doing things to fit in or because you really want to, you can drive yourself mad.' She stopped, before adding: 'Depending on your definition of mad, of course.'

'You found all of this out from an RE teacher?'

She giggled. 'No, he just made me think about it. I think he was having a bit of a game with me. I was always trying to offer the opposite view to other people, so he figured he'd see how I liked it. He was right though. I went away and read all sorts.'

'. . . *It's normal for you to keep believing. A year from now, five years, ten years: you still believe he might return . . .*'

Andrew thought how Jenny had copied his explanation in an attempt to comfort Elaine Carr about her son. She would have felt lost otherwise, so mimicked something she'd seen. It also explained why she was so good in certain situations and a spare part in others. If she'd witnessed something similar before, she would know how other people handled it. If she hadn't, then she had no idea. Perhaps that was why she seemed to read him so well – because they spent so much time together.

'I know what you're thinking,' she said.

Jenny's words sent a tingle slithering along Andrew's back, until she broke into a giggle and then it sounded as natural as she'd probably meant it.

'What?'

'You're wondering if that means I worry about people being hurt. That's what's wrong with psychopaths, they really don't care if other people are in pain.'

'So what's the answer?'

Jenny twisted in her seat to face him, even though Andrew was still focusing on the road. 'I told you, I'm not a psycho.'

'So you do care about other people?'

'I'd feel bad if I saw someone being attacked, or hurt. I just don't really get on with that many people. Plus I'm happy by myself.' She paused to drain the rest of the drink and then scrunched up the can with a metallic screech. 'Is that okay?'

'Of course.'

'Still, I could have just said all of that because I'm completely self-aware of my own condition and I wanted you to feel empathy for me. That's what a *real* psycho would do.'

Andrew stared at the road, not knowing what to say.

Jenny's girlish laugh broke the mood again. 'I didn't do that, by the way. I know I'm weird – but you did ask.'

Andrew wondered if he would have been better off not knowing.

22

There was no kind way to put it: the Eccles housing estate on which Kristian Verity was last known to have lived was a complete and utter hole. At the front of the development was a graffitied road sign with a double O converted into a pair of breasts. Rusting shopping trolleys lined a wall next to a row of boarded-up shops, with the customary group of tracksuit-clad youths hanging around smoking. Next to their feet was a gold-coloured cardboard box full of Special Brew – not even the cheap supermarket knock-off version, but actual Special Brew. It must be someone's birthday.

The sat nav continued to direct them through the winding labyrinth of roads. Each time Andrew hesitated, the female voice stroppily demanded he perform U-turns in inappropriate areas and then took her time offering an alternative route. The mardy cow.

Kristian Verity's house was a two-bedroom place in the middle of a terrace. Every other house was either 'for sale', 'to let', or boarded up. The rental car was the newest vehicle on the road by at least ten years and the moment Andrew parked, a moped that sounded like a jumbo jet chuntered past.

Andrew nodded towards the house. The window frames were thick with grime, net curtains blocking any view of the inside. The front door was rotten and wet at the bottom, even though it hadn't rained all day. It looked like a good boot would easily put it through, the only surprise being that no one had bothered to try. Stuck to the wall between the door and window was a 'to let' sign, with a 'for sale' on either side.

'Was this definitely the last place he lived?' Andrew asked.

Jenny eyed the street, taking in the grim scene. 'It's all I could find.'

Andrew knocked on the door just in case but there was no answer. When he turned, Jenny was on her mobile phone.

'Hello, is that Walker, Walker and Walkden? I was hoping to arrange a viewing of one of your properties.' She held her hand up to prevent Andrew from saying anything, dimple on display again. 'I was hoping for today, really. It's a bit of an emergency. I know it's a Saturday but we're really struggling.' She read out the address and then waited. 'That's the one.' Pause. 'I know where it is – we're right there. Like I said, it's a bit of an emergency.' Jenny checked her watch. 'As soon as you can would be great. We're *really* interested in renting it.' Pause. 'Brilliant, thanks very much, we'll be waiting.'

She slipped the phone back into her pocket. 'They're going to be about forty-five minutes. Not bad, considering.'

Andrew raised his eyebrows. '"*Really interested*"?'

'They're estate agents. They're used to the odd white lie, or a dirty big black one.'

They sat in the car avoiding the elephants in the

vehicle: Jenny potentially being mentally unstable and Andrew not wanting to talk about Keira. What a pair they were.

A little over half an hour later and a souped-up Vauxhall Look At Me with a personalised number plate – PL4YER – screeched to a halt behind Andrew's car. The thumping bass went silent at the same time as the howling oversized exhaust. A man in a shiny grey suit with a thick Windsor knot strangling him jumped out, clutching a plastic folder underneath his arm. Fake tan, chunky watch, shiny shoes, slicked-back dark hair, sunglasses in November, a bit of a simple look on his face: definitely an estate agent.

Andrew and Jenny climbed out of the car, with her unexpectedly hooking her arm through his, all teeth and dimples.

'Thank you *so* much for coming around so quickly,' she smiled. 'Like I said on the phone, we're really interested.'

The estate agent showed them his best fake grin – which was actually pretty good – and then fiddled with a set of keys, before shouldering the front door open with an ungainly grunt.

There wasn't a lot he could say because the inside was as much of a dump as the outside. The hallway had a green-grey carpet that smelled of old trainers, with the smallest of the upstairs bedrooms reeking of cannabis.

The agent stood in the doorframe, umming, erring and blaming it on 'incense', but he wasn't fooling anyone, including himself.

Andrew and Jenny took the full tour, peering into the bedrooms, trying not to pull faces at the mouldy green bathroom and wondering why no one had cleaned the cooker in seemingly ever. Apart from the carpets, curtains and an occasional lampshade, there was nothing in the house.

They eventually ended up back by the front door, the agent's skin colour switching from mahogany brown to Oompa-Loompa orange as he realised this was going to be a harder sell than he suspected.

Jenny was still hanging onto Andrew's arm. 'What happened to the last tenant?'

The agent skimmed through his file, clearly trying to avoid eye contact. 'There were a few issues.'

'What sort of issues?'

'They're sort of . . . confidential.'

'How do you mean, "sort of"?'

The agent pressed himself against the front door, swagger disappearing in front of their eyes. Confidentiality clearly wasn't his strong point. 'To be honest, it was a single guy who upped sticks still owing money. He left all of his stuff here and we had to clean everything out. We were going to leave the furniture but it wasn't in the best of states. There were books, clothes, and all sorts – mainly junk. We tried to trace him but he wasn't answering the phone, plus there was no next of kin listed on his form and no partner.'

'Did you find out what happened to him?'

'Nope.'

'So what happened to his stuff?' The agent glanced down at his pad again and Jenny quickly added: 'I'm wondering what we'd do if we moved in and he came back.'

The agent nodded shortly, one hand dropping into his pocket, the scent of a result closer again. 'Some of the grimmer things went straight to the tip. There were food wrappers and all sorts. After we'd emptied it, we had to get cleaners in. Everything cost the agency a fortune. The landlord lives abroad and we're financially responsible for the tenants. Everything else is in storage. No one seems to know what to do with it. We're trying to find out if we can ditch it or if we have to wait for a certain length of time.'

'Did you call the police about a possible missing person?' Jenny asked.

'They said there's nothing to go on. People go missing all the time and I'm not sure they even came out.'

Andrew hadn't said a word, wondering if chatting up gullible ego-types was something Jenny had taught herself. She was certainly good at it.

Jenny squeezed Andrew's arm slightly, gazing up longingly at him for a moment. 'We've got loads in storage, mainly my things: clothes, shoes, all sorts. There was a fire in the house next to us and we're desperate to settle somewhere. Storage is really expensive, though. Which company are you using? We're after something cheap – everyone tries to rip you off these days.'

The agent didn't think twice before replying: 'It's nowhere special. There's a garage out the back of our main office. Everything's in there.'

Jenny squidged Andrew's arm again – a sure sign that trouble was on her mind.

23

Winter had fully arrived in the north of England. The wind was whipping along the River Irwell, hunting along the canals and sealing Manchester in its arctic tendrils. Andrew was wrapped up in a thick olive-green jacket he'd bought from a shop in the Northern Quarter. The man behind the counter had assured him it was authentic army wear, straight from the battlefields of Afghanistan to his shop. Andrew couldn't have cared less if it had come from some knock-off factory in Stockport – it was bloody warm. Jenny was wearing a dark beanie pulled down over her plaited hair, with jeans and a dark jacket. They sat in his car on a side street, watching the pub crowd on their way out for the evening: a mix of middle-class couples ready for a nice meal, with stag and hen parties giggling their way down the street like howling packs of wolves.

Andrew tried to sound as firm as he could. 'We really shouldn't do this.'

'Pfft.'

'Will you stop doing that?'

'Doing what?'

'Making that noise.'

'What's wrong with it?'

'It's really difficult to argue against.'

A troop of men dressed as nurses bounded along the

end of the road, braying and laughing. Pairs of hairy legs were sticking out of short blue or white dresses, half of them in stockings, looking like escorts for those on a budget. They must have been utterly frozen.

'It's up to you,' Jenny said, in a distinctly 'I-don't-know-what-the-problem-is' way.

Andrew sighed. This was going to be another one of her ideas that ended up with him in a brothel, or somewhere similar.

'You're absolutely sure there are no security cameras?'

'I went for a wander around the back of the estate agent's earlier. It's a staff car park with a giant garage in the corner. There's a bottle bank, overgrown trees, that sort of thing. Everything's in shadow.'

Another sigh. Andrew was beginning to annoy himself. 'We can go and have a look. Just a look, mind.'

The car doors clunked open and closed, then the indicator lights plipped on and off. In the distance another couple hurried past hand in hand, with the male practically dragging his heel-shod partner behind him.

Jenny led the way, almost skipping across the main road like a slightly giddy ninja wearing a backpack. Sirens were going off in Andrew's mind – bad idea, bad idea – but Jenny was right in the sense that if they wanted to trace Kristian Verity, this was where events had directed them.

She skirted around the side of Walker, Walker and Walkden, through a dodgy-looking archway and onto a crumbling patch of tarmac. Jenny was right about something else: the garage was in shadow, as was everything else. Andrew gave his eyes a moment to adjust and then strained to see through the gloom in the direction she'd headed.

A giant oak tree towered overhead, swaying in the wind, its branches like a gangly teenager trying to cop a feel at a party. Hedges surrounded two sides of the car park, with the estate agent's on another and the back of an office on the fourth. Above, the moon was bright, wispy thin clouds skirting past, leaving a hazy blue glow.

'Over here.'

Jenny was standing in front of a giant eyesore: speckled thick walls, a corrugated steel roof and a battered, well-scratched garage door. For breeze-block enthusiasts, this would be right up their alley. Andrew joined her by a person-sized normal door next to the garage one.

'Do you reckon it's locked?' she asked.

'Obviously.'

'Let's try.'

Jenny reached for the door handle but Andrew grabbed her arm. He reached into his back pocket and passed her a pair of nitrile gloves. 'Think about it.'

So much for just looking.

She slipped them on and then pulled down the handle and pushed. It didn't budge a millimetre.

An overgrown hedge was covering the side of the garage: winding, scratchy vines wrapping themselves around the fabric of the building. Jenny peeped around the corner and then pressed her back against the garage and started to sidestep along its length.

'Where are you going?'

'You said we were coming here to have a look, so I'm looking.'

'That's not what I meant.'

'Pfft.'

Andrew watched her disappear behind a tree trunk, her slender frame arching and bending around the foliage. He leant against the side of the garage and checked his phone: 21.33. In a flash, he remembered what he was doing this time the previous day with Courtney. His decision-making really wasn't up to much at the moment.

'Psst.' Jenny's stage whisper.

Andrew tried to gaze through the bracken around the edge of the garage but couldn't see anything other than tight clumps of branches.

'What?'

'Come and look.'

Andrew had already squeezed himself past the first set of branches before he stopped to ask himself what he was doing. Who was supposed to be in charge?

A sharpened pincer of wood flashed through the darkness, narrowly missing Andrew's face as he tried to force himself through a gap between the garage behind and the bushes in front. Jenny had made her way silently, but he was snapping every twig going.

Andrew found Jenny in an unexpected clearing a metre or so in diameter. She was on her tiptoes, gloved hands pressed against the browning glass of an ancient single-paned window. To the right of the centre, a tree branch had grown straight through the glass, creating a jagged hole.

She spoke in a whisper but there was mischief in everything she said. 'Can you give me a piggyback?'

'Why?'

'Why do you think?'

'You're not breaking in.'

'If the window's already open, then it's not breaking, is it? I'm only going to have a look – that's what you wanted to do.'

'I meant have a look at the outside.'

'What's the problem with having a look at the inside? That estate agent told us they were only storing a bunch of Kristian's stuff that he'd left. They don't want it and neither does he.'

'It's still breaking and entering.'

'I'll give you entering but I'm not going to break anything.'

'I don't think that's how the police are going to see things.'

'How will they know? This is like the end of the earth – a dingy little car park hidden behind some office blocks.' Andrew couldn't argue that point. Jenny turned and placed her hands on his shoulders. 'Crouch down then.'

Andrew did as he was told, still tutting, but hoisting her onto his shoulders and then standing tall. He grunted, largely because he thought he should. Jenny weighed hardly anything. He angled his head up, cricking his neck but watching as she eased the tree branch out of the hole in the window and snapped it in half. Carefully, she reached through the gap, straining downwards and scrabbling on the inside.

'What are you doing?' Andrew hissed.

'Trying to get hold of the latch. It's all rusty. Hang on.'

She lifted herself slightly upwards, putting more pressure on Andrew's shoulders, the heels of her trainers digging into his chest.

'This actually hurts.'

'I've almost got it.'

There was a clunk and then a joyous giggle of glee. Jenny carefully removed her arm from the hole, avoiding the rough edges of the glass, and then wedged her fingers in the gap in the window frame and tugged it open.

'Victory!'

Too late to go back now.

Jenny readjusted her backside, scooting backwards and forward and nearly making Andrew topple. He grumbled again, peering up as she clicked the latch into place, leaving a narrow gap.

'You're not going to fit through there.'

'I'll fit.'

Jenny wriggled again, dropping her backpack on the floor next to Andrew and then twisting, bending herself through the narrow space like a high jumper but with the grace of a gymnast. With one final push, she was through with a clatter of wood and the sound of something metallic rolling across a hard floor.

'Jenny.'

No answer.

Andrew pushed himself onto tiptoes, trying to peer through the latched window. He whispered her name a second time but there was still no reply. From the clatter as

Jenny flopped inside, she could have landed on anything. He tried calling her name again, slightly louder this time, but she still didn't reply. Andrew peered up at the gap. When he was a teenager and could eat whatever he wanted without it instantly appearing on his waist, he might have been able to squeeze through if he held in his stomach and didn't mind his clothes getting torn. Now he had no chance.

He picked up the rucksack and pressed his back against the breeze-block wall again, sliding his way towards the front of the garage, grumbling as he moved, cracking more twigs and generally scratching his hands to pieces. The coat wasn't helping either. It might be warm but it was also adding a few pounds to his weight and centimetres to his size.

After a final slash of branch on flesh, Andrew emerged back into the car park, rubbing his cheek. He squinted towards the arch but there was no one there, or in the vicinity. Andrew edged along the front of the garage watching his feet before jumping back with a high-pitched shriek as the door opened in front of him.

Jenny emerged, eyebrows pulled down. 'I thought you wanted us to stay quiet.'

Andrew's heart was pounding irrationally. He breathed out heavily. 'You scared the shite out of me.'

'All I did was open the door.'

'When I was right next to it!'

'How was I supposed to know? Are you coming in?'

Andrew had a final glance around, figured he was already on unsteady ground legally speaking, and so followed her in. He slipped on his own pair of gloves and then closed the door behind them.

The inside was dark; vague, barely visible shapes cluttered around the edges of the room. From nowhere there was a flash of light and Jenny was using her mobile phone as a torch. Andrew reached for his, realising his chest felt tight from the claustrophobic clamminess of the space. The air was thick with damp, sticking to his tongue and making it hard to swallow. As the light from Andrew's phone joined Jenny's, he gulped back a phlegm-filled cough.

The corner of the garage was flooded with a pooling puddle of water, drips plopping from the ceiling despite the lack of rain. Piled close to the door were stacks of brochures and magazines, the corners curled and floppy. Andrew scanned across the top one: 'Boom shack a lack: How the days of recession are over'.

The piles continued to the far wall, as if someone had emptied a skip-full and bundled it into nearly neat stacks. The cover date on the closest one to Andrew was from eighteen years previously. Jenny had lifted a plastic sheet and was looking underneath, pulling items out of boxes and returning them.

'See anything?' Andrew hissed.

'Junk.'

Against the next wall, there were towers of boxes that weren't as damp as everything else around and weren't covered in dust. Andrew held his phone between his teeth and then reached up to lift down the first. He nudged an office chair that had no back with his knee, sending it spinning until he dropped onto it. The damp immediately soaked through his trousers.

Inside the box was an assortment of tat, but Andrew knew instantly it was Kristian Verity's. Sitting on the top was a leather-bound book with a large pentagram on the front.

'Jenny.'

She splish-splashed her way across the sodden ground, the light from her phone zipping across the space. Andrew put the box on a dryish patch of floor and reached up for the next one. In all, there were seven boxes, drier and less dust-covered than everything else around them. One box at a time they began hunting through the assortment of items Kristian Verity had left behind.

Jenny held up a rubber-stopped vial of sand but Andrew could only shrug as he pulled out a silver cross hanging upside down from a chain. He rummaged down to the bottom of the same box, removing what looked like three chicken bones tied together with a neat red bow.

'Is this magic stuff?' Jenny asked.

Andrew assumed so but didn't know enough about it. Then he shuddered, thinking that the bow could be holding together any sort of bones, not just from a chicken.

One of the boxes contained nothing but candles and an incense burner. As Andrew delved deeper to make sure they weren't missing anything, Jenny opened the next one, immediately holding up a pair of hedge clippers with a vicious curved blade. The light from her phone glinted ominously from the sharpened edge.

'Did he even have a garden?' she asked.

Andrew shook his head. He didn't but three of Nicholas Carr's severed fingers had been found in the woods. Next to the clippers was a serrated knife in a leather sheath, piled on top of a damp laptop that definitely wouldn't work and a dark silky gown.

From the next box, Andrew pulled out a couple more magic books; a type of doll made from straw, with fine strands of wool holding it together; and then a collection of thin twigs bent and tied into a circle with three more attached in the shape of a triangle within it. Andrew held it up for Jenny to see: first Nicholas, then Lara, the natural bowl of the woods, his office door, and now Kristian Verity.

Jenny responded by holding up a framed photograph. Andrew put the symbol back in the box and used his phone to illuminate the picture. Water must have seeped into the box, getting into the space between the glass and the photo, because the ink had started to run. Instead of a normal photograph, there was a greenish-brown smudge across the lower half, with the top part smeared except for a face.

'Do you think that's Kristian?' Jenny asked.

Andrew peered at the figure: curly dark hair, with a narrow face and a single spindly arm next to the water stain. Clearly visible on his wrist was a dark circle with an out-of-focus shape that was almost certainly a triangle. He was only seventeen or eighteen.

'Maybe. How old is he now?'

'Thirty-six.'

Because of the way the ink had run, it looked as if there

were two Kristians, frizzy black mops of hair running into one another before the water had seeped across the rest of the picture. Jenny put it into her backpack and then picked up the symbol made from twigs and dropped that in too. Andrew didn't object.

With two boxes remaining, they took one each. Inside Andrew's were more magic books, the pages damp and sagging. Jenny pulled out a smaller fake leather-bound book and started fingering through it.

'It's his address book,' she said. 'I guess he didn't like using his phone for that.'

'Anything interesting?'

'You can hardly read it – it's really wet and the ink has run.'

Andrew took out the next book from his box but it was even wetter than the first. It was hard to breathe again, his throat sore from the clogged atmosphere.

All of a sudden, Jenny sat up straighter, her eyes meeting Andrew's through the dusk. 'What was Lara's last name?'

'Malvado or something like that.'

Jenny turned the book around, her thumb pointing to a soggy lined piece of paper and one word written in neat block capital letters: 'MALVADO'.

24

Andrew pulled into his parking space underneath Beetham Tower, took Jenny's backpack from the boot, and headed for the lifts. Floor minus two was a mass of parked vehicles, varying in wealth from the not too bad to the really sodding expensive. His footsteps reverberated around the space, echoing from the low ceiling. Andrew stopped by the pillar closest to the lifts, turning in a circle and hoisting the bag onto his back. There was no one there, yet the stain of what he'd done on the past two evenings was weighing upon him. He couldn't really blame Jenny; she was young, excitable and sometimes reckless. He was supposed to know better and yet tonight he'd rooted through items that weren't his and last night . . . well, he shouldn't have done that either.

The lift dinged into place and Andrew stepped inside, thumbing the button for his floor and leaning against the wall. The compartment chuntered upwards, metal grinding against metal, sounding as if it could drop at any moment. If it did, whoever found him would have a fun time going through Jenny's bag, wondering what the Miss Piggy zipper pull was all about, along with the circle and triangle symbol made from twigs.

Ping!

His lift journey the previous night had definitely been more fun.

And expensive.

The corridor leading to Andrew's floor was as quiet as usual. In the distance, one of the overhead lights was flickering. Andrew stepped out, looking both ways. Something didn't feel quite right but he wasn't sure what. He checked the number on the wall: definitely his floor. In the opposite direction from his flat, there were the faint sounds of someone's television on a little too loudly. You had to have money to get a place this high up, so people were used to doing what they wanted. Well, as long as they abided by the rules in the residents' agreement. No noise after eleven, no slamming doors, tie your bin bags before dropping them in the rubbish chute, avoid outdoor shoes on wooden floors, respect your neighbours, no farting in the lifts: the usual sort of thing.

As Andrew continued peering from side to side, he realised it wasn't as quiet as he first thought. Behind one of the other doors, someone was playing the Stone Roses, with a woman's giggling voice as the backing vocals.

Aside from the odd nod in the lift – the universal signal that you didn't care who the other person was – Andrew didn't talk to any of his neighbours, not that they went out of their way to talk to him either. It was just the way things were. Jenny would love it here.

Andrew moved along the corridor towards his flat, convincing himself he was just uneasy from what he'd been up to. He dug into the pockets of the jacket, trying to remember which one his keys were in. If it was a genuine army coat from Afghanistan, they sure had a lot of pouches in which to keep their stuff. He finally found them in one of the inside pockets, pushing the key into the lock before he heard a scrabbling from his right. Andrew turned too late, glancing up as the fist flew towards his face. He tried to duck but the blow caught him on the side of the cheek, sending him careering back through the now-open door as the shape of a familiar man loomed over him.

25

Andrew skidded backwards, trying to get his balance on the hard floor. He managed to shrug off the backpack but the coat was cumbersome and heavy, leaving him struggling to stand.

In front of him, the man closed the door with a quiet click. He was dressed entirely in black, with bollock-crunching steel-capped boots, waterproof trousers, a leather jacket and thin, dark gloves. Andrew tried to scramble away but the figure was on him, a fist thumping into his ear, once, twice. Andrew's head began spinning from the blows, his balance thrown as he finally managed to roll himself away.

Stewart Deacon stood tall in the space between Andrew's leather sofa and the wall, fists clenched. It was Andrew's first proper look at him in person. On the trails to the Huyton brothel, the tinted windows of Deacon's car had prevented him seeing much of the actual man. He might have been in his fifties but he had the toned, athletic body of someone twenty years younger, the leather of his jacket straining from the bulge of his upper-arm muscles. He was shaped like a wedge: wide, heavy shoulders with a narrow, trim stomach and greying short dark hair with no hint of stubble.

Very deliberately, he slipped a knuckle-duster from his pocket and slid it across the fingers of his right hand.

'Good evening, Mr Hunter.'

Shite.

'You do know there's CCTV downstairs and throughout the building,' Andrew said.

'Is there indeed?'

'If you leave now, we'll let it lie here.'

Deacon's face cracked into a boyish smile. '*We'll?*'

'What's the best you think can happen?'

The intruder polished the bridge of the knuckle-duster with his gloved thumb. 'Oh, I know what the best I think can happen is. I wonder how thick that window is.'

Andrew glanced backwards towards the huge expanse of glass behind him. Manchester was brighter than the previous night, a pulsing mass of northern partygoers enjoying a Saturday night on the lash. Andrew managed to throw off the coat, which at least gave him a degree of mobility, although Deacon looked the stronger and fitter. Andrew patted his trouser pocket for where he usually kept his mobile phone before realising it was in the coat he'd just tossed to the floor. The apartment's phone was next to Deacon's shoulder on the wall.

'Whose life have you been out poking your nose into this evening?'

Andrew didn't answer, edging sideways into the open-plan living room, hoping that if Deacon followed him, he might be able to double back around and get to the front door. His ear was pounding from the blows to the side of his head.

'I asked you a question, Mr Hunter.'

'What do you want me to say?'

'I'm a self-made man. I built my companies from the ground up. I employ lots of people, I've made people money, I've paid taxes. Who are you to say that I'm doing anything wrong?'

'I don't judge people.'

'Really?'

'Really.'

'What sort of life must you have? Spying on people, following them, sticking your nose in?'

'I try my best not to do that.'

'That's not what I hear.'

Andrew slipped in between the coffee table and sofa, the seat between him and Deacon, who still hadn't moved from the door. It was the only way in or out and he knew it. Andrew carried on moving, sitting in the armchair and spinning to face the intruder. Deacon was running his finger along the knuckle-duster again.

'I think you should go,' Andrew said.

He was hoping for a reaction, any reaction, but Deacon was calm. 'You'd like that, wouldn't you?'

'I really would.'

'How many people's lives have you ruined?'

'That's not what I do. I go out of my way to avoid cases like that.'

Deacon held his hands up to indicate the apartment. 'This is pretty smart for someone who avoids doing work.'

'This place wasn't paid for by the business.' For a few

moments neither of them said anything. Andrew stood and stepped across to the kitchen. 'Drink?'

No reply.

He poured himself some water and leant against the sink, sipping slowly as he eyed Deacon across the room. He tried to tell himself he wasn't scared but he could feel the acceleration of his heart, his instinct telling him to find a way out, even though there was only one. He knew the window was thick and fully reinforced. A person was never going to go through that but the intruder and his knuckle-duster could do a lot of damage.

The liquid was cool and refreshing, sharpening his mind. There was little chance of fighting his way out of here and apparently no opportunity to escape, so he had to talk the other man down instead.

He turned to rinse the glass out, eyes skimming across the rack of knives. The tallest one was serrated and used for cutting bread but the next one down was razor-sharp and four inches long. It would certainly be a leveller in a fight and he'd no doubt get in a swipe or two, but did he really want to go down that route?

He waited for a few moments, allowing Deacon to see the knives, and then turned, not reaching for one.

'Are you going to leave?' Andrew asked.

For the first time, Deacon hesitated. 'If you say you don't really do this type of job, then what about me?'

'What about you?'

'Why are you following me around? Taking pictures, writing reports . . . ?'

'That's what I was asked to do. If I'd known straight

away it was because you were having an affair, I would have turned the job down. It was because you were disappearing and no one knew where.' Andrew stepped back towards the living-room area, away from the knives. 'It's just a job. Believe it or not, I try to help people.'

'That's how you justify it? "It's just a job"?'

'It is.'

Deacon was shuffling on the spot now, heavy shoes clattering on the wood underneath. 'I've heard some interesting stories about you from my son. About the things you were telling my wife.'

'I didn't realise he was there.'

'That's not the point. You think you're smart, do you?'

'Not particularly.'

'I know where you live, where you work.'

He finally took a step towards Andrew, away from the door. The sofa was still between them, not quite a knuckle-duster-proof barrier but marginally better than nothing. Andrew wondered if he should have taken a knife after all. If he moved now, he could still get there first – but what would he do then? He'd not been in a fight since school and he'd got his arse kicked then. Fish Lips Nixon had attacked him from behind and then climbed on top of him, punching him in the back of the head until other students pulled him off. That was all because one of Andrew's friends had coined the nickname 'Fish Lips'. Before and since, he'd somehow managed to avoid physical conflict.

'I know where *you* live and work,' Andrew replied.

Deacon was resting on the back of the sofa, one

dramatic lunge away from grabbing Andrew. His eyebrows were dark, unlike his grey hair, almost meeting in the middle as they sloped downwards into a V. His eyes were unblinking.

'Is that a threat?'

'No. Was yours?'

'Yes.'

Andrew started to shift sideways, back to his original plan of rounding Deacon and getting to the door first. The problem was that Deacon was moving sideways too. Andrew stopped shuffling, using the armchair as a shield.

'Everything that's happened is really an issue for you and your family,' Andrew said.

Deacon nodded, lips pursed. 'Is that right?'

Andrew's eyes darted to the knuckle-duster and back again. 'What are you going to do? If you beat me up, I'll be able to tell the police your name, so you'd have to kill me. If you do that, there'll be a huge police investigation. I'd be shouting and screaming, so people upstairs, downstairs, left, right, and across the hall would hear. They might raise the alarm – even if it's just to complain about the noise. There are security cameras downstairs, so you'd have to find a different way out. Even if you did, there are cameras on the streets around here, then more traffic cameras nearby. It's a Saturday night, so there are loads of people out there and somebody will see your face. If you somehow escape all of that, the first thing the police will do is go through my records. They'll look at cases involving people who've had unhappy outcomes and you're the most recent. Even if there's no evidence to say you were here, you'll still be the first person they visit. They'll want to know where you were tonight. They'll check your number plate against the recognition cameras they have around the city to see if you might have driven here. They'll look at CCTV on the buses, check with taxi firms, all that stuff. One way or another, they'll find out. None of that even touches on any DNA evidence. You've got gloves on, so no fingerprints – but if you're going to beat me to death, that's going to be messy. There'll be blood all over you, not just your clothes, the parts of your skin that are showing and in your hair. Are you confident you could wash all of that away before they come? Or how about if a hair from your head somehow comes loose and they find it? Perhaps it already has?'

Andrew stared at him defiantly, hoping his list of reasons not to kill him were enough.

Deacon held his gaze, not wilting but not stepping forward either. Perhaps he'd already thought all of those things through? He could punch Andrew in the larynx with the knuckle-duster first of all to prevent the noise and then beat him to death. If he had a cap to cover his hair, the cameras wouldn't pick up much and, as for the chances of somebody outside spotting him, they wouldn't even remember how many drinks they'd had, let alone the bloke in the cap hurrying past.

In a flash, Deacon lunged for his jacket pocket. Andrew stumbled backwards, expecting to see a knife or a gun, but instead there was a bundle of money. Deacon tossed it onto the chair between them, rolls of crumpled twenty-pound notes unfurling and tumbling to the floor.

His voice was low and growling. 'There's your dirty money. It's nothing to me and you're just a posh rent boy. Take it and stay away from me and my family.' He slipped off the knuckle-duster and put it in his pocket, turning to leave. 'If you get in my business again, Mr Hunter, next time you won't see me coming.'

SUNDAY

26

Andrew's head was pounding as he jolted awake in the morning. He'd been sleeping on the opposite side to usual, avoiding putting any pressure on his well-thumped ear. He stood in front of the wardrobe mirror tilting his head to the side, trying to force his eyes to rotate at an impossible angle to see if there was any bruising. It wasn't working, but from the little he could see, apart from a bit of reddening, there wasn't a mark on him. It was typical; if you were going to get the crap kicked out of you, the assailant should at least have the decency to leave you looking like you deserved a bit of sympathy.

The headache tablets in the bathroom cabinet had something about 'fast-acting' plastered on the front but they weren't quick enough for Andrew's liking. How come when he was coming through reception with a woman there was a security guard there to give snide looks, yet when someone who wanted to kick his arse came along, they'd handily nipped off for a toilet break?

Andrew thought about calling the police but they hadn't even pulled their collective fingers out about his car yet, so what good would it do? So far, they'd decided they didn't have any evidence from the actual vehicle to say who had set fire to it, although the good news was that the damage was only cosmetic. It was now at a local garage waiting to be resprayed and would be ready for pickup on Monday.

His only other option was to sidestep the official procedures and call the detective sergeant he knew. That would still be a tough call: 'I kind of had my arse kicked because I let a teenager overhear me talking to his mother, can you ride to the rescue?'

All things weighed up, it wasn't worth it. She'd probably laugh.

Head still pulsing, Andrew stumbled through to the living room and pulled open the curtains. It was a decent-looking day for November, the clouds bordering on white but with a glaze of frost on the tops of the surrounding buildings. He watched a small group of fun-runners jogging through the streets far below, up at a ridiculous time for a Sunday. If God had meant people to do exercise on the seventh day, he definitely wouldn't have rested himself.

Andrew slumped on the sofa, letting the folds of leather envelop him. It had come with the apartment but really was comfy. He picked up Jenny's backpack and emptied everything they'd borrowed/liberated/stolen onto the coffee table. The largest item was one of the magic books. The cover was made from a damp-feeling brown leather, with an almost faded gold pentagram etched into the material. The pages had a spongy texture but the contents were similar to what they'd seen in the books underneath Nicholas's bed: symbols, Latin-looking words, apparent spells and curses, plus information about bones, plants and herbs. In many ways, it didn't matter whether magic was real – Kristian Verity believed it was and perhaps Nicholas and Lara did too.

As well as the book, there was the heavily smudged photograph of Kristian as a teenager, the straw doll, the wrapped-up bones and the twig symbol. Andrew peered around the room, trying to remember what had happened to the contacts book. It had definitely been put into the bag. His head still felt heavy, as if he was moving in slow motion. Eventually, he spotted the small black book on top of the radiator in the kitchen. He didn't remember putting it there, so it must have happened in a moment of clarity not long after Stewart Deacon left the previous evening.

The broiling heat had dried out the pages but most of the contents had been destroyed by the clogginess of the garage. Andrew leafed through to one of the words which was clear: MALVADO, as visible now as it had been in the clingy atmosphere the night before. Lara's family name was clearly known to the magic fanatic. Richard Carr had told them Lara was orphaned but it was now time to start trying to find out exactly who her parents were – and how long ago they died. Malvado was certainly a strange enough name.

With Lara's name being in Kristian Verity's contacts book, it meant two men connected to her had disappeared.

Andrew continued flicking through the book. There were many fragments of words and names and a few half-visible phone numbers but much of it was unreadable. The once-blue ink was now a pale mauve, draining into the margins and pooling into a dirty, dark smudge.

From the entire book, there were only three more names Andrew could make out, and he wasn't entirely sure he had those correct. The spidery handwriting wasn't helping but he pieced together the names Esme Graham, James Wicker and Brian Oswald, alongside partial addresses. If he'd had only the names, he would have left them for Jenny the next day but Andrew wasn't too bad with the computer system.

The laptop he took home could connect to the information system in his office, with all traffic routed through a proxy so that it didn't look as if he was based in Greater Manchester. Everything on the hard drive was encrypted and he'd been assured by the tech geek who put it in that no one – even the police – would be able to access it without the key. He didn't have anything to hide but who knew when it might come in useful. Jenny had given the entire setup her own seal of approval too, although he'd turned down her offer of getting someone she knew from her old course to try to hack in.

After first using the Internet, Andrew called the guy who ran credit checks for him. Despite his contact grumbling about the fact it was a Sunday 'and sodding early too', Andrew finished up with three most recent addresses for the people who might know Kristian Verity. They were all in the Greater Manchester area – not around the corner but drivable.

Andrew downed a couple more headache tablets, drank so much water he knew his bladder was going be plotting payback for later, and then decided to do something productive with his day.

*

A small army of young teenagers slumped along the pavement as if a zombie apocalypse had happened overnight. Their arms hung limply by their sides, chins low to their chests, sullen aimless stares into the distance. Andrew drove past them, checking the address he'd written down and parking under a lamppost.

Apart from the zombies, no one in their right mind was out and about in the icy conditions on a Sunday. The sane members of this particular Bury housing estate had locked themselves inside, turned the central heating on, and were currently sitting around with their feet up watching cookery programmes. What they definitely weren't doing was driving around trying to track down people from a missing man's largely destroyed address book.

Andrew watched his footing carefully on the frost-covered pavement, treading one step at a time towards the house that apparently belonged to Brian Oswald. Each step felt as if he was walking a perilous tightrope that could end up with him on his arse at any given moment. Winter had well and truly arrived, late this year. Usually it kicked in about the end of September and then hung around the north of England until April, like an annoying drunken uncle that wouldn't leave on Christmas Day.

Brian Oswald's property had a set of steps leading up a ridiculously steep slope to the house at the top. Andrew held onto the rail, negotiating one step at a time. The area was shaded by an overgrown tree on the opposite side of the road, viciously combining to make it colder and more frozen than the other houses.

The front door was opened by a scraggy-looking

woman, with wet dark hair kinking off in all directions as if she'd just unplugged herself from the national grid. It was going to take more than a comb to tame that. She peered over Andrew's shoulder towards the road, valley-like furrows in her forehead.

Andrew tried to sound as polite as he could possibly manage. 'Is Brian in?'

She brushed a matted clump of hair away from her face, flashing a wedding band in the process. Presumably this was Mrs Oswald.

'Who's asking?'

'I'm one of his old workmates. I was in the area, so thought I'd pop in and say hi.'

It was just about plausible but she didn't budge from the door, her emotionless stare making it clear she had her suspicions. 'Which job?'

'From the call centre in town. We both got laid off at the same time when they moved the work out to India.'

That had been easy enough to find out from the credit check and an Internet search, with Mrs Oswald's face finally cracking into something that was only around eighty per cent hostility.

She was chewing either the inside of her mouth or some gum. 'He's not in.'

'Any idea when he'll be back?'

'Nope.'

'Do you know if it'll be today?'

More chewing: 'Nope.'

'Is he working . . . ?'

'He's just away.'

224

'On holiday?'

'Just away.'

This was going well: the type of responses Andrew had got from women when he was a teenager but with marginally less disdain. Mrs Oswald stepped backwards, one hand on the door ready to close it in his face, jaw bobbing up and down.

Andrew reached forward, trying to at least get something from his morning jaunt. 'When did he go away?'

'Can't remember.'

'Is there any way I can get hold of him?'

'Nope.'

She nudged the door until there was slim crack but didn't close it entirely. Andrew moved back a step, carefully, still watching her. Mrs Oswald's eyes hadn't left him.

Andrew waited on the edge of the top step, his ear hurting from a mix of last night's blows and the wind. 'If Brian's not here, perhaps you could answer something for me. I don't suppose you know the name Malvado, do you?'

Her eyes finally darted away from his, the door opening slightly as she peered both ways along the street. In a flash, the door was closed with a solid click but her flinching reaction gave Andrew the answer he needed.

27

That meant there were three men connected to Lara's name who were missing – but that was only part of the story. Kristian Verity was single, some sort of loner, so it was unsurprising no one knew he had disappeared until the rent stopped being paid. With Brian Oswald, the woman who answered the door knew who he was, and was probably married to him. If he was missing, then why wouldn't she have reported it? If he wasn't missing, why the secrecy over where he was and how long he was likely to be away?

Andrew drove around the edge of the city to the outskirts of Oldham. He was so convinced that everyone connected to the name Malvado was missing that he stared in surprise when Esme Graham answered 'that's me' when he asked for her. She was in her late forties, skinny, with a taste in clothes similar to Lara's and long black hair to match.

He thought of asking Esme about Kristian Verity and the names in his contacts book, perhaps even Lara, but held back for a reason he wasn't sure of. Something was definitely going on and announcing himself as a private investigator was only going to alert people to the fact that he was trying to find out what.

He twisted back towards the road, speaking over his

shoulder. 'Have you ever thought about switching energy suppliers?'

Esme's eyes narrowed as she closed her front door a fraction, staring at him in the same way Mrs Oswald had done. He felt her gaze flitting across him, trying to weigh up who he was. Andrew didn't have an ID badge, clipboard, tablet computer or anything else on him that might be used to identify himself or pass on information. It was the first thing he'd thought of.

'What did you say your name was?'

'I didn't. I think I might have the wrong house.'

Andrew turned to walk away but could feel her staring at him, knowing he'd lied about who he was. Jenny might have been able to dig herself out of the situation but Andrew wasn't that good an actor. As he moved his way down the path towards the car, he spotted a small collection of items in the corner of the garden, almost hidden by the shade of interconnecting hedges. Attached to a small stump of wood was a thin twine of rope tied into a circle with a triangle stitched into the centre.

Scrumpy had said that the symbol was associated with the occult. It was appearing all too regularly in Andrew's life: first Nicholas's wrist, then Lara's, the woods, within Kristian Verity's possessions and among the people he knew. Not to mention the charcoal version drawn on Andrew's office door. Whatever the occult involved – genuine evil, magic, something to do with the devil, or a figment of people's imaginations, Andrew was beginning to feel intimidated by it. The web of people he'd stumbled across were connected by it, with everything stemming back to Nicholas and his girlfriend.

The final name from Kristian Verity's book was James Wicker, whose address already had Andrew questioning whether he should go there by himself. He lived on a rough estate sandwiching Longsight and Moss Side.

Long, ugly rows of red-brick terraces stretched along both sides of the road, with grubby, battered vehicles parked half on the pavement leaving a narrow gap for people to manoeuvre their cars through. A dab hand with a paintbrush must have been through towards the end of the summer because each of the houses had their window and door frames painted a bright, blinding white. It was a nice try but didn't distract from the unsightliness of the area.

Andrew waited at a junction, allowing a car to pull out, but everything looked the same in all four directions: rows and rows of neglected housing. Even the woman on the sat nav seemed to have given up trying to decipher the jumble of streets, insisting Andrew was at his destination, even though he was outside a pizza shop. He pressed the button to turn it off, instead relying on old-fashioned methods. He pulled up next to a bloke who was carrying a black bin liner across the street and lowered the driver's side window, asking for directions. The man pointed behind Andrew, offering vague assertions that it was 'somewhere on the right', which only marginally helped.

With the road so tight and the number of cars hemmed in nose-to-tail along its length, performing a U-turn was an impossibility, so Andrew made his way along the parallel street, reaching the end and finally spotting the street sign he'd been looking for.

James Wicker's end-terrace house was in pretty decent shape compared to some of the others in the row. His windows were clean for a start and the 'no junk mail' sign next to the letterbox hadn't been defaced. Andrew knocked on the door and waited.

At the far end of the street, there was the sound of giggling as a car pulled up and three young girls climbed out in pretty pink dresses, dancing their way into one of the houses. Attached to the front door were pink and red balloons and a 'happy birthday' banner.

Oh for the days when birthdays were celebrated, not dreaded.

Andrew tried knocking again but there was still no answer. He clicked open the letterbox, nudged the bristles aside and stared into the empty hallway. The walls were a crisp magnolia, with an insurance-invalidating set of keys attached to a hook on the left-hand side. If James's keys were inside, then he probably hadn't left the house, so where was he? Andrew was about to stand when something caught his eye at the back of the hall. The narrow gap didn't give him much space through which to peer but what he could see was spotless: no junk lining the edges of the hall, no rubbish bags, strewn coats, random shoes, or anything else.

Except for the dark pool of liquid that had soaked into the brown carpet at the edge.

At first Andrew had thought it was a trick of the light but there was only a faint sliver of white from the wide-open internal door.

Andrew moved around the side of the house, running his hand along the brickwork. A cobbled alley separated James Wicker's row from the one behind. Green wheelie bins lined the cut-through, with one on its side, spilling pizza boxes and polystyrene takeaway tubs into the centre.

The wall at the back of the house was crumbling, with rough edges across the top and brick dust on the floor. Andrew lifted himself over the waist-high gate into the back yard, which certainly wasn't as clean as the inside of the house. A rusting metal barbeque was built into one side of the shed, the grille lying flat on the floor in a puddle of soil. Around the edges were more disintegrating bricks and three unopened bags of cement.

Andrew had taken three steps towards the back door when the smell hit him: like backed-up, overflowing toilets in a cut-price restaurant but much worse. Andrew stepped backwards, cradling his stomach and taking some breaths of clean air as he realised his eyes were actually watering. He was almost certain what the smell was. He knew he should walk away and call the police but felt the unexplainable urge to see for himself.

He took a deep breath and pulled his coat up to cover his mouth, which was as useful as trying to soak up water from a bathtub with a tissue. A single-ply one.

The stench seeped through Andrew's nostrils, tickling the hairs and leaving him worryingly close to retching. He pressed himself against the window, using a hand to shield the glare but unable to peer past the net curtain. Bloody things.

The smell was too powerful to be coming through a locked house and solid walls, so there had to be an opening somewhere. Andrew stepped back, taking another breath and covering his mouth with his hand. The windows were all closed, upstairs and down, but he realised he'd missed the obvious. Flaking black paint coated the back door but there was a small gap between its darkness and the white frame on the inside.

After another breath, Andrew dashed for the door, bounding through it with a shove of his shoulder. The last person to leave via the rear hadn't bothered to lock up, which only added to Andrew's fear of what the smell was.

He found himself in a kitchen, the once-clean black-and-white tiles now speckled with rat excrement and chewed remnants of food. The smell might be keeping people away but it wasn't worrying the rodent population. The draining board was overflowing with unwashed dishes, with a pool of dirty brown water in the sink and the steady drip-drip-drip from the tap adding to the already brimming sludge.

Andrew stepped across the kitchen, holding his nose with his fingers. A door opposite opened directly into what he assumed was the living room but it was hard to know for sure because it was so dark. Andrew fumbled for the light switch on the wall close to the doorframe, using the inside of his sleeve to prevent leaving fingerprints, just in case.

Dim yellow light flooded the room as Andrew stepped backwards towards the doorway, seeing everything he needed to from where he was. A man was lying flat on the floor, torso bare, arms and legs spread wide, eyelids closed.

Andrew spotted the tattoo on his inner wrist: a circle with an upside-down triangle in the middle.

It wasn't the only symbol in the room.

The hairs on the man's chest had matted together from the circle of blood carved into his torso. Shreds of flesh around the cut were splayed outwards, the dark red, almost black, liquid pooling towards the other doorway leading into the room. Within the circle was a crudely sliced triangle, punctuated by a round hole in the centre of his chest where someone had staked him like a vampire.

28

Andrew sat in the pub, a pint of something cold, dark and cloudy in his hand, enjoying the sensation. He'd deliberately chosen somewhere that would be bouncing, even on a Sunday night. There were always places in the student area around Oxford Road that would be rammed, regardless of which day of the week it was.

He was sitting at the bar, taking in the rest of the space. At one end, groups of lads were lining up to play pool, arguing over whether the winner should stay on or if people could actually play against their mates. At the other, the dance floor was rocking. Sunday night was Manchester music night, with a Stone Roses tune bleeding into an Oasis track. The DJ had already worked his way through songs from Joy Division, New Order and the Happy Mondays and was promising that the Smiths and Charlatans would be up soon.

Sod you, world – this is how we do music in Manchester.

It was the type of place Andrew had loved when he was a student himself. Now he looked like someone's dad, there to pick up an errant daughter and slipping in a quick pint as he waited.

Still, at least the music was good, and he had company.

Jenny was sipping from her own pint, some fruity, cidery thing that everyone was into nowadays. When he'd called to ask if she was up to much, he hadn't even realised she lived around the corner.

'Sorry . . .' he said.

Jenny nudged him with her elbow, leaning in so he could hear her over Liam Gallagher's amplified twang. 'Stop apologising, it's fine.'

'I didn't know who else to call.'

'I don't mind. I was sitting at home reading one of my old textbooks.'

Andrew wanted to believe she was joking but knew she wasn't. 'I'll pay for your time.'

Ick, that sounded bad.

Jenny frowned at him. 'Don't be a dimwit. We're out as mates.'

A ball from the pool table shot over the top of the cushion, landing with a solid thump on the ground and started rolling towards the dance floor. A lad with a baseball cap scurried after it, apologising as he crouched and fished it out from underneath a stool. Its female occupant turned and pushed him away in annoyance as he held the ball up in an attempt to prove he wasn't just trying to look up her skirt.

Jenny was still smiling, watching the room like him, learning from people. Andrew downed a third of his pint in one and rubbed his ear. It had been such a long day that he'd almost forgotten about being slapped around the night before.

She nudged him with her elbow again. 'Are you going to tell me about it properly then, or are you going to grump all evening?'

'I'm not grumping!'

'It looks like it.'

He had another sip of his drink, leaning in to speak into her ear. Some things definitely shouldn't be shouted.

'After I saw the body, I dashed out the back and called the police. They wanted me to wait, which was unsurprising really, and then there were sirens everywhere, people in white suits, all sorts. They even sent out an ambulance, which was a bit late considering the poor bastard had a massive hole in his chest.'

'And they took you to the station?'

'Right. I told them who I was and there was an immediate groan. They love it when private investigators get caught up in things. They offered me a solicitor but there wasn't much point and I have a bit of an idea about what I'm doing. I told them I was looking into a missing persons case and thought James Wicker might be able to help. I mentioned Nicholas Carr but didn't go into too much detail and they didn't ask anyway. I told them I smelled something bad and that the back door was already open – which is all the truth.'

'What *didn't* you tell them?'

Andrew squirmed on his stool, rotating it back towards the bar and having another sip of his drink. 'I didn't tell them that I got James Wicker's name from a contacts book we took from a locked garage.' Jenny laughed, actually giggled, as if it was funny. Andrew kept talking over her. 'I didn't talk about Lara at all, or give them the Malvado name. If they want that, it's all around for them. I told them I was looking for Nicholas. They should know she's his girlfriend.'

'What about connecting Nicholas to the dead guy?'

'I said I'd heard Nicholas was interested in magic and that James was too. I left it at that. I didn't lie, which is the main thing.'

'Why didn't you tell them the truth about everything?'

The final bars of Oasis ebbed into a Chemical Brothers track, with accompanying strobe lighting. It was like being in a full-on interrogation, the bright beams thundering into Andrew's eyes. Emptying his thoughts was the reason why he'd asked Jenny to meet him, so he could hardly complain.

Another sup: 'Because I don't really know what we have. Lara's last name and that circle symbol is about it. I don't want to send them off on a wild goose chase and I don't want to look like an idiot.'

Jenny nodded. 'Fair enough.'

It really wasn't; someone was dead, after all, their flesh brutally whittled apart.

Jenny polished off her cider with a large gulp and a clatter of glass on the bar. 'You're not a suspect, are you?'

'No, the body had been there for a few days. They were asking me about Friday night but I was with somebody then.'

'Who?'

A pause. 'Someone . . . I think they were just covering their arses anyway. It's not like they really thought I'd killed the guy.'

Andrew finished his drink and then spent ten seconds

flapping in the general direction of the barmaid. There really was no cool, calm or collected way to try to get the attention of someone serving behind a bar. It was either look like a fool, or not get served. He paid for the drinks just as the Chemical Brothers morphed into the Smiths, with the dancing masses adapting impressively to the audacious change of pace.

Jenny screeched her stool closer to his. 'What do you think's going on?'

Andrew had been thinking of little else since he'd smelled the stench of decay at James Wicker's house. 'There's a whole host of magic types who are either missing or dead but perhaps the strangest thing is that no one's linked them until we stumbled across it. We're seeing those occult symbols everywhere. Lara's name is mentioned in Kristian Verity's book, but he's missing. Her own boyfriend is missing. There could be loads more people named in his book who have disappeared.'

'If someone like Brian Oswald is missing, though – properly disappeared like Nicholas – why wouldn't his wife have reported it?'

Andrew shrugged. 'I don't know. Perhaps she's scared? I mentioned "Malvado" and there was definitely something there.'

'So we're back to Lara?'

'I suppose, or her family. She's meant to be an orphan.'

'I can do some digging tomorrow. I was struggling last time though – all I could really find were the odds and ends Lara has on social networks, which wasn't much. As a general people search, there were loads of Laras but not many Malvados. None, really. Her family history was largely non-existent too.'

'So who is she? It feels like there's a hidden community to do with that symbol.'

'Like a cult?'

The word hung in the air, interposed by Morrissey singing about double-decker buses. If there was some sort of local black magic group, then he and Jenny were caught in the thick of it, the charcoal markings on the office door a warning that now felt more and more ominous.

'Perhaps . . .'

The thought was clearly now in Jenny's mind. 'Say there is a cult and they're responsible for people going missing, perhaps even human sacrifices – things like that. Wouldn't somebody have noticed? The man you found had a circle carved into his skin and a massive hole in his chest. It's not the type of thing that happens every day.'

At first Andrew thought someone had bumped into him but then he realised his phone was buzzing. He stared at the flashing name on the screen. 'Oh for . . .'

'Who is it?'

'Richard Carr.'

Andrew hurried towards the exit and relative peace of the street. The call was much the same as their conversation outside his office, with Richard fishing for information about whether there had been any progress in finding out what happened to his son. Andrew tried to be as diplomatic as he could, even though it was almost ten o'clock on a Sunday evening. Richard continued talking about his wife and how she was taking everything badly, but there wasn't a lot Andrew could do. It took almost ten minutes for Andrew to finally shake him off, pledging that he'd ignore the call the next time, or at least until he had something he could report.

Back inside the pub, another Oasis track was blaring. A new group of lads were on the pool table, pound coins piled next to the centre pocket.

Andrew slipped back onto his stool and had a sip of his drink. Jenny leant towards him. 'Okay?'

'He's just anxious. I don't know if he's worried about money, or if us being involved is making things worse. They might have been starting to get through it and now we're around asking the same questions that didn't get answered nine months ago. You can't blame him, I guess.'

Jenny's knee was pressing against his, the music feeling louder than before as she leant across to bellow into his ear. 'I don't know anything about black magic.'

'Me either.'

'Are we going to have to talk to someone who knows what they're on about?'

Andrew nodded, feeling uncomfortable. Ever since Scrumpy had mentioned the word 'occult', he'd had a feeling they'd end up at this point. Perhaps that was why he'd continued pushing at the case, even though it was seemingly a series of unconnected events? He'd only gone to Scrumpy on the off-chance and then followed up Kristian Verity on a whim. He might not have kidnapped or killed anyone but, in some ways, he'd engineered his way to this moment.

Jenny cupped her hands around her mouth, shouting. 'Do you know anyone?'

Andrew nodded again.

'Who?'

'My ex-wife wrote her dissertation about the Pendle Witch Trials.'

MONDAY

29

Andrew's car looked in a significantly better state post-fire than before someone had covered it in flammable liquid and thrown a match onto it. As well as respraying the bonnet, the garage had serviced the vehicle, checked everything over, and given it a thorough clean inside and out. Andrew wondered if the same process would apply if he set fire to a few more of his things – the oven in his apartment could certainly do with a clean and he didn't fancy that. Perhaps arson was the way forward?

The journey out of the city, south through Cheshire, used to be familiar. Whenever Andrew and Keira were visiting her childhood home, they would ignore the motorways and opt for the country roads. Manchester was a network of jammed inner-city highways and the M60 ring road. It was refreshing to get away from that into the hedge-banked narrow lanes.

Red triangle signs for ice and animal crossings littered the sides of the road, with black-and-white chevrons on the tight, dangerous bends. Masochistic cyclists blitzed their way along the windy pot-hole-ridden roads, leggings and thermals practically sprayed on as drivers flashed alongside them.

The area near Delamere Forest was a collection of leafy hamlets and villages. The further Andrew got from home, the greater his sense of déjà vu. He'd been on these roads in happier times, when car journeys with the woman to whom he was once married were spent singing along to the radio and discussing plans for the future. Now this *was* his future and he was by himself, their ideas long since abandoned.

He followed the signs towards the little village to which she had once introduced him. As well as the picture-postcard bridge crossing the babbling stream, there was a country pub with a thatched roof. The chalkboard outside advertised hot food and a friendly atmosphere, which sounded good – although Andrew didn't know of any pubs who openly publicised cold nourishment and a riot waiting to happen.

The village store was closed, with a 'back at one' sign pinned to the glass. Around the corner was the only cafe, a pretty little cottage with a brown picket fence and rows of picnic tables on the lawn. Given the conditions, their placement was optimistic to say the least.

The bell over the cafe door tinkled as the waitress glanced up from her book towards Andrew in clear bemusement that someone had come in. She was the only other person there, a creeping smile appearing on her face as if she'd forgotten what to do when customers entered.

Andrew ordered a cappuccino, treated himself to a short-bread slice, and then sat at one of the small round tables listening to the whoosh and burr of the coffee machine. He peered at the clock over the front door; he was fifteen minutes early. After delivering his drink to the table, the waitress perched herself on the edge of the counter and started to talk about the weather – every Brit's get-out topic of conversation. If there was nothing else to blather about, the temperature and/or the rain was always a given. Andrew played along, before she returned to her book. He sipped his coffee slowly, taking a newspaper from the rack near the front door and keeping a close watch on the clock.

At a minute past the time they had agreed to meet, the bell jangled again. Andrew's eyes shot up expectantly from the paper but it was a mum with a pushchair, struggling her way inside. A young girl clambered out of the buggy, staring at Andrew before her mother ruffled her hair and asked her what she wanted.

They stayed for twenty minutes, in which time Andrew ordered a second coffee, worrying if he was going to struggle to sleep because of too much caffeine. The coffee machine whooshed again, the waitress continued reading, the mother and daughter left in a gust of freezing air blowing in from outside.

Tick-tick-tick.

Keira was late. Not just by a minute or two but by half an hour. Andrew looked at his phone. He hadn't missed a call and there were no messages. He couldn't blame her; he and his ex-wife hadn't spoken in almost eight years and now he'd called her after ten o'clock on a Sunday night asking for help. It was no wonder she'd fobbed him off with a time and place to meet and then not bothered. What else did he expect? He deserved to be stood up.

Andrew left a few dregs in the bottom of his mug, finished off the crumbs of the biscuit, and then started reading the paper again. Five more minutes.

Which was what he'd told himself ten minutes ago.

He had reached the lifestyle section in the centre for a second time when the door rattled again. For a few moments, he didn't dare look up, focusing on the newsprint but not taking in the words. He sensed the waitress moving, heard the shuffle of feet and a woman gasping as she moved out of the cold.

Andrew finally allowed himself to peer upwards, taking in the silhouette of the figure in the doorway, making himself believe what his eyes were telling him. There were a few more crinkles around her eyes, her hair was shorter and lighter – but it was undoubtedly the woman he'd walked away from eight years previously, lying that he didn't love her.

SEVENTEEN YEARS AGO

30

Andrew Hunter sat at the table in the corner of the university refectory, drumming his fingers. The man opposite peered up from his baked potato, eyebrows raised.

'Can you stop that?'

'What?'

'The finger-tapping thing. It's really annoying.'

Andrew did as he'd been asked, not realising he'd been doing it in the first place.

His flatmate, Gideon, continued to shovel baked beans into his face, dribbling a trail of orange juice onto his black T-shirt. It dawned on Andrew that this was probably why no one bothered to pay them any attention. Or, to be more precise, no *women* bothered to pay them any attention. If he'd been placed in halls with a potential rugby captain, an elite teenage specimen, he could have ridden on that person's coattails when they went out. Instead, he was stuck with Gideon, his posh accent, appalling dress sense, enhanced sweat glands, and disgusting culinary habits.

'Whrre jouff wannv gotooonicht?'

And he talked with his mouth full.

Andrew continued watching the door, wondering if someone from his course was going to come in. Anyone he might be able to have a conversation with that didn't involve illnesses or diseases Gideon had endured over the years.

'Pardon?'

Gideon swallowed this time. 'Where do you want to go later?'

Somehow, Andrew and Gideon had slipped into the routine of going to one of two pubs close to their halls pretty much every night. Both were dives, neither contained any interesting people (girls) and the only thing they had going for them was that they were both cheap.

University really wasn't what Andrew thought it was going to be. His course was dull, the only friends he'd made weren't the sort of people he'd usually be bothered about, the Manchester weather was awful, and he was haemorrhaging money.

Gideon scratched at his armpit, exposing a dark circle of sweat. '. . . I was thinking we could go to the union. They're putting on a karaoke night . . .'

Ugh.

Andrew knew he was kidding himself, Gideon wasn't the problem – he was. It wasn't in his nature to go out of his way to talk to strangers. He'd never been good at small talk, or making friends. The reason he hung around with Gideon was because they were so alike: both social misfits, awkward around both sexes, struggling to know what to say.

He stood abruptly. 'I'm going to get something to eat after all.'

Andrew didn't wait for Gideon to reply, making his way around the scattered chairs and picking up a tray. He headed to the back of the line, behind the exact kind of rugby-type he wished he'd been placed in a room with. The student towered over him, bulky wide shoulders blocking the light. He was the sort of person who would know where all of the cool people (girls) hung around, and it definitely wasn't going to be karaoke nights at the students' union. That had dregs of society written all over it.

The surrounding noise was almost overpowering: trays clattering, plates banging, cutlery scraping and the non-stop chatter, chatter, chatter of the massed students.

Andrew continued edging ahead as he felt a group of young women slot in behind him, moaning about one of their other flatmates.

At least it wasn't just him.

He finally reached the front and opted for a potato with chilli. There weren't too many other options – pizza, chips, some sort of brown sludge masquerading as a stew. It was like being back at primary school but with higher prices.

Because there weren't enough queues in the world, Andrew joined a second one, waiting to pay. At the front, a blonde girl was digging through a small purse, picking out coppers as she haggled with the person on the counter about how much she owed. The rugby-type was already eating his pizza, munching his way through half a slice in two bites.

Andrew risked a small glance behind towards the women, peering over their shoulders towards the back of the refectory as if he was really looking at someone else. There were three of them, all normal-looking – not the protesters with dreadlocks who sat outside the library banging on about some cause or another; not the giggly ones who'd be fawning over the rugby-type. Normal was good.

He twisted back as the lad behind the girl at the front offered her ten pence to make up the difference.

'Andy!'

Instinctively Andrew spun towards where the sound had come from. As he did, his plate skidded across the polished tray, flipping over the rim and slopping a large mound of chilli over the girl standing directly behind him before smashing on the floor with a thunderous crash.

For a moment, everything stood still.

The student at the front of the line stopped counting her pennies, the mass of chattering voices was silenced, forkfuls of food waited in mid-air – and everyone turned to look.

The young woman behind Andrew stood with both hands in the air, mouth gaping in shock. She was wearing a fitted pink top that now had a trail of brown slurry dribbling down it.

Everyone stared.

Everyone.

If aliens had landed in the centre of the room and started performing anal probes, there would have been fewer people watching than there were looking directly at Andrew.

Then the chattering began again.

'. . . Did you see that? . . .'

'. . . Wow, what a dickhead . . .'

'. . . Oh my God, I'm so glad that's not me . . .'

'. . . What happened? . . .'

'. . . Who is that idiot? . . .'

'. . . Did he just puke on her? . . .'

Then the laughing began.

The girl's friends had leapt backwards in an attempt to avoid the splashback but she hadn't moved, hadn't even screamed. She had highlighted brown hair in a loose ponytail, big blue eyes with long eyelashes and a yoghurt pot in her hand. She was also dripping with stinking brown chilli, staring at him, mouth still open.

Andrew stared back. 'Er . . .'

'You could start with sorry.'

Andrew reached for the pile of napkins on the counter, stretching towards her but stopping himself mid-reach when he realised he was about to start dabbing at her chest.

'Er . . .'

One of her friends leapt forward, grabbed the paper towels and began patting away the worst of the spilled food.

Andrew finally managed a full sentence. 'I'm really sorry.'

The friend with the towels turned to him, sneering. 'What a complete prick. How clumsy are you?'

'I know, I'm really sorry. It was an accident. I heard my name and turned and it just . . . went all over.'

The queue was moving again with people sliding around Andrew to get to the front, each glaring at him as if he was about to throw food in their direction too. From

253

the kitchen, a haggard-looking cook, who had likely seen it all before, shuffled out with a mop and bucket.

The young woman was still watching Andrew, mouth finally closed. There was a small dark dot of a birthmark next to the curve of her lips. 'What's your name?'

'Andrew.'

'Do you normally throw food over people?'

Over her shoulder, Gideon was peering around the corner, bemused grin on his face. Around the rest of the room, knives and forks were scraping again, chatter back to normal.

Move along, folks, nothing to see here.

It wasn't the worst thing Andrew had ever done in his life. When he was seven or eight, his next-door neighbour had taken him, her own son, and half-a-dozen other children to the park on a scorching day in the summer holidays. He'd run around, gone on the swings, climbed the frame and used the slide over and over.

Then he'd scoffed down two packets of Chewits for lunch.

After his neighbour offered to push them all on the roundabout, Andrew had staggered off, head spinning, stomach grumbling, and promptly thrown up all over the woman.

This was close but it wasn't quite in the same league.

Andrew thought about her question. Usually he would apologise, tell her he definitely didn't usually throw food over people, apologise again, and then slink off to his dorm hoping no one he knew – or anyone who knew the people he knew – had witnessed it. Except for Gideon, of course, but that was unavoidable.

Instead, with the situation as bad as it could probably be, Andrew decided to do something he never did: say what was actually on the tip of his tongue, as opposed to what he thought the other person might want to hear.

The young woman was still eyeing him, brown stain looking somehow worse now that the remnants of the chilli had been dabbed in by her mate.

'I only usually throw food over people on the weekends.'

The food-slathered girl and both of her friends stared at him some more, mouths open – and then her face cracked and she laughed. She stepped over the broken plate and the mound of wasted food and offered her hand.

'Hi, I'm Keira.'

31

Sometimes, the nicest dreams are far worse than nightmares. In the unconscious imagination, the most wonderful things can be created: soaring, sweeping cliff faces; endless, perfect beaches; gravity-defying waterfalls. But it is always the people that stick most strongly in the mind: imaginary friends, acquaintances, even lovers, who appear and then disappear alongside the devastating realisation that they were never real to begin with. The only thing remaining is a struggle to remember what they looked like, why they were so appealing, and quite why an insentient part of yourself felt the need to construct them in the first place.

Although she was real, Andrew had thought of Keira as that dreamlike paradigm for much of the past eight years. He remembered the things they had done together: the laughs, nights in and out, the places they'd been. The other experiences and the reason why he left her were cast aside as if they'd never been there in the first place.

He thought of the chilli and potato stuck to Keira's top as now she stood in front of him wearing a pink coat. Her hair was completely blonde, cropped short to her ears in a bob that was curling slightly inwards. She was perhaps a little thinner and there were definitely more lines around her face, but they gave her features a striking lived-in sense, as if she had gone places and experienced things.

She unfurled a rainbow scarf from around her neck and unzipped the coat, breathing a final mist of cool air before closing the door with a second rattling of the bell. After the briefest of glances in Andrew's direction, Keira headed to the counter, walking in the way she always had: shuffling without fully picking her feet up, as if gliding. Her voice was a tiny bit deeper than he remembered but it could have been because of the cold outside. She ordered a latte and a cookie and then floated across the cafe, scraping back the metal chair and sitting opposite Andrew.

Andrew tried to look at Keira in a not-looking-at-her kind of way: glancing over her shoulder towards the window and the door, focusing on the empty table beyond for no reason, picking up his mug and peering around it. Then, finally, he gave up and simply watched her.

Her eyes were bluer than he remembered, the colour of exotic oceans in far-flung places of the world that he'd seen on television but never been to.

Or perhaps he was just a soppy so-and-so?

Probably that.

'Hi,' she whispered.

'Hi.'

'Sorry I'm late, I couldn't get away . . .'

'It's all right. Thanks for coming – I wouldn't have called if I didn't need help.'

The waitress stepped across with Keira's order, before returning to the counter and her book. There was a delicate clank of mug on saucer, followed by a slow sip of milk froth and then a clumsy, confidence-sapping hush. Andrew could barely remember why he was there.

Keira was peering at him over her cup, a hint of an upwards crinkle to her lips. 'You've lost weight.'

Andrew peered down at his stomach. Since he'd last seen her, he had eaten loads, exercised a bit, gained weight, lost weight, obsessed over it, not cared about it – the usual. His words felt stuck, scraping somewhere at the back of his tongue, unformed.

'You too . . .'

Ugh. Awkward.

Keira returned the cup to the table. 'So what do you want?'

With the lack of small talk, Andrew followed Keira's lead, fumbling with his satchel and pulling out a cardboard wallet but not opening it. There was a lot he wished he had the courage to say but if she didn't want to bring it up, then he couldn't either. 'I'm working on something and there are links to the occult.'

Keira yawned, covering her mouth with a flapping hand. 'It's been a long time since I thought about anything like that.'

'That's still more recently than me.'

'What's wrong with the Internet?'

'We tried that. It's hard to know what's accurate and what's been written by excited teenagers who've been to the movies. Plus you can't just search for "black magic expert".'

'*We?*'

Oops.

'My assistant and me.'

Her eyes hadn't left him, searching for hidden meanings, the presence of which even Andrew wasn't sure about. 'I only studied European history,' she said.

'But we both know what your dissertation was about. You knew all sorts about cases involving witches and dark magic at the time. You don't just forget that, do you?'

The peppering of freckles on Keira's cheeks was slightly darker than it used to be. Perhaps she'd been on holiday?

She had another sip of her coffee. 'What do you want to know?'

Andrew took out a pen, and drew an upside-down triangle within a circle on a napkin. Keira glanced briefly at it but seemed a little confused.

'What are you showing me?'

'That symbol's been following me around. I've seen it on tattoos and someone drew it on my office door.'

She grimaced slightly, almost pained. 'It's only a symbol, a bit like a pentagram but a little more traditional.'

'Does it mean anything?'

'Not really. Some say certain combinations of shapes show power but it's all about belief. All sorts of different sects or people might have their own interpretations about various icons or numerology. It's so broad that I'm not sure what I can tell you that wouldn't be on the Internet.'

Andrew now understood why she'd winced. This was small-fry and, from her point of view, an excuse for him to contact her after such a long time.

'When I say that symbol's been everywhere, it's about a teenager who went missing. He and his girlfriend had that tattooed on their wrists. Three of his fingers were found at this site in the woods where there's a natural bowl shape. Around the edge, there are three trees, like a triangle.'

Keira pursed her lips for a few moments, then pulled the napkin back towards her and peered at the symbol again. 'I can't really remember properly . . . but you've got three points of a triangle and three fingers . . .' She rubbed an invisible blemish on her cheek, clearly trying to think back. '. . . I remember something from one of my books about this nineteenth-century thing in southern Europe. People would have their hands and feet removed in a sort of ritual. It was something to do with the Bible saying that Man was created in God's image. Believers did it to desecrate that image.' She ran her hand through her hair. 'I'm sorry – I really can't remember any more.'

Andrew paused, thinking through what she'd said. 'Southern Europe?'

'I think so.'

'Have you ever heard of the name "Malvado"? We did search for it but, aside from its Portuguese origins, we were struggling.'

Keira replied but it took Andrew a few moments to realise she had done so in a foreign accent. She smiled at him as she finished with a flourish – 'Mal-va-do' – rolling the word around her mouth. 'It *is* Portuguese,' she added, 'but that means it's Brazilian too. More or less, it means "evil".'

Lara Evil: like Doctor Evil but with more eye make-up. Something felt wrong.

Keira continued, more confidently this time. This was something she clearly knew about. 'Portugal began colonising Brazil in the 1500s. They exported their language and used African slaves to help them mine gold and diamonds. By the eighteenth century, they were transporting millions of pounds around the world and home to Portugal. With all that to-ing and fro-ing, all sorts of folk tales and myths were exported to mainland Europe. Malvado *does* mean evil but you could easily translate it as "devil", "Satan", or something like that.'

'Was there a myth about something named Malvado?'

'How much do you know about devil-worship?'

'I only practise at weekends if that's what you're asking.'

For the first time, Keira smiled with her eyes, not just her mouth. Almost as quickly as the sparkle appeared, it was gone again. She straightened herself and continued. 'People think it's dancing in a field but it's more nuanced than you might imagine. In many ways, the idea of Satanism is about anarchy, disrupting the normal structure of society. Christianity is broken down into all sorts of sects and factions. Even at its very base, there are Protestants and Catholics. Then there are Quakers, Evangelicals, Baptists and so on. It's hard to say that Christianity is any one thing. Devil-worship is much the same. Most wouldn't even believe in "God" or "the Devil" in those senses. It's more about the forces of nature. But others would and they'd have their own rituals. If you think of a Christian communion, breaking bread and drinking wine, it symbolises the body and blood of Christ. A devil-worshipper might do something similar. There are all sorts of accounts dating back to the dawn of time about black masses – where people drink the blood of a cloven animal, like a goat. Christians might say the Lord's Prayer, or litanies to keep them safe. Satanists might do the same, so their chants or rituals are no different in the sense that they're reciting something they believe in. It's all about faith.'

'How would that tie in to Malvado?'

Keira paused to have a bite of her cookie just as another couple entered the cafe in a bluster of freezing air. They knew the waitress's first name, ordering drinks and snacks and then sitting close to the counter, chatting.

After another mouthful of coffee, Keira continued: 'The important thing to remember is that the devil takes many forms.' She burst out laughing, putting a hand over her mouth. 'Sorry, that's not what I meant. I sounded like a fundamentalist Christian for a moment.' She took another sip of her drink, still smiling. 'What I was trying to say is that every culture has its own demons – in most cases, more than one. There are long lists of devils – Mephisto, Abbadon, Eligos, Valac – all sorts. One of the myths brought back from Brazil was of Malvado. He was a deity who ruled over the woods—'

The gasp had slipped from Andrew's mouth before he'd realised: an actual connection from Nicholas to the place where his fingers were found.

Keira nodded but continued. 'Malvado would supposedly appear to weary travellers or others seeking refuge, promising them eternal life in exchange for their soul. It's like a nursery rhyme, not the type of thing anyone would think to take seriously now, but I suppose things like that have diluted over time. Now there are horror movies everywhere, then it was just the power of storytelling. If you knew how to really tell a tale, then you could make anything sound intimidating.'

'How would that have found its way here?'

'Patience!' She smiled at him – with her eyes again,

actually enjoying telling the story. 'I don't really remember much more about the Brazilian origins but I do know a sort of cult built around Malvado in Portugal. There are documents going back to the nineteenth century of groups setting themselves up as a community living in the woods. They would capture homeless people and sacrifice them to their god of the trees. There was a big scandal at the time. As for how it found its way here . . . assuming it has, then I suppose in the same way as anything else: either passed down through generations, or it's an idea that immigrated.'

'Is it something that's widely known about?'

The other man and woman picked up their drinks and offered a loud 'thank you' to the waitress. They said 'hi' to Andrew and Keira, clearly mistaking them for another couple and making brief small talk about the conditions, before crossing to the table closest to the window.

Keira finished her drink and pointed to the mug. 'Are you buying me another?'

'Um . . . sure.' Andrew reached for his wallet. 'What do you want?'

'Peppermint tea.'

Andrew paid for the drink and sat back down. Keira finished her cookie and checked her watch, though didn't comment on the time. 'It's definitely not *that* widely known of, especially over here. I suppose if you went to Portugal and asked if they knew about the Pendle Witch Trials, then you'd see blank faces. Over there, seven people were executed for various offences involving witch-craft in what roughly translates as the "Black Evil" trials: "Mal Preto", or "Malvado Preto". It's not massively known about but it was one of the things I studied as supplementary information for my dissertation.'

Keira's tea arrived and the rest of the table was cleared, leaving a small trail of cookie crumbs across the polished surface. She dunked her teabag a few times and then gave it a poke with the spoon.

'Has that helped?' she asked, not looking up from her mug.

'Massively.'

Andrew was thinking about the reaction of Brian Oswald's wife to the name Malvado. At the time, he thought she'd flinched because of a link to Lara but it might be that she was more worried by the legend.

He watched Keira stirring the drink, knowing she'd never drunk peppermint tea when they'd been together. It had been eight years and was such a small thing but it seemed strangely affecting that he'd missed out on something she now enjoyed. How had she discovered it? Did she drink it regularly?

She still didn't look up, the greeny-brown pigments from the teabag completely discolouring the steaming water. 'Can I help with anything else?'

'Have you ever heard of anyone having the last name Malvado?'

Keira's eyebrows bowed in the centre. 'I don't think so. I'm probably not the right person to ask – but people would baptise or christen themselves as a devil's child. That's not just related to devil-worship. Think of a name like "Christenson": literally, "Son of Christ". At some point, someone decided to take that name.'

'So their last name wouldn't really be Malvado?'

'I doubt it. They'd have an actual birth name. If you had those Portuguese roots, you might call yourself something like "Andrew do Malvado", which is "Andrew of Evil". Of course, you'd probably lose the "do" part.'

That explained a lot. They had struggled to find out very much about Lara Malvado, likely because that wasn't her real name. Instead, she'd taken – or been given – a name that roughly translated as "Lara of the Devil" or "Lara of Evil".

Keira sipped some of her tea, checking her watch again. Andrew knew he only had a few more minutes to talk to her. He thought about everything he'd wanted to say over the past eight years – the explanation of why he'd walked away and how he'd regretted it from the moment he told her they were finished. He thought of how he could best put it into words, sentences that might not make it feel so brutal.

In the end, he could only come up with a pathetic: 'So how is everything?'

Keira put down her cup and started to laugh, not because she found it funny but because she understood how pitiful he was being.

'Is that your way of asking if I'm seeing anyone?'

'No.'

'You do remember that you left me?'

'I know.'

'And you know that it's really unfair for you to call?'

Her eyes didn't move from the table, her voice croaking on the final word, giving the merest hint of the heartache Andrew knew he had caused.

'I'm sorry. I didn't know who else to ask. You've really helped.'

'How is Manchester?'

'Full of traffic, of people. It's built up a lot since we were at uni. There are glass-fronted things everywhere and neat little restaurants. If it wasn't for the weather, it'd be really nice. When the sun's out, it's incredible.'

Keira abruptly dropped the spoon into the mug, leaving at least a third of her tea. 'I've got to go.'

'Oh . . .'

They both stood at the same time but Andrew couldn't bring himself to look into her face, just in case she was upset. He'd spent the past eight years convincing himself she was better off without him. Perhaps she was, but he still couldn't bear to see her unhappy. For a few moments, they stood awkwardly a step away from each other. Then they had an even clumsier shoulders-in, arses-out hug that lasted barely a second.

Keira hauled her coat back on and rewrapped her scarf. She picked up her bag and then stepped away from the table. Andrew wanted to say something meaningful but ended up fumbling in his satchel for a slightly crumpled business card.

'Can I give you this?' he asked.

Keira took it, skimming the details. 'Why?'

'I don't know . . . I suppose . . .' He sighed. 'I don't know . . .'

She pocketed it, muttered something Andrew didn't catch – and then turned and walked out of his life again.

32

The journey back to the office was a long, frustrating one. The pretty hedges were now towering monstrosities blocking the light. The tight, picturesque roads were now an utter pain in the arse – why didn't they just tarmac the entire countryside, stick in a ten-lane motorway and be done with it?

By the time he got stuck behind a tractor for the third time, Andrew was in the mood to return to his apartment and go back to bed. Sod Lara and whatever nutty deity she thought she was representing.

As he reached the outskirts of the city, away from the greenery, the icy roads, the peace, and Keira, Andrew began to feel a little better. Regardless of anything he'd managed to mess up by not being able to get a proper sentence out in front of his former wife, he felt as if he had a vague idea of what might be going on with Lara.

'Vague' being the key word.

Any positivity immediately left him as soon as he walked into the office. Sitting on opposite sides of the desk, cups of tea in hand with Bourbon biscuits on a plate between them, were Jenny and Violet Deacon, chatting away like old friends at a weekly mothers' meeting.

The memory of Stewart Deacon and the knuckle-duster was suddenly at the front of Andrew's mind.

'. . . If you get in my business again, Mr Hunter, next time you won't see me coming . . .'

It was a shame Stewart hadn't told his wife to stay away, not that Andrew had mentioned it to Jenny either. It wasn't that he particularly responded to threats but the case was over and they had delivered the report to Mrs Deacon. As far as he knew, there was no need for them to be involved again.

Jenny and Violet both peered up as Andrew entered. 'I told you he wouldn't be long,' Jenny said with a smile.

Violet was dressed a little more sensibly than the last time Andrew had seen her, wrapped up in jeans and a thick jumper, with a large winter coat, hat and scarf hanging on the stand close to the door. The dark rims around her eyes made it look as if she hadn't slept in days.

Andrew nodded towards the door, looking at Jenny. 'Can we have a word?'

Violet gazed between the two of them, the conversation hastily cut short.

Down the stairs and back outside, Jenny was in the process of separating the top half of a Bourbon from the bottom. Across the road, Tina the receptionist offered them a small wave, simultaneously cradling a phone between her shoulder and ear while typing on the keyboard.

They both waved back and then Jenny turned to Andrew. 'How was it?'

'Interesting. But what's Violet Deacon doing upstairs?'

The first half of the biscuit had disappeared. 'It's probably best that she tells you herself. Why?'

'Her husband came to my flat on Saturday night with a knuckle-duster.'

'Oh . . . did he . . . ?'

Andrew touched his ear, feeling the area where he'd been punched. 'He made it clear he wasn't happy. It's my own fault for going to their house in the first place. I was trying to rush things through and didn't bother to ask about who else was there.'

'Did you talk to the police?'

He shook his head. 'I thought it was going to be all over with.'

Jenny pushed herself onto tiptoes, the remaining half of the biscuit dangling from her mouth. She reached up and twisted Andrew's head to the side, like a worried mother about to lick her fingers and dab a smear of mud away from his face. Andrew instinctively pulled away.

'Hold still,' she scolded, mouth still full of the remaining biscuit. Given the amount of sugar she put away, it was a miracle she wasn't bouncing around like a hyperactive sumo wrestler.

'It feels fine.'

'I'm just looking.'

Jenny brushed forward his ear lobe and then ran her finger along the area where it joined his head. Andrew flinched but she had a grip like a toddler with a rattle.

'Ouch.'

She released his face, leaving a stinging sensation around his ear where her fingers had been. 'Stop being such a baby. There are blobs of dried blood. Didn't you clean it?'

'It hurt.'

'There's a bit of a cut but it doesn't look too bad. You should have said something last night.'

Suitably chastened but without an explanation, Andrew led Jenny back upstairs, where Violet was sitting in the spot they'd left her in, munching on a Bourbon on the other side of Jenny's desk. Andrew wheeled his chair around and asked how he could help.

Violet seemed more defensive in front of him than she had been with Jenny, crossing her arms and angling her body away. 'Did you get your car sorted?'

'Yes.'

'I asked Jack if it was him but he kept saying he didn't start the fire. He said he went for a walk and wasn't around. I'm not pretending that's definitely what happened but I don't know what else I can do. He really is a good kid.'

'It's over with now.'

She glanced towards Jenny; clearly this was something they had already spoken about. 'It's not really. Since you were around last week, Jack has been changing.' She sighed, plucking out one of the pins that had been holding her hair into a bun. It dropped down to her shoulders and she started to bundle it up again. 'It's mainly happened because of his father. After you'd been around on Wednesday, Stewart came home early from work because Jack had called him. It's my own fault for asking you to come to the house instead of coming here. I didn't want to leave Jack at home by himself. I should have realised he'd be able to overhear.'

Andrew wasn't going to argue – he'd been guilty of not checking too.

Jenny stood. 'Do you want another tea?' She waggled her empty Mr Men mug in the air and Violet passed hers across. Andrew shook his head. If he kept downing hot drinks at this rate, he'd either need a leg bag, or spend the rest of the afternoon working from a toilet cubicle.

Violet turned back to Andrew. 'I thought Stewart was going to want a big row about things but he didn't even talk to me. He pulled up outside, picked up Jack, and then they went out.'

'What time was that?'

'Late afternoon.'

That must have been after Andrew had caught Jack following him and Jenny to the Carrs' house – something else the teenager's mother didn't know about.

'They were gone for about three hours,' Violet added. 'When they got back, neither of them spoke to me. I assume Jack told Stewart about you being there and the report but I don't really know what they spoke about. Neither of them have talked to me since.'

'Not at all?'

'Not a single word.' She stopped to swallow. The smile on her face when it had just been her and Jenny was long gone. She was ageing in front of him: chin sagging to her chest, body sinking into the seat. 'When they got back, I asked Stewart if he wanted to talk but he brushed past me. I asked Jack if he wanted something to eat but he didn't acknowledge I was there.'

Jenny returned, putting two mugs down on the desk

and resting a reassuring hand on Violet's shoulder, simultaneously making eye contact with Andrew. He could sense her telling him that she'd learned this from watching other people. It was a strange moment of honesty conducted entirely in silence. Andrew didn't believe in telepathy but he did know that people who were familiar enough with each other could read a mere flicker of an expression as if it was a full conversation. He'd once had that with Keira and now there was a connection to Jenny: not romantic, just . . . different. Andrew wasn't sure he understood it, or her.

He offered her the smallest of nods to say that he got it as Violet turned to give an appreciative 'thank you'.

'Can I get you anything else?' Jenny asked.

After a shake of the head and a sip of tea, Violet continued: 'At first I thought it would just be that night. Stewart went off to work the next morning but he's normally up early, so it's not unusual for me not to see him. Then Jack went out for the day too. But even when they're home, they'll only talk to each other. It's like I'm not there. It's been like that since Wednesday . . .'

Andrew let her tail off, wondering if she'd fill the silence. When she reached for her tea, he cut in: 'How can we help?'

'I know I said last week that I was going to see things out but . . .' Another glance at Jenny. '. . . I think I was kidding myself. I suppose I always was. I wanted to keep things together for Jack but it has to be a two-way thing. I probably shouldn't have gone about things the way I did by having Stewart followed but I guess I always knew it might come down to this. To answer your question, I'm going to file for divorce and I'd like everything you might be able to find out about my husband. I know you told me where he'd been the other day but I want to know if there's anything else. Does he actually have a mistress? I want a solid case for divorce that he won't be able to get out of.'

'Didn't you say you did the accounts for his businesses and could bring him down?'

'Perhaps that was a bit of bravado. I do the business accounts and there's plenty in there that could cause trouble but I'm not one of the directors. I'd only end up harming myself – and Jack – because if Stewart was arrested, the business accounts would be frozen and then investigations take a really long time. What I need is the truth about our personal lives and then I'll have a more straightforward case.'

'. . . *If you get in my business again, Mr Hunter, next time you won't see me coming . . .*'

Violet sounded genuine: a woman at the end of her tether. But Andrew didn't like getting involved in these types of cases anyway, let alone when he'd been physically warned off.

Violet slowly rolled up the long sleeve of her jumper, not saying a word but exposing a row of purple finger-shaped bruises at the top of her right arm. The colours flowed outwards like a circular rainbow, creeping around the curve of the saggy skin of her bicep.

Andrew glanced at Jenny, who was watching Violet. He knew it was a form of emotional blackmail, using the injuries to tug on his humanity. The awareness didn't stop him feeling sorry for her, though.

'Was that done by your husband, or son?'

'Stewart.'

'Have you told anyone else?'

She shook her head. 'A son needs his father to be around, doesn't he? Us separating would be hard on Jack but having his dad carted off would be worse.'

Andrew tried looking at Jenny again and this time she met his eyes, though there were no hidden messages. 'Your husband and I had a bit of a run-in the other evening,' Andrew said.

Violet almost jumped out of her chair, pressing forward and slopping some of her tea over the lip of the cup. 'What did he do?'

'He was waiting for me at my flat—'

'How did he know where you live?'

'I don't know but he knew about what had been going on with you hiring me.'

'What did he do?'

'Not much, mainly make threats.'

She nodded knowingly. 'That's Stewart all over . . . well, recently. In the old days he was fine. As soon as the business took off, he was a different person. At home, he'd fume at rivals he thought were trying to get one over him and he'd be so paranoid that they were out to get him. If ever someone got a contract that he didn't, or undercut him at an auction, he'd brood on it for weeks. Eventually, it got to the point where we couldn't have a conversation because it would always end up degenerating into an argument where he said I wasn't supporting him. Then he started getting aggressive.'

She paused to finish her drink, voice lowering.

'We were out for a meal one evening but another property developer was in the bar. Stewart spent around an hour glaring in his direction and then followed him outside for some reason. I went out a minute or so later but by the time I got there, Stewart was already pointing fingers and mouthing off. I didn't even know the other guy, but in the end he snapped and had Stewart up against the wall by the throat. Stewart was struggling and kicking but the other guy was one of those deceptively strong blokes where they don't look that big but they're all muscle, no fat. I was screaming at him to let Stewart go and he did but that was the end of everything, really. Stewart shrugged me off and went to get a taxi and we never spoke about it again. He was a different person and I suppose that's when it started with him and his other women. He was more aggressive but smarter with it. He'd still shout and swear but he'd never risk anything getting physical with someone bigger than him. If you stand up to him, he slinks back to where he came from.'

'I'm not sure why you're telling me this . . .'

Violet breathed out heavily. 'I suppose I've just had enough of it all. This last week has proved to me that it really *is* over with. I hope you can help. I don't need much – just proof of what he's doing. I know you did that previous report but he could easily argue he wasn't getting up to anything untoward in that place out in Huyton.'

That's what Andrew had feared at the time. He thought

of Keira and how he'd react if someone was harming her in the way Stewart was treating his wife. He'd thought that these types of infidelity cases were exactly what he wanted to avoid, so he could concentrate on those where he could help people. Here, he could help at least one person . . . he just had to be very careful.

Andrew waited until Violet peered up from the desk and was looking at him.

He always was a soft touch.

'I'll see what we can do. But you might have to give me a few days because there's something else I've got to deal with first.'

TUESDAY

33

As Andrew approached Lara's block of flats, a young twenty-something wearing a tight cardigan and even tighter cord trousers was on his way out, presumably in an effort to find a mirror or a clothes shop. Andrew offered a thin smile and the student held the door open for him, not bothering to query who he was.

By the time he reached the top of the stairs, Andrew could hear raised voices coming from inside the flat. The female Alex's voice was by far the loudest: '. . . all I want is for you to stop going through my things!'

Male Alex was giving as good as he got: 'I've not touched your stuff.'

'I had six corner yoghurts in the fridge and now there are only five.'

'So what?'

'So you're the one that's always going around stealing other people's food.'

'I am not.'

There was a slam of something fleshy-sounding on the wall. 'Everyone knows you do. Sophie caught you stealing her HobNobs the other week.'

'That was different.'

'How?'

'I was pissed and they were sitting there in the cupboard!'

'You're such a pig.'

'You love it, babe.'

Wallop – flesh on skin this time. 'Stop calling me that. And I really *don't* love it.'

There was a slam of a door and then hush. If Jenny did know what she was talking about – which Andrew wasn't convinced of – then the two Alexes probably should just do it to get it over with. If Jenny was wrong, then they should probably be separated before one of them murdered the other.

Andrew waited just in case there was going to be more arguing. Stuck to the railings was the same flyer asking people to get in touch about the apparent rat problem. This time he noticed Alex's name and email address on the bottom. There were more 'Vote Dave P for President' posters overlaid with the picture of someone's hairy arse but also a scattering of 'Don't vote Dave P for President' banners with a picture of Postman Pat. There was definitely a private joke going on.

When he was sure the row was over, Andrew knocked gently and the door was soon opened by the female Alex. She blinked in recognition. 'Oh, it's you.'

'Is Lara in?'

Alex pulled the door open further and nodded towards the end of the hallway. 'See for yourself.'

Nothing appeared to have changed inside, with the fridge still buzzing like an aeroplane coming in to land and an underlying smell of curry that seemed to be part of the walls.

Further along the corridor, Andrew stopped outside

Lara's door and knocked gently. Her voice sounded from the inside. 'Who is it?'

'Andrew Hunter. I was hoping we could have another chat.'

There was a shuffling, a 'hang on', and then the door opened a crack, revealing a single, blinking eye.

'What do you want?'

'Have you got ten minutes?'

'Why didn't you call?'

'I'm here on a whim. I only need a few minutes.'

It was a lie; Andrew had wanted to catch her when she wouldn't have had time to prepare for his arrival.

She swore under her breath. 'All right, give me a minute.'

Before he could answer, the door clicked closed, leaving him to lean awkwardly on the side wall.

It took Andrew a few moments to realise that the young woman who emerged from Lara's room was actually the person he was there to see. Apart from the long, dark hair, she looked completely different: make-up-free and wearing jeans with a heavy coat.

She didn't even glance at Andrew as she headed for the main door. 'Come on, let's go.'

Andrew did as he was told, following her downstairs, past the array of posters into the lounge area where she had apparently had her rant about Harry Potter.

Five vanilla-coloured sofas were scattered around the room, each with amber beer stains and copious amounts of fluffy yellow stuffing pouring out. Fixed to the widest wall was a large, flat television with a series of scratches along the front panel and a remote control connected to the bottom with string and what looked like five or six rolls of sticky tape. A printed card was pinned underneath, reading: 'Save the world by saving electricity. TURN IT OFF.' Predictably, the red dot indicating standby glowed directly above it.

On the wall, there was another photocopied sheet asking people to contact Alex if they saw a rat, plus many more of the vote/don't vote posters.

Lara fell onto one of the sofas, with Andrew sitting nearby, not too close. She picked up the remote control and muted a cookery programme that was bordering on pornographic, with lingering shots of a female chef sucking on a jam-dipped spoon.

'You can't keep coming here,' Lara said.

'I don't intend to. Hopefully I can leave you alone after this.'

Lara glanced away from the television towards Andrew, suddenly interested. 'Have you discovered something?'

'I'd like to ask you what you know about black magic.'

Her mouth bobbed open but only for a second before she composed herself again. Without the heavy make-up, her face seemed capable of stronger emotions. Her eyelid was twitching and there was a sense of vulnerability that hadn't been there before as she scratched at her cheek.

'Why are you asking?'

'There were books about the occult in Nicholas's room.'

'Really?'

If Lara was faking it, then she was good – the word popped straight out.

'They were under his bed.'

'Oh . . . was there anything else?'

'Like what?'

She started to say something but stopped herself. 'I don't understand why you're here. You're supposed to be finding out what happened to Nicholas. Have you discovered something, or not?'

'That's why I was hoping you could tell me what you know about magic.'

Lara was scratching her cheek again, eyes nervously glancing to and from the door as if she was worried someone was going to come in. 'Why? Because of the way I usually dress? You think that makes me some sort of wiccan?'

'No, I'm asking because of the books. Nicholas wouldn't have had them if he wasn't interested and you were his girlfriend. It's natural to think you'd know something.'

He was trying to be diplomatic but could see why people had told him about the arguments between Lara and Nicholas. Everything about her body language screamed rage. She was leaning forward, top lip curled, fists balled.

'How do you know they were his?'

'Who else's would they be?'

Lara frowned, shaking her head. 'I don't know – you found them.'

'Did you ever hear him talking about the occult?'

'No. That type of thing is just for kids with their vampire movies, isn't it? Nothing for grown-ups.'

'Didn't you have an argument with people in this room, saying that magic was real?'

Lara leapt off from the sofa, instantly furious. She poked a black fingernail into Andrew's chest with surprising force. 'Are you spying on me?'

Andrew flinched in pain, trying to pull away without raising his arms. 'No.'

She edged back, weapon-like finger crooked and poised. 'So how do you know that? Have you been following me?'

'I heard from someone.'

'Who?'

'I don't think I should say.'

'I want you to leave.' Lara was on her feet, grabbing his forearm and trying to pull him towards the door. Andrew didn't fight but didn't go with her either, remaining on the sofa.

'Lara . . .'

'I'll call the security office. You're not allowed to be here unless you're invited.'

'I need to ask you about your name.'

She stopped tugging Andrew's arm, standing over him instead, hands on hips. 'What about it?'

'Where does Malvado come from?'

'It's what I'm called . . .'

'Is it really? That's what it says on your birth certificate?'

'What's it to you? You're supposed to be finding out what happened to Nicholas, not spying on me. I—'

She stopped as a young man with straggly shoulder-length dark hair appeared in the doorway wearing obscenely tight running shorts, a vest that clung to his slender frame, fluorescent yellow running shoes and socks pulled up to his knees. He glanced between Lara and Andrew. 'Everything all right?'

Lara dismissed him with a wave of her hand. 'Piss off and mind your own business.'

'I was only—'

'Well, don't.'

The jogger had one last look at them and then pissed off to mind his own business. Lara sat back on the sofa close to Andrew, her voice lower, not wanting to attract attention.

'Why does it matter what I'm called?'

'What does Malvado mean?'

'It was just a word I liked.'

'So you started using it as a last name?'

'People have nicknames all the time – so what? I just chose my own.'

'But why that one?'

Unconsciously, Lara was rubbing the area of her arm where Andrew knew the circle symbol was. 'My dad used to use it . . .'

'Oh . . .'

Andrew didn't know what to say. They'd been looking for information about Lara's parents and the name 'Malvado' for days with little luck. All they knew was what Richard Carr had told them in the first place: Lara was an orphan. He hoped she would fill the gap but Lara wasn't going to give up any information she didn't have to.

'Is your dad—'

'He's dead if that's what you're asking but it's none of your business.'

'Do you know what Malvado means?'

Lara was scratching at her cheek again, leaving a red mark. 'It's just a word – I told you. What's it got to do with Nicholas?'

Andrew reached into his pocket and took out the napkin from the previous day on which he'd drawn the circle with the upside-down triangle. He passed it across. 'Do you know what this is?'

A shrug before she screwed it up.

'It's on your arm. Nicholas had one too.'

Lara tugged down her sleeves, even though they were already around her wrists. 'So?'

'I'm only asking what it is.'

'It's just a logo we liked. Why's it so important? Is this what gets you off? Harassing young women, like that one you brought here last time?'

'It's an innocent question.'

'Do you think you're some sort of super-cop? I've already had all of this from the police and his parents: everyone looking at me as if I'm lying. I told you what happened the night Nicholas disappeared and don't understand why you're still here.'

'Because I want to find out what happened to your boyfriend.'

'So what have you actually done? All you do is keep coming here and asking stupid questions. I can dress how I want, have any tattoos I want, read what I want. It's nothing to do with you.'

'I'm not trying to say it is.'

Lara's features scrunched together with a new ferocity,

like an angry turnip but with the wild-eyed gaze of some-one who could cause some serious damage. This was a different, more focused type of anger; no elaborate finger-waving or posturing. There was no show: just her and him.

'You should be *really* careful about what you stick your nose into.'

The room felt colder and Andrew could see what other people had tried to tell him about the fierceness of Lara's arguing with Nicholas and her flatmates. Her stare was a traction beam from which he couldn't escape.

'What do you mean?'

'I think you know.'

'Tell me.'

'Some forces go far above you.'

Andrew sucked on his bottom lip, not entirely sure how to respond. 'Is that a threat?'

'Take it how you want.'

With any pretence of a civil conversation now over, Andrew stood, ready to leave. Lara continued glaring at him and then stormed through the open door, heading towards the stairs without looking back. He followed her into the hallway but she was practically running, taking the stairs two at a time and bounding around the banister at the top of the first flight. Moments later, a door slammed above.

Andrew turned in a circle, taking in the tatty space. There were more posters on the walls and windows and one of the overhead lights was flickering furiously. A shiver bubbled along his spine but not because of the cold. Lara's send-off certainly sounded like a threat and had been genuinely chilling. He still didn't know who had drawn the occult symbol on the office door but he'd spoken to Lara on Thursday evening to ask if they could meet, and the symbol had likely been sketched sometime overnight. It also didn't seem true that she could have chosen 'Malvado' as a last name, or nickname, by chance. Keira had indicated that believers could use it to symbolise 'daughter of', which felt more plausible. What *did* sound genuine was that she'd got the word from her father, but Jenny hadn't been able to find out anything about him, including how long Lara had been an orphan.

He was about to leave when he noticed what a row of the vote/don't vote posters were covering. Almost completely hidden was a row of cubby-holes, used to store mail for each flat. Andrew slowly looked around but the area was clear. He brushed aside the flyer and delved into the pile underneath number eight. At the bottom, buried under a mound of unopened post for the male Alex, was a single brown envelope with the university's logo in the top right corner. Printed on the front was Lara's full name. Exactly as Keira had predicted, it was not Malvado.

34

Jenny was wearing her glasses again. Andrew had never managed to figure out if she really needed them, or if it was a fashion statement.

She peered over the top across the office towards him. 'It's a really sad-sounding name. I feel a bit sorry for her.'

'Do you?'

Jenny shrugged, not so sure. 'Sort of. It's an expression, isn't it?'

Lara Loveless did have something of a forlorn-sounding name. In many ways, it was no surprise she wanted to change it, but that didn't mean she had to opt for Malvado.

'Anyway,' Jenny continued, 'it's been a lot easier trying to find things since you phoned in with her real name. I found her dad almost straight away – he's called Franklin and died a year and a bit ago. There's a two-line obituary on the *Manchester Morning Herald*'s website about him, saying that he left behind a daughter named Lara.'

'How did he die?'

'Lung cancer.'

'How old was he?'

'Fifty-six.'

'Did you find out much else about him?'

Jenny's collection of Bourbon biscuits was still going

strong – unless she'd brought in more, which was definitely possible. There was a scattering on a plate next to a folded-over half-full packet.

She held a biscuit in front of her face, looking puzzled – something incredibly rare for her. 'Can I ask you a question?'

Andrew was slightly confused himself; she didn't usually ask permission, she just went for it. 'Sure.'

'We both think there's something not quite right about Lara. I don't know if that means she was responsible for Nicholas disappearing, or if she killed him or anything like that, but why don't you just ask her?'

'Ask her what?'

'Ask if she was responsible. Instead of tiptoeing around it, say it outright: "Did you kill Nicholas?" or "Did you do something to make him go missing?"'

There was no hint of mischief on Jenny's face. She popped half the biscuit in her mouth, staring at him.

'I can't do that because we're not the police. We might need her to cooperate with us again later today, or tomorrow, or the next day. I could go storming in and accuse her of all sorts, but if she tells me to get lost and won't engage again, then I've achieved nothing. You've got to walk a really fine line.'

'But isn't that the nature of the job?'

'It depends how you choose to do it. I could stick to following cheating husbands and wives and never have to talk to anyone. By choosing to go for other kinds of cases, I'm setting myself up – ourselves up – for a lot of complicated situations where you can't talk to people in the way you'd like. You have to be tactful around them and understand they might be using you as much as you're hoping to use them.'

The second half of the biscuit was devoured as Jenny nodded shortly, before turning back to her screen, apparently satisfied. 'There's a lot of information about Franklin Loveless. He sounds like quite the character.' She beckoned Andrew over so he could see the computer screen over her shoulder. She flicked through a selection of webpages, showing a collection of colourful posters. 'He was a bit of a local celebrity when he was younger. Someone's uploaded a scan to the Internet from a programme of this variety act he used to be involved with. There are singers, magicians, comedians, impressionists: the usual. They used to perform in a few smaller music halls and theatres a couple of times a week. It seems quite local – Manchester and Liverpool were the biggest cities but there were a host of smaller places around Lancashire and Yorkshire. Franklin used to do a mind-reading act.'

'How long ago was this?'

Jenny ummed as she fiddled with the on-screen document. 'Over thirty years ago. He would have been in his twenties at the time, so before Lara was born.'

'What exactly did he do?'

'It's hard to tell because it's a promotional thing. Look at his picture.'

Andrew peered around her to see a figure in a top hat and long black cape, arms outstretched extravagantly, like a penguin that was particularly pleased with itself. Franklin had a long, thin face utterly unlike Lara's but there was certain similarity.

'You can just about tell Lara's his daughter,' Andrew said. 'Same nose, same eyes. I saw her without the make-up today.'

'All the programme says is that he'll read your mind and help you speak to long-lost loved ones. I guess it's one of those cold-reading things. I have no idea why people fall for it.'

The printer whirred and Andrew collected the pages from the programme, flicking through them at his own desk. The show sounded very old-fashioned but understandable in the context that it was before the days of widespread satellite and cable television. For a few quid, people got a night out and a host of entertainers. If half the acts bombed, the punters were still happy because of the sheer number of performers. Aside from the photo of a youthful Franklin and the brief description, there was little else. Jenny was probably right that he was a cold-reader. Ask if there's somebody in the audience whose name begins with J, pick the oldest one and then blabber about how their mother or father had a message for them and you'd have people in the palm of your hand. It would be even easier in the remnants of the industrial market towns it seemed like they toured. Tell a few people that money was coming their way and they'd go home happy.

Andrew glanced across to Jenny. 'Is there much else?'

'Not really. There's a big gap until the next thing. How much do you know about tarot?'

'Only what was in that James Bond movie with the voodoo.'

She looked at him blankly.

'Have you never watched a James Bond film?' he asked.

'No.'

'Okay, well, I don't know very much about tarot other than it's some sort of card thing where people claim they can read your future.'

'That travelling act was thirty-ish years ago and probably ran for two or three years. Fourteen years ago, Franklin Loveless was sent to prison. I found two different news articles from the time and another from a year or so later when he's referenced from a separate story about someone else going to prison.'

'What did he do?'

'Fraud and tax evasion. He pleaded guilty, so no big trial. He was forty-two at the time. What's interesting is that it's really unclear how much of it was actually him. It talks about his wife, Hari Loveless. They ran some sort of mystic business from their house in Cheetham Hill. He'd do the mind-reading, talk-to-your-dead-relatives thing and Hari would give tarot readings. They weren't done for that, they were picked up for not declaring all of the income.'

'How long was he in prison for?'

'I'm not entirely sure. He was sentenced to three years.'

'What about Hari?'

Jenny's dimple made a reappearance as she reached for another biscuit. 'That's the interesting thing. It looks like he pleaded guilty to take all of the blame. In the article it mentions that charges were dropped against Hari Loveless because "prosecutors did not want to deprive her of the ability to raise her four-year-old daughter".'

'Lara.'

'I suppose. The ages would match.'

'So Lara grew up with her dad in prison for at least a year. That must have been tough.'

Jenny continued without acknowledging it. 'Hari Loveless died six years ago in a car accident. There's quite a lot about that on various news websites – it was that which helped me find everything else. She was driving on Mancunian Way when a lorry flew across the central barrier and crashed into her head on. The other driver had been working through the night and there was a prosecution of him and the company he worked for, plus they redesigned the entire stretch of road. The series of articles runs over a year or so but most of the detail is in the court reports. Hari was killed instantly but her twelve-year-old daughter was in the back seat. Firefighters worked for over an hour to cut her free. She's not named in any of the reports, probably because she was only twelve, but the age fits Lara.'

Andrew found himself tugging unnecessarily at his sleeve as Jenny paused. 'Her father went to prison when she was four and she was in the back of the car when her mother died in front of her . . .' He blew out loudly. '. . . poor kid. It's no wonder she flips to being furious in a moment. If I'd been through all of that by the time I was twelve, I'd be a mess too. And with her father dying last year too. It's a wonder she managed to get herself to university.'

He stopped for a moment, remembering that she'd chosen the name Malvado for herself.

'There's more,' Jenny added, almost impatiently. 'At the bottom of one of these reports, there's a bit you should read.'

She passed a print-out across from the *Manchester Morning Herald*. Andrew scanned through the details at the top about the accident but he felt a tingle as he reached the second page.

'"The accident is the latest in a string of misfortunes to hit the Loveless family. Eight years ago, Franklin was sentenced to three years in prison for fraud offences, plus this year is the thirtieth anniversary of Franklin's brother, Mark, disappearing on his eighteenth birthday. He was never found."'

Andrew peered up, meeting Jenny's triumphant gaze. 'Lara's uncle disappeared on his eighteenth birthday?'

'That's what it says. Bit of a coincidence, isn't it? Mark was two years younger than Franklin.'

'How would the police have missed it?' Jenny didn't reply but Andrew wasn't asking her anyway. 'The Malvado name-thing might have confused them because she would have been an orphan when Nicholas went missing but still . . .'

He reread the date on the report. Mark Loveless would have gone missing thirty-six years ago, so it wasn't beyond the realms of possibility that it might have been missed in among the police workload. He and Jenny had only got this far by going in one big circle, finding out the significance of Lara's chosen name, discovering her original name, tracing her parents and then uncovering a solitary news report. At the time Nicholas disappeared, he and Lara were both eighteen – relatively normal teenagers out for a drink on his birthday. There were no particular reasons to dispute her side of the story, plus, unfortunately, people went missing all the time. Most cases would never be reported by the media, with the police making the basic checks and then hoping for the best. If the person's bank cards, SIM card or passport were never used, then there wasn't an awful lot they could do. With Nicholas, they had got somewhere with the severed fingers find but digging up the woods was expensive and time-consuming. They would have hoped to quickly find a body but when it didn't show up, it was no wonder someone had pulled the plug.

Andrew read the article for a third time before he remembered something Keira had told him.

'. . . All sorts of different sects or people might have their own interpretations about various icons or numerology . . .'

He spun in his chair to face Jenny. 'Did you find anything else?'

'That's all I could see about the Loveless family. Now we've got the name, I can do the usual, credit checks and the like.'

'Mark Loveless disappeared on his eighteenth birthday thirty-six years ago. Nicholas Carr went missing on his eighteenth birthday this year. What if there was another eighteen-year-old who disappeared exactly in the middle?'

35

It was perhaps no surprise that Andrew and Jenny couldn't find anything from exactly eighteen years ago. If they'd known the name of whoever might have disappeared, they would have had something to go on. As it was, they didn't have access to police records and the Internet didn't prove very useful. There was no official list of missing people and a host of charities with incomplete records. There definitely were eighteen-year-olds who vanished in the year they were looking at – every year in fact – but they had too little to go on.

Jenny sat chewing on a pen, presumably as a replacement for biscuits or cakes. She suggested searching for the names they'd been able to make out from Kristian Verity's contacts book but they threw up nothing. Even Kristian Verity himself produced no results. The only thing they were sure of was that Lara was the sole remaining Loveless family member and that two people connected to her disappeared on their eighteenth birthdays. Not only that, she'd chosen to name herself after a sort of mythical devil-like figure.

More pen-chewing, which couldn't be healthy. Andrew would probably have to fill in a health and safety clearance form in case there was a danger of her choking to death on it, or getting plastic poisoning, something like that.

She eventually removed the pen. 'Do you know what happened to my backpack?'

'The one we had at the garage?'

'Exactly.'

'It's still at my flat. I keep meaning to bring it in.'

'Can we fetch it?' Andrew must have pulled a disapproving or confused face because she continued straight away. 'It's not for me. I'd like to check something that we, er, borrowed from Kristian Verity's stuff.'

Andrew didn't have any better ideas but Jenny had never been to his flat. He could say he would pick up the bag and return it to the office but that would make it obvious he was trying to avoid taking her there. He didn't necessarily have a problem with Jenny being in his living space but it felt like worlds colliding: home and work life uncomfortably close.

Still, he didn't have much choice. 'Let's go.'

Andrew found it hard to press the key into the lock of his flat without pausing to make sure there was no one else around. He peered over his shoulder and leant back, gazing towards the end of the corridor: the corner from which Stewart Deacon had appeared a few evenings previously.

Next to him, Jenny sensed his unease. She nudged him gently with her elbow. 'You okay?'

He turned the key and pushed ahead. 'Yes.'

Inside, Andrew stood to the side, waiting for the inevitable reaction. Jenny followed him in and started unzipping her jacket before feeling the magnetic pull towards the window. She crossed the floor, footsteps resonating, until she was in front of the glass, staring across the entirety of the city. Visibility was good, buildings and roads stretching into the distance, with the frosted fields far beyond.

'It looks so different from up here.'

'I know.'

'I wonder if I can see where I live.' Jenny slid her way along the window, her hand shading her eyes as she gazed past the Arndale shopping centre, Piccadilly Gardens and the prison, before turning towards Oxford Road and the universities, which were just out of view. She pointed a thumb. 'It's off that way somewhere.'

Andrew smiled. She looked like an adult with her hair down, tights, skirt and a coat, but the moment anyone saw the view for the first time, they became a child in wanting to spot where they lived.

Jenny had seemingly forgotten the reason they were there, walking in an echoing circle around the combined living room and kitchen. Andrew suddenly felt embarrassed by it all: posh leather sofas, an all-glass coffee table, a too-expensive coffee machine with so many knobs, he didn't know what half of them did. Then there was the customary large television and surround-sound speakers. He'd spent so much on everything and barely used any of it.

As she continued walking, Jenny stopped in front of a painting hanging to one side of the television. Most of the canvas was unpainted white but in the centre there was a gothic-looking spidery figure, undoubtedly female, painted from the back. She had a flowing black dress, with tendrils dribbling down to the far reaches of the canvas. She was gazing into the distance of the picture, where there was more white.

'What is it?' Jenny asked.

'I'm not really sure. I was in a gallery in Liverpool and liked it.'

'I like it too. She has the whole world ahead of her.'

Andrew had seen the painting every day for many years and that was exactly why he liked it: the cleanness of the white canvas coupled with the darkness of the woman. In his mind, the figure was staring into a future of infinite possibilities. He was uncomfortable that they thought the same about it – as if Jenny was scratching away at his thoughts, his soul. This was why he hadn't particularly wanted to bring her here.

Jenny continued staring at the artwork, taking a step forward to have a closer look at the textured blobs of paint. When she turned, he could tell something had changed slightly. Her big brown button-like eyes were now full of questions.

Andrew didn't want to hear her say the words, so answered anyway. 'Yes, I've got a bit of money.' She held her hands out to the side, no doubt wondering why he didn't spend his days at home enjoying the view. Or go on holiday and not come back. He'd heard it all before. 'If you want to know why I still get up and come to the office every day, it's because I like it. I suppose I like people.'

He'd not seen it before but now recognised the irony

that Jenny had told him she was the opposite, not under-standing people and, to a large degree, not wanting to.

She turned away from the painting towards the window again. 'Did you win the lottery?'

'If only.'

'Did you inherit it?'

'In a manner of speaking . . .'

There was no escaping the fact he was going to have to tell her now. Jenny was gazing directly at him, pulling the information from his mind. Andrew sat on the sofa, falling into the comfortable, warm, soft leather that prickled his guilty conscience every time he went anywhere near it. Jenny joined him, sitting in the opposite corner and folding her legs as if it was story time. In many ways, it was.

'I did something bad. I didn't steal the money and it's not like I killed anyone but still . . .'

She placed a hand on his knee and, for a moment, it felt as if she was a mate reassuring him. Then he wondered if she'd seen someone else do that in a film and was merely doing what she thought she should.

'You know I used to be married to someone named Keira but I've never told you what happened when we broke up. We met at university . . .' He counted on his fingers. '. . . sixteen or seventeen years ago. We were together for most of our three years there but come from completely different places. Not just geographically – I grew up on a council estate, her dad inherited wealth of his own and then made even more. He worked in the City in London but owns this huge place in Cheshire, among others. After me and Keira had been going out for a little while, she took me down to meet her parents. Her mum was fine but her dad . . . well, he wasn't.'

Jenny removed her hand from his knee and started chewing her fingernails. 'Why not?'

'He didn't like who I was. From his point of view, a man should be able to look after his wife and family. He wanted her to go off with one of the sons of someone from his banking or country-club crowd. He wanted grandchildren.'

'Did he tell you that?'

Andrew smiled weakly. 'Eventually. At first, he'd just blank me. It was pretty clear he wasn't pleased but, from his point of view, he thought his daughter was having some university fling and that it would be over by the time she took her exams a couple of years later. We were only nineteen or so at the time.'

'But you stayed together?'

'There was no reason not to. We always had a good time. I felt as if I could actually be myself around her and she probably felt the same. She would have grown up in that environment of being expected to live up to certain standards, so there was probably a hint of wanting to do her own thing too.'

'What happened when you graduated?'

'Wait here.'

Andrew headed to the chest of drawers in the bedroom. The top drawer was full of boxer shorts and socks, like any self-respecting person's. Everyone knew the top drawer was for underwear and he was nowhere near enough of a maverick to break that taboo. The middle drawer was nightwear but the bottom drawer was an assortment of everything else: belts, ties, a pack of tiny pants his parents inexplicably bought him for Christmas one year, some maracas he once bought on holiday when he'd taken leave of his senses, and everything in between. Buried underneath a handmade pocket game of backgammon he'd never used was the small box Andrew was looking for.

In the living room, he handed the hardened red velvet tub over to Jenny. She popped it open and took out his wedding ring.

'The day after Keira's final exam, we flew to Las Vegas and got married. It was her idea because she knew that if we planned anything, her father would stop it. They didn't even know we'd gone. We didn't bother hiding anything when we got back. My parents were a little disappointed we'd not told them but were otherwise delighted. At Keira's house, it wasn't quite like that. In front of me, her dad said she'd thrown her life away and that he hadn't brought her up to make such stupid decisions. It went on and on until we eventually left. They didn't speak for about six months after that.'

'Wow.'

Jenny was still running his old wedding band through her fingers. It was white gold, thick and heavy. She placed it back in the box and handed it over. Andrew put it on the coffee table.

'After six months, her mum got in contact and they slowly drifted back together again. It wasn't as if her dad liked me but he just about tolerated me because it enabled him to see his daughter. There was a strange sort of truce for a few years. Keira did a small amount of teaching and then went back to study for her Master's. I did a little bit of work for her dad's bank. It was at a time where it felt like he was judging whether I might amount to what he wanted me to. I think her mum made him sort things but I wasn't happy and went into social work. That's what my criminology degree was partly for but it was at a time when councils were cutting their budgets, so it was really unstable. I ended up doing odds and ends of private staff profiling for companies, which was awful. I was trying to get back to the social work but it was always a struggle. Then we started to think about children.'

'How old were you then?'

More counting on fingers.

'Twenty . . . *seven* – I think. Around there. We'd been married for five years and were still living in Manchester. We'd been renting this place in Chorlton – nothing special but nice enough. We were at that age where everyone around us was buying houses and having kids. Because we were married, we were getting the question all the time. When they were talking to Keira, people would do that thing where they tilt their heads and touch their stomachs, then say, "It must be your time soon?" Either way, we were thinking about it ourselves but didn't have the income. I was still struggling between jobs and she had a Master's degree with no one interested in hiring her. She thought we might be able to ask her parents for a bit of money – not loads, just enough for a deposit on a house to get us going. In terms of what she would have been due as an inheritance, it was nothing. Her dad still wasn't keen on me but we figured that we'd been married for five years and together for almost eight, so he'd had time to get used to it.'

The memory still felt raw but so close that it could have been yesterday. Andrew could picture their old house. In many ways, he wished he still lived there. It had a homely feel to it, unlike his apartment, which had the amazing view and state-of-the-art appliances, but none of the warmth.

'We went there one Sunday and Keira asked them over lunch. Her dad was all right at the time. He said he'd think about it, which was better than an outright "no". Later that afternoon, Keira's mum wanted to show her something upstairs – I don't really remember – but it left her father and me alone. That's when he said he didn't want me married to his daughter because he thought I was a scrounger who wasn't good enough for her. He said the fact we'd asked for money proved I wasn't up to looking after her. He wasn't shouting, it was as calm as I'd ever seen him. He added that if I thought he was going to stand by and watch us destroy his family name by bringing children into the world then I'd have another think coming.'

'How could he stop you?'

Andrew snorted a disbelieving laugh. 'I've been thinking about that ever since but it's difficult to describe unless you know him. He's a big guy anyway: taller than me, with big shoulders – you know the type. It's not just that though. You know those people who walk into a room and everyone turns? He's like that. There's something about him you can't put into words. When he looks at you, it feels as if you're the only two people in the world. But if he doesn't like you, that makes it the worst thing you can think of.' He swallowed, before adding: 'I know that sounds stupid.'

Jenny didn't reply but reached out and rubbed his arm.

'Anyway, he said that he'd find a way to break us up before we ever had a child. He said he'd do whatever it took. He was staring at me as he said it. I don't know if it was a threat – "Whatever it takes" – but it sounded like it. He said he'd destroy my life, that he knew a lot of people and he'd make sure I never got a job. He said he'd do his homework and make life hard for the people around me, like my parents.'

'He actually said that?'

'He said he'd look into buying the houses around them and then renting them out for the lowest price possible. He wouldn't have cared if the places got trashed but it would have made their lives a misery.'

'Did you believe him?'

Andrew let out an even deeper breath, sending a patch of hair at the front of his face flapping into the air before dropping back into place. 'I don't know . . . I did then. I probably still do. It's hard to know. I've not seen him since that day but I can still picture what he looks like. Were you ever scared of monsters under the bed as a child?'

'No.'

Typical.

'Okay, well, I feel a bit like that, like there's this thing in my past I can't quite forget. For months after, I'd see bigger, older guys in suits from the back and think it was him.'

'What did you do?'

'He said there were two options. One, he'd destroy my life; two, he'd pay me to go away.'

Andrew waited for a shocked reaction that didn't come. Instead, Jenny's gaze held steady. He couldn't work out if it was the type of thing she might have expected from him, or if she didn't understand the implication.

'He said he'd give me a lump sum of money but the condition was that I had to break up with Keira and make it completely final. I had to tell her I didn't love her and didn't want children. I couldn't leave things open that there might be a reconciliation. Not only that, I only had twenty-four hours to decide. If she hadn't gone to them saying it was all over by the end of the next day, then he'd put things into place to ruin me.'

This time Jenny did react but it was more mechanically than he might have thought: a simple nod. 'So you took the money?'

He hung his head. 'It didn't feel like I had a choice. When I saw Keira yesterday, that was the first time in eight years.'

'Do you still love her?'

Andrew rocked back. It wasn't that the question was utterly unreasonable, more that Jenny had been so blunt in asking it.

'I don't know,' Andrew lied before moving on quickly. 'I used the money to buy this place and didn't do much for a few years. Then I decided I should probably do something, so set up the business on a bit of a whim. It was vaguely related to what I studied. I didn't really know what I was doing at first, then someone I was supposed to be following killed herself and I decided it wasn't something I could do half-arsed. That pretty much brings you up to date.'

'Wow. You're really interesting.'

'Er, thanks.'

Andrew was sick of talking about it. He'd hardly told anyone that story and now he was going to have to go to the office each day and sit across from someone who knew what he'd done. He'd taken money over the person he loved. Who did that?

Wanting to change the subject, he picked up Jenny's backpack from behind the armchair and passed it over. Jenny unzipped it, lips still pursed thoughtfully, although she didn't seem to know what to say.

For once.

She took out the photograph of Kristian Verity and shuffled closer to Andrew, holding it out so they could both see. It was still as hard to make out as it had been in the first place, the ink running to the edge of the frame.

'What do you think?' Jenny asked.

'About what?'

'Look at the photo.'

'I am.'

'Look again.'

Andrew had seen it before but did as he was told anyway. There was still a soil-coloured smear across the bottom but what they had assumed was Kristian's teenage face was clear at the top, a wiry bob of hair draining into a dark puddle of ink, as if someone had knocked a glass of liquid across a fresh watercolour. Next to him was an identical blob from where more liquid had pooled, making it look like Kristian had two heads.

Unless . . .

'Could he have a brother?' Andrew said.

'They look exactly the same,' Jenny replied. 'I was thinking twins.'

36

Jenny had already searched for details about Kristian Verity when Scrumpy had given Andrew the name. If he was a twin, there was nothing recent or obvious to say so. What she did have was a long list of addresses attached to an extended credit history, the census, and electoral records. He had certainly moved around a lot but not apparently out of Greater Manchester.

They didn't know exactly how old Kristian was in the photograph but it couldn't have been older than seventeen or eighteen. The closest address to the office was one from sixteen years ago, when Kristian would have been twenty. Unfortunately, when they arrived to see if there were any long-term residents that might remember him, the houses had been knocked down and replaced by a supermarket.

There was only one older address Jenny had been able to find. When he was nineteen years old, definitely older than in the photograph, Kristian had lived on an estate bordering Hulme on one side and Trafford on the other. It wasn't much to go on but marginally better than nothing.

As Andrew parked the car, they realised quite how grim the area was. The house on the end of a row of semi-detached properties was burned out, with black sooty marks around the window frames, heavy metal plates bolted over the doors and windows, and criss-crossing black and yellow tape with 'do not enter' signs.

Andrew asked Jenny to wait in the car as he walked around a large patch of mud and approached the house that Kristian had apparently once lived in.

No answer.

Next door, a weary-looking woman in her twenties answered, dark hair scraped back mercilessly, baby cradled over her shoulder.

Andrew nodded towards the adjoining house. 'Hi, do you know if anyone lives next door? I'm trying to track someone down.'

'Who?'

'Kristian Verity.'

'Never 'eard of him.'

'Perhaps they might have done? Do you know when they'll be back?'

She started patting the baby on the back. 'They never answer the door. They assume everyone's from the benefits office, popping around to see if they can walk. They can, by the way. Last summer, when they were pissed, they were running up and down the garden.'

The baby started to shuffle, with the woman reaching for the door handle.

'Is there anyone on this row who's lived here for a while?' Andrew spoke as quickly as he could. 'Twenty years or so?'

The woman pointed a thumb towards the end of the row opposite the burnt-out house. 'Try Sheila three doors down. She's been here forever. Just be careful – she's got *problems*.'

'What sort?'

She juggled the baby and door handle, using her free hand to indicate someone drinking from a bottle. 'She loves a scoop or ten,' was all she said before closing the door with a thud. Moments later, there was a click of the key turning.

The sky was beginning to darken, with the ridiculously short hours of daylight almost over already. There were two times of the year Andrew dreaded: mid-summer with the long days and parades of drunken buffoons who thought they could drink for hours on end. At least that came with the consolation of being warm and sunny. Mid-winter was just shite all around: dark and cold with everybody – justifiably – complaining about how dark and cold it was.

Andrew signalled to Jenny, who clambered out of the car and rounded the patch of mud before joining him at the end of Sheila's driveway. A black cat darted across the path ahead, leaping vertically onto the house's windowsill and then skulking up and down, watching them carefully, daring them to come closer. There was a white spot on his head, with patchy pepper-coloured fur intermingled with the black. Andrew had a single foot on the driveway when the cat began hissing. His other foot brought a louder sound of displeasure and a raised paw, hooked claws on show.

Bring it on, pal.

In a war between human and feline, this one in particular, Andrew knew there was only going to be one winner and it wasn't him.

He took two steps back.

'What are you doing?' Jenny asked.

'That cat's going to kill us.'

'It's a cat. What's the worst that can happen?'

'It could skin us alive.'

'It really couldn't.'

Jenny stepped confidently onto the driveway. The edges had largely crumbled into the surrounding hedgerows, with weeds growing through the disintegrating tarmac.

Hissssssssssss.

'Oh, sod off.'

Andrew didn't know if cats understood the mechanics behind sodding off but the hissing black and white fur ball certainly didn't seem to. Jenny continued walking as the spitting noises went on. Reluctantly, Andrew followed her, keeping both eyes on the cat in case it leapt towards them. If nothing else, Jenny would make a good human shield, not that he told her that.

Hissssssssssss.

'Yeah, yeah, whatever,' Jenny said.

She was standing barely two metres from the cat but wasn't even looking at it as she rang the doorbell. Andrew waited awkwardly by her side.

Jenny glanced sideways at him. 'Are you hiding behind me?'

'No.'

He was.

If Malvado actually did exist and ascended from the depths of hell to claim the earth, Andrew doubted he'd make as much noise as the cat was doing.

Jenny rang the bell a second time and then knocked. It

was another thirty seconds before the sound of something moving came from inside. The door opened a crack, an eyeball appeared, and then it snapped shut again. Andrew and Jenny exchanged a shrug and then he tried again.

'Sheila? Is that you? I was hoping you could give us a few minutes of your time. I'm not selling anything if that helps.'

The door opened a thin crack again, revealing a blood-shot eye and matted strands of greying brown hair. 'Who are you?'

It took him a moment to pick up on her pronunciation. Like a Rottweiler with a Manc accent.

'My name's Andrew and I was wondering if you've ever heard of someone named Kristian Verity. I think he used to live on this rank.'

The door opened a little further, revealing a figure ravaged by age, sunbeds and an aversion to water. Sheila's hair was so dirty, it had partially matted into natural dreadlocks. It really was something when that wasn't the most striking part of her appearance. Her skin was the colour of tea if it was made with eight teabags that had all been left in, plus it had shrivelled so much that she looked like one of the dodgy potatoes found at the bottom of the bag that supermarkets snuck in there because nobody delved that deep before buying.

Her eyes flicked both ways, taking in Jenny before she stuck her head out of the door, turning towards the window and the angry cat. Instead of reeling away, Sheila hissed back, adding: 'Oi, you're doing ma napper in. Skanky bastard thing.' She slapped a hand on the windowsill and the cat, realising it had met its match, ran for it. Andrew felt like doing the same.

Sheila pushed past Jenny, heading back towards the door. 'Come in then.'

The house reeked like a tobacco factory, with brown nicotine stains on all of the walls and the ceiling. It was so stale, so clogging, that Andrew was instantly coughing.

Sheila led them through a door into the living room, which was in more of a state than the hallway. If she'd been living here for twenty years, then Andrew doubted Sheila had changed a thing. There were brown cord-covered armchairs and a grimy maroon carpet with so many cigarette burns that it looked like some sort of modern art installation.

She fell into a wooden rocking chair and started clicking her fingers in Jenny's direction. 'Oi, you, girly, can you scav me a fag?'

'I don't smoke.'

Sheila pointed at Andrew. 'You then – let's have a fag.'

'I don't smoke either.'

'Aww, give over. No one sodding smokes any more. What's wrong with y'all?'

She was wearing a pink onesie made from a soft blanket-like material. At one point it would have been soft and comfortable, now it was covered in flecks of cigarette ash and miscellaneous food stains.

Sheila delved into an unseen inside pocket and pulled out a packet of cigarettes. 'Gonna have to smoke my own then, aren't I?' As she rummaged for a lighter, she nodded at Jenny again. 'Got anything to drink?'

'Sorry.'

A nod at Andrew.

'Me either.'

'Bah! Useless. I've got some bangin' stuff of my own.'

Cigarette lit, packet and lighter dispatched into the nether regions of her onesie, Sheila reached across to a cabinet and took out a bottle of Coke. As soon as she unscrewed the unsealed lid, Andrew could smell the alcohol, which was surely enough to get a shire horse drunk. If horses could get drunk. She took a swig, grimaced, and then started rocking herself in the chair.

'Who was it you were interested in?'

'Kristian Verity.'

'He owe you money or something?'

'No, I'm just trying to find out a few things about him. I believe he lived a few doors down when he was eighteen or nineteen and I'm told you were living here then.'

Without removing the cigarette from her mouth, Sheila started counting on her fingers. 'I've been here . . . eight, nine, ten . . . er . . .' She was one step away from removing her shoes when Andrew interrupted.

'Do you at least recognise the name?'

A puff of smoke spiralled into the air. They could fix her driveway with the amount of tar on the ceiling.

'Aye, little lad, big hair. Looked like a tit . . .'

'Right. Do you know if he had a brother or a twin?'

'. . . then after him it was that Paki pair. We hounded them out, then it was that guy with the car . . .' She clicked her fingers in Jenny's direction. '. . . something or another. I can't remember. He always had engine parts out front.

Then those poofs, then the Smiths. I'm not sure who's in there now. Nobody ever talks to their neighbours any longer. Rude bunch of bastards.'

Andrew doubted it was the people who'd moved in and out that were the problem.

'But you remember Kristian Verity?'

'Aye.'

'Do you know how long he lived here for?'

'Dunno – year or two. They come, they go. Like that song.' There was more finger-clicking in Jenny's direction until the cigarette ash crumbled onto her crotch. She brushed it away and then took the cigarette from her mouth.

Andrew was doing his best impression of somebody who had patience. 'Do you remember if he lived by himself?'

'No, there was that other one, wasn't there? Two of them.'

Jenny didn't flinch under another brutal bout of finger-clicking. Considering Sheila's alcohol and cigarette consumption, there was every chance the toxic combination meant that she saw two of everything. She certainly wouldn't be the best of choices as a high court witness. She swigged more of her Coca-Cola, yawned, scratched her crotch and then puffed some more on the cigarette.

'What's his name,' she added. 'Edam-something? Eagle? It begins with an E.'

Andrew was thinking that it almost certainly didn't begin with E when Sheila clapped her hands together. 'Emil, that's it. Kristian and Emil Verity. Nice lads, kept themselves to themselves, just looked a bit stupid.'

Pleased with herself, Sheila reached for her Coke bottle again. Andrew was about to ask something else when he saw a flicker of movement over her shoulder. In the back corner of the room, nibbling on the edge of the carpet without a care in the world, was a rat. Andrew thought about saying something but didn't want to risk putting off Sheila when she was finally coherent enough to be of use. His eyes darted sideways to Jenny's, who had been watching the rat too. She offered a small, unconcerned shrug, but then she had been happy to take on the cat as well. She seemed unnaturally calm, even smiling slightly. She really was borderline crazy, or whatever the correct medical term might be. For now, crazy was accurate enough.

'Can you remember what happened to Emil?'

Sheila started scratching her head, sending an avalanche of dried scalp flakes cascading onto her lap. 'It was ages ago, wannit?' Another drink. 'Course that's what made the brother move out. He couldn't stay around after that, could he? Poor guy.'

The rat scarpered towards the kitchen.

'What happened, Sheila?'

'Awful, wannit? Police up and down 'ere, knocking on doors, asking questions. People round 'ere don't like the police with their yap, yap, yap. Never came to anything, did it? Not like they sorted it out. Course, that was all years ago now.'

'Sheila, what happened?'

He was running out of ways he could phrase it.

'That's exactly what they were asking. I told them then I didn't know. That's what we all said. He just disappeared. One minute he was there, the next he was gone. Poor git had just turned eighteen too . . .'

37

It was dark by the time they got in the car again. Andrew had to concentrate to remember his way to the main road, where lines of white and red lights were stretching into the distance.

'I'm going to be late getting you back,' Andrew said.

'It's fine, just leave me at the office. I left some of my stuff there and I've got some typing to finish.'

'You can do that tomorrow.'

'Pfft. It's not like I've got anything else to do. Besides, this is *exciting*, isn't it? Thirty-six years ago, Mark Loveless disappeared. Eighteen years ago, Emil Verity went missing. This year, the same happened to Nicholas Carr. They're all connected to Lara or, at the very least, her family.'

Andrew wasn't sure he approved of the relish in her voice when she said 'exciting' but it was true to a degree.

'What do you think's going on?' she added.

They were stuck in traffic again, so Andrew had no chance to be alone with his thoughts. 'Keira told me that Malvado could be translated as a devilish figure. There was a sort of occult group that built up around him in Portugal at one point. All sorts of cults live on in various forms, some far bigger than others.'

'Like the church?'

'Well, I wouldn't put it like that but maybe. Kristian

319

had "Malvado" written in his contacts book, which might have referred to Lara or her father – but could have been the name of the devil-figure too.'

'Lara wasn't even born when her uncle went missing.'

'I know.'

'If the Malvado thing was her dad's project, she could be continuing it after he died. But that's a lot for someone who's not even twenty.'

'I know.'

'And why are other people from Kristian's contacts book going missing, or getting killed?'

'That's one I don't know.'

Andrew continued edging the car towards the city centre. Jenny was checking the pockets of her coat, saying she was hungry. He'd never known anyone eat as much as her, let alone as much junk food. When there was nothing to be found, she started biting her fingernails again.

'Should we call the police?' Jenny asked.

Andrew had been thinking that himself. 'It's complicated because I'm not sure what we actually have. We found a book in a garage we shouldn't have been in, so we can hardly hand that over. Most of the words are smudged anyway and then there's an assumed surname of a teenager. My ex-wife helped us connect that to people interested in the occult but all of that is only second-hand information. Also, we were hired to find Nicholas and we're nowhere near doing that – we just have a couple more missing people and poor old James Wicker, who was carved to pieces in his own house.'

'Hmm . . .' Jenny didn't sound so sure. 'What did you think of that rat?'

'I don't know how you were so calm. It was all I could do not to jump up and run off screaming.'

'Yeah, but you're scared of cats.'

'I don't know how you can call that thing on the windowsill a cat, it was practically demonic.'

Jenny wasn't listening, but still talking about the rat: 'It was so tame, I can't believe that was the only one. Mad Sheila must have got used to having them around.'

'Ugh.'

Andrew wondered what the female Alex would make of the far more obvious rat problem at Sheila's house. As he did, he suddenly felt cold, a tingle fizzing from his finger-tips up and down both arms as if someone had flicked a switch, and suddenly he knew at least some of the answers.

'Jenny, can you do me a favour?'

'That depends on what it is, but probably.'

'If I drop you back at the office, can you call Richard Carr and ask him to meet me there in a couple of hours? Once you've done that, go home – you shouldn't spend all night working.'

'I don't mind.'

'That's not the point. Go and have fun.'

'Fine, but why do you want me to call Richard?'

'I've got to visit Lara again. I think I've got something.'

'What?'

'I might know what happened to Nicholas Carr after all.'

38

Getting into the block of flats in which Lara lived was even easier than usual. A tearful girl was holding the door open with her foot while having a blazing row with someone apparently named 'Gary' on her mobile phone. With the device wedged between her shoulder and cheek, she had both hands free, one of which was cradling a cigarette, the other making elaborate unhappy arm movements, as if she was at a particularly downmarket ballet recital.

'. . . I don't care if she's the bloody Queen, Gary. If it wasn't for Michelle seeing you down that alley, I wouldn't have known . . . Yeah right – as if! There's no way you were going to text me afterwards . . . Bollocks were you. What were you going to tell me? "Sorry I fingered that girl out the back of Wetherspoons?" What did you think I was going to say? . . .'

She offered Andrew a weak smile, flicking cigarette ash into the gutter and stepping aside to let him inside as he wondered which Wetherspoons.

The hallway was quiet but cold. There had been a purge of the voting posters, which had been replaced by various adverts for end of term parties and the sci-fi/fantasy club calling for new members. Alex's 'has anyone seen a rat' poster had been defaced by someone replacing the 'r' with a 'tw', with all of the pull-off tabs at the bottom ripped away.

By the main door, the girl's cigarette was almost finished, as was the conversation and relationship. By now,
his name had been altered from Gary to something else
with four letters. Upstairs, Andrew knocked softly on the
door of Lara's flat. There were no raised voices this time as
male Alex opened the door, still topless, his ribs poking
through his pasty skin. In damning evidence, he was
halfway through a HobNob, which might or might not
belong to the Sophie that Andrew had never met.

The prosecution rests, your honour.

'Y'all right, man?'

'Is Lara in?'

Alex stood to the side, holding the door open. 'Dunno,
mate. Loads of people have gone out.'

Andrew strode to the third door on his left and waited
until Alex had closed the front door and disappeared into
his own room. When it was quiet again, Andrew knocked
on Lara's door.

He heard shuffling from inside and then Lara's voice:
'Who is it?'

'Andrew Hunter, I—'

'For God's sake, what do you want now?'

'A few minutes of your time. It's about Nicholas.'

At first, he didn't think she was going to answer but
then she uttered a quieter, 'What about him?'

'I'd rather not do this through a door . . .'

More scrambling. 'Wait there.'

There were muffled sounds of complaining, a wooden
thump, the sound of the latch being pulled down and,
for a few moments, nothing. As a breeze blustered through

from the kitchen, Andrew felt very self-conscious: he was a bloke in his mid-thirties and for the third time in a week, he'd arrived in a student hall of residence. It really wasn't right – especially as he'd turned up unannounced the last two times. Hopefully this time would be the last. It would be if he was right . . .

'It's open.'

Andrew pushed the door, waiting as it swung slowly inwards. Lara was sitting on her bed in the back corner of the room, wedged in between the two walls. She was fully made-up, all pale skin and dark eyes, wearing a black sweatshirt which covered her skirt, with tights and scuffed Doc Martens. Andrew waited close to the door, feeling even more uncomfortable at being in her room. At least he'd had Jenny with him the last time he'd been in here. The blind was closed, with the overhead bulb showering a pathetic amount of light into the too-dark room. The walls were still splashed with drapes and throws, as the built-in wardrobe at the bottom of the bed overflowed with clothes that bulged against the black curtain.

Lara really was fearsome when she scowled, for which Andrew didn't really blame her.

'What do you want this time?' she asked, not attempting to hide her annoyance.

'I can't stop thinking about the Malvado thing with your name.'

'I told you it was just a word I liked.'

'I know, but you also said it came from your father, Franklin Loveless.'

Her eyebrows twitched slightly but the rest of her features didn't move. 'So?'

'I understand that your parents were interested in magic and related things – the tarot and mind-reading – but that's relatively harmless compared to the occult associations of the name Malvado and the symbol you have tattooed.'

'I told you that Malvado was just a word.'

'You also told me to be careful of digging too deep and we both know it's not true about what that name means.'

'Who says?'

'I do.'

Lara gritted her teeth but kept her tone calm. 'I think you should leave.'

'Is it a coincidence that your uncle Mark disappeared when he was eighteen too?'

For a few seconds they stared at each other and then Lara screwed her feet underneath herself, the bedcovers scrunching around her boots.

She spoke slowly and deliberately, not breaking eye contact. 'What are you trying to say?'

'That there's something going on. Every eighteen years, an eighteen-year-old goes missing. Thirty-six years ago, it was your uncle. Eighteen years ago, it was someone named Emil Verity.' Her eyes widened slightly in recognition. 'This year, it was Nicholas. There might be more people in between – maybe it's every three years that someone goes missing? Every year? I don't know.'

Lara's lips were pressed together. Her voice was barely a whisper. 'I thought I told you to be careful.'

Silence.

Andrew took a step further into the room, feeling cold. Lara squirmed as far into the corner as she could, all elbows and knees. Tiny.

'At first I thought it was something to do with you,' Andrew said. 'The name Malvado kept coming up and I thought it was your real name. Then the symbol that's tattooed on your wrist kept appearing everywhere. Nicholas has it; it's on a book I found that belongs to Kristian Verity; someone drew it on my office door.' Lara opened her mouth to protest but Andrew didn't give her the chance. 'That's not it at all, though, is it?'

'No.'

'Can you answer something honestly for me?'

'Maybe.'

'Is Malvado *really* just a word that you liked?'

She nodded slowly. 'It was my father's thing. After he died, I wanted to do something for him. Loveless isn't a very good name. It makes people think strangely of you.'

Which was the first thing that Jenny had said. Andrew knew he should have listened then.

'What about the tattoo?'

'That was my dad's too.'

'Why did Nicholas get it?'

'I asked him to.'

Andrew nodded, believing her. He sat on the corner of the desk and turned to face the wall behind the bed. 'Nicholas, you can come out now.'

39

Nothing happened.

Lara's mouth dropped into an O, eyes darting from Andrew to the wall to the wardrobe and back again.

'If it's any consolation,' Andrew said, 'it was nothing you did. I saw a rat today. A real one: teeth, claws, hungry eyes. When I first met Alex – the female one – she said she heard the scuttling of rats in the walls. She also said you'd argued to get this room. When I was here the first time, I spotted there was a wider gap between your room and the bathroom than between the other rooms. The rest is a bit of guesswork.'

A rat started scraping the wall next to the bed. Andrew and Lara stared at the built-in wardrobe, where there was a ruffle of clothes, a swish of curtain, and then the rodent revealed himself as a ghost that was distinctly un-rat-like.

Nicholas Carr had lost weight compared to the photo his father had given Andrew in the first place. His dark blond hair was still messy, as if he'd just got out of bed, but there were flakes of plaster in it too. He stared at Andrew, seemingly unsure what to make of the situation. He was wearing jeans and a dark hoody with a sandy rash of stubble across his face. Without speaking, he crossed until he was in front of the door, sandwiching Andrew in the middle of the room. The only concession he made was a shrug in his girlfriend's direction. His right hand was covered in a black glove, the middle finger spaces flat and limp.

Andrew looked from Nicholas to Lara and back again. 'It sounds like the pair of you owe Alex some food.'

Nobody spoke until Lara giggled, which was utterly out of character considering how she'd been the rest of the time. Nicholas smiled tightly but said nothing.

To satisfy his own curiosity, Andrew brushed aside the curtain at the front of the wardrobe. A thin wooden board was resting to the side, with a hole in the wall leading into the space between the bedroom and the bathroom. It was no wonder people had complained to Lara about her loud music in the first few days of moving in – that had been to conceal the sound and effort it took to saw out the patch of wall.

Andrew sat on the desk chair, turning to face Nicholas. 'How long have you been living here?'

His voice was a low murmur. 'Since Lara moved in.'

'Presumably, you only disappear into the walls if someone needs to come in here?'

A shrug.

'Do you ever go out?'

Lara and Nicholas exchanged a quick glance before he replied. 'Who do you think drew that symbol on your door?'

'Oh.'

'So you don't know everything,' Nicholas added.

'Clearly not.'

'Have you told my dad yet?'

'No.'

Another swift peep at each other. 'I get out more than you think. With the hood up, nobody thinks any differently of you around campus. The downstairs door is always open anyway.'

'Were you here the first time I came around?'

Nicholas shook his head. 'We knew you were coming because you phoned ahead.'

That made sense. It was no wonder Lara had asked him question after question about what he'd found out. She had to feed it all back.

'How did you know you wouldn't be spotted coming and going?' Andrew asked.

Lara shrugged. 'It's easier than you think. There are so many students here, going in and out at all hours, that no one gives you a second look most of the time. There are always people around who don't live here.'

The female Alex had told Andrew something similar in the kitchen. It was the same when he was a student – flats and blocks filled with people who didn't live there: friends, classmates, boyfriends, girlfriends. No one had paid him any attention on the occasions he'd visited the halls. Strangers were expected.

He glanced between the two of them, unsure how to phrase things. In the end, he took Jenny's advice and went for it. 'So what's going on?'

Lara and Nicholas were staring at each other, perhaps waiting for the other to take the lead. Nicholas replied. 'How about you tell us what you know?'

Andrew took a breath. He didn't know who he should

be addressing. Lara was in one corner, Nicholas in the other blocking the door. He didn't really know what had been going on and wanted to watch the reactions of them both but was going to have to choose. He also wondered if Nicholas's placement was deliberate. There was no way for Andrew to leave without going past him.

He opted to watch Nicholas, giving himself a moment to take in the young man's features. He'd certainly aged since the photograph Andrew had seen. As well as losing weight, he'd let his hair grow. The tufts of stubble made him seem more grown-up but there was something else too: a hardness to his stare and the way his left arm hung by his side. The right one was limp, betraying his missing fingers, but the left was primed, fingers slightly crooked as if ready to fight – which might well be the case.

Andrew tried his luck anyway. 'I'm guessing the pair of you were caught up in something you didn't really know about.' He nodded at Lara. 'Your father was involved in the occult in a way you didn't understand. I don't know if he was the one in charge of the group, or if it was Kristian Verity. You took the name Malvado and had the tattoo done, thinking it was honouring your dad. Perhaps you were even a part of his group, thinking it was a bit of fun, or that it was just about anarchy. You didn't realise that the other people in that group took it far more seriously than that.' He motioned towards Nicholas. 'When you turned eighteen, they decided they were going to use you as some sort of sacrifice to Malvado. They might have even thought you'd go along with it? They took you out to the spot in the woods where the trees and the land are laid out like the symbol. Perhaps they even cleared the earth to make it like that? Anyway, somehow you got away and Lara's been hiding you ever since.'

He stopped, waiting for confirmation that he was right or wrong. Neither would have surprised him. Nicholas's gaze flickered to the back corner of the room before returning to Andrew, waiting for more. Andrew gulped. He could feel sweat forming under his chin and around the back of his neck.

'What else?' Nicholas asked.

'I don't know.'

'You do.'

'Well . . . I'm only guessing here but I'm assuming you didn't take too kindly to any of that. While you've been hiding, people connected to the group – to Lara's dad – have been going missing. Kristian Verity's not been heard from, Brian Oswald doesn't seem to be at home and I found James Wicker dead in his own living room with that symbol cut into his chest. There are probably others too.'

Nicholas nodded slowly, reaching into the back of his trousers with his left arm and pulling out a large knife. The tip was pointed, glinting in the overhead light, with angled razor-like serrations cut into the blade.

40

Nicholas twisted the knife in his hand. Andrew had no idea if he was originally left- or right-handed but it didn't appear to be a problem for him now. Andrew remembered the night he'd seen a man set on fire but that was nothing compared to this. He wasn't in danger then, he was now. Sweat was flowing along the back of his neck as he wondered if his body was going to be found with perspiration stains in the armpits of his shirt. What a way to go that would be. Then he wondered what on earth was going on in his mind. As if that was important.

Nicholas's eyes left Andrew, darting towards Lara, who was sliding along the bed towards the wardrobe.

'Don't be a dickhead,' she whispered harshly.

Nicholas frowned at her and then returned the knife to the back of his trousers. He peered back at Andrew but didn't seem all there, fingers twitching as if he wanted to feel the blade again. 'Who are you going to tell?' he asked.

Andrew held his hands out, trying to appear open. 'No one. People will understand what you did – and that's if you want to tell them. I can stay quiet.'

He didn't actually know if that was true but it was better than saying he was going to go straight to the police.

Nicholas and Lara turned to each other again, trying to

weigh up what they should do. Lara shrugged. 'He seems all right.'

'My dad . . .'

'I don't know. Just . . . not here.'

Andrew was unsure what was going on. 'It's okay. You're safe now. Kristian Verity's disappeared, hasn't he?' He chose the word 'disappeared' carefully. 'Whoever's in charge has gone. Who else can be after you?'

Nicholas spun to face Andrew, eyebrows meeting in confusion. 'Verity?' Nicholas said.

'He was in charge, wasn't he? He collected all the books and had details on everyone.'

'He's not the one who tried to sacrifice me. He was one of the sheep.'

Andrew realised Lara and Nicholas were both staring at him and knew he'd missed something. 'Who then?'

His only other thought had been Lara's father, but he'd died naturally before any of this had happened.

Nicholas reached towards the back of his trousers again but he didn't take out the knife. 'I thought you knew?'

'Knew what?'

'That's why I followed you in the first place; why I set fire to your car. I was trying to warn you off.'

'That was you?'

'So you've been in the dark the whole time?'

Andrew stared between the two young people wondering what they were talking about. He'd clearly overlooked something that should have been obvious.

'I don't know what you're talking about,' Andrew said. 'I thought you were part of the Malvado group and then taking your revenge when you realised what the truth was?'

'That's sort of true,' Nicholas replied, 'but the person in charge was never Lara's dad or Kristian.'

'Who was it then?'

'You do know what "Carr" is short for?'

'No.'

'Cardozo – it's Portuguese. My dad hired you because he wants to finish what he started.'

41

'. . . You have to be tactful around them and understand they might be using you as much as you're hoping to use them . . .'

Andrew's mouth flopped open. He'd been used the entire time. He'd even told Jenny that the job had an element of using people and then missed it. What a fool.

'I told your dad to meet me at my office later,' Andrew whispered.

Nicholas took out the knife again. 'Let's go then. He and mum rarely leave the house – they're really careful because they know the rest of the group have been disappearing. It's why he went to you. He knew I was getting closer to him and wanted me found. At the time, I was spending some time on their road, trying not to be noticed by the neighbours, hoping they'd leave themselves open. For ages, it didn't look like they went out by themselves. Lara hired a van so that I could wait but we were out of money and it was the final day when I followed him to your office. I was hoping I'd get a chance where he'd be on his own but he was really careful.'

'It's not a game, Nicholas. You can't just go around killing people.'

Nicholas's eyes flared; he didn't reply because he didn't need to. Everything that had happened to him had left him detached from the world around him. He was solely focused on revenge against those who'd led him here. Andrew could see it from his gaze: the idea of killing excited him.

'Nicholas.'

The young man shook his head, drifting back into the room. 'What?'

'Are you saying your father was looking for you, and you were trying to find a moment when he was alone?'

'I suppose. The final straw came when Oswald went missing the weekend before last. Dad would have known I was close then. They'd long-since changed the locks at the house. As the rest of their group continued to disappear, he knew I'd be coming.'

Andrew turned to Lara. 'If that was true, why wouldn't one of them go after you?'

'They only suspect I might be involved – only you know for certain. We used to argue a bit, so they were never sure if we were together or not.' She glanced up at Nicholas, smiling sheepishly. Andrew could only imagine how trivial those petty squabbles were now. 'Also, why do you think I go out of my way to look so different? No one ever fails to notice you when you're walking to lectures like this. I don't go out after dark and I'm always close to groups of people. Even if they knew for sure, there's not much they could do.'

Andrew felt as if he needed a long lie-down on a very comfortable bed. He'd completely lost the plot, metaphorically and literally. He rubbed his head. It felt like he was close to completing a jigsaw but the final few pieces he had to work with belonged to a separate puzzle.

'You're going to have to explain some of this to me.'

Nicholas was bobbing on his tiptoes, ready to go, but Lara moved across to him and tugged on his sleeve. 'We can give him ten minutes.' She leant up and kissed him on the cheek, before sitting on the corner of the bed and turning to Andrew.

'My dad got me involved in his circle of friends before he died. I'd always known the name "Malvado". He brought me up with this nursery rhyme about how Malvado was a Brazilian prince. He tried to take food from the noblemen to help feed hungry peasants but was killed by the King's men in the woods. That night, his spirit returned and took vengeance on the sleeping soldiers and from then on, his essence patrolled the forests, protecting those who needed it.' She glanced at Nicholas, then back to Andrew. 'Yeah, I know.'

Andrew couldn't judge. If you were brought up being told Santa Claus or the Tooth Fairy were real, then you believed it because you trusted your parents. That was before you started thinking about religion. It was as Keira had told him: everything was about faith.

Lara rubbed at her face, accidentally smudging some of her eye make-up. 'I don't know when I stopped thinking it was real but I believed it all for a while. Growing up, he taught me about our ancestors. He said that we were cursed as a family, destined to be without true love for eternity because one of my great-great-great-uncles was a witch-hunter or something like that and that he massacred innocent people. That's where our name came from, which is why I wanted to change it. When I was fifteen or sixteen, he started taking me to these gatherings in the woods. I thought it was a bit silly at first but . . .' She peered at the floor. '. . . I saw things that I couldn't explain. You think it's all chanting and being immature but there's more to it than that. Words are powerful.'

'What did you see?'

She croaked slightly, reaching out for Nicholas. He perched on the edge of the computer desk, putting the knife down next to him and taking her hand in his left.

'Just . . . *things*. I want to believe they were tricks but I don't know how they would have done it. There was a fire and we would ask Malvado to show himself, to guide us. It was scary.' She squeezed Nicholas's hand. 'That's where we met. Nicholas's father was the person in charge of it all, and his mum was involved too. For a little while, we were into it. That's when we got the tattoos and I used to wear this upside-down cross. After a while, it seemed a little silly.'

'What about the books under Nicholas's bed?'

The two teenagers looked at each other. 'Nothing to do with me,' Nicholas said.

They must have been left by Richard as just enough of a nudge to put him and Jenny on the path that had led him here.

Lara continued the story: 'When my dad found out he had cancer, he wanted me to take his full place in the circle.'

'Circle?'

'That's what they call it: the Circle of Eighteen. Malvado was a young prince – he was killed when he was eighteen.

338

I was scared by what I'd seen in the woods but didn't know what it was all about. Like you said, really.'

'What did happen?'

'It's more or less what you were talking about. Because Malvado was eighteen, we believe—' She stopped, coughing and squeezing Nicholas's hand again. '*They* believe that the number is sacred. The circle needs eighteen people and every eighteen years, they sacrifice an eighteen-year-old. It's supposed to provide Malvado with new blood to help restore him to his former glory. We only found that out on the night when Nicholas had to go missing.' She rolled up her sleeve, revealing the scars of her circle tattoo with the triangle inside. 'I got this done before any of that.'

Andrew nodded at Nicholas. 'Is that why you disappeared on the night you turned eighteen?'

'More or less.'

Lara cut in: 'It happened pretty much as I told you. We didn't know anything about it but Nicholas hadn't been feeling well. He walked me home and we said goodnight. I was living at home by myself at the time.'

Nicholas took his hand back and crossed his arms as best he could. Andrew tried not to stare at the flattened section of his glove where he once had fingers. 'I think my mum or dad put something in my food earlier that day. My stomach was in agony but I thought I could walk it off. I texted my mum to say I was on my way but it took me a while to get there. When I did, the lights were still on, which was unusual. I often got home late and they'd be in bed. I went through the front door and my mum was in the living room. I remember saying hello, and then . . . I have no idea.'

'What do you mean?'

'I guess they used some sort of drug or that chloroform stuff to knock me out. The next thing I knew, I was in the woods, tied to a tree.'

Andrew motioned towards Lara. 'Were you there?'

She shook her head. 'I didn't know anything about it.'

'Weren't you one of the eighteen?'

'Exactly – we're guessing they only had seventeen there. They would have known I wouldn't go for it.'

'There are lots of rituals,' Nicholas said. 'Lara and me saw animals being sacrificed but never anything more. I think they were building us up to it. On that night, my parents were there. It felt cold and there was the dry lightning going on. They thought it was a present from Malvado. I was in the clothes I'd gone out in, jeans and a hoody, but there was something in my mouth so I couldn't speak. My dad was telling me I was the chosen one and that it was an honour. They were wearing the same brown robes they always did and were chanting. I knew some of the words but not many.' He held up his right arm. 'Then they started to take my fingers.'

'What were they going to do with them?'

'I don't know.'

'A friend told me that some groups connected to the occult removed hands and feet because God created us in his image and it was to desecrate that.'

Nicholas's face was blank. If that was true, it was the first he knew of it. He closed his eyes, reaching for Lara again. 'I only remember it in flashes. Perhaps I was blacking out but it could have been because of the weather. It wasn't raining but the thunder was getting louder and there were these really bright white flashes that lit up the trees. It actually didn't hurt that much when they took my fingers – I assume they'd given me something but who knows? I remember my dad taking my third finger. He held it in the air, letting the blood drip. I thought he was going to eat it for a moment but he started saying these words I didn't understand, then there was this enormous *boooooooooom.'*

Nicholas's eyes popped and he held his hands out wide as he tried to explain how loud it was without raising his voice.

'It was like the sound was everywhere. I could feel it pouring through me, like my whole body was shaking. As that happened, the lightning lit everything up. It was like when someone shines a torch in your eyes but so much brighter. I couldn't really see for a few seconds, my eyes were full of pink and green stars, but then it all came clear in a flash. Because the thunder and lightning was so close, everyone had hit the ground. They were holding their ears and rubbing their eyes. I was about to start struggling when I realised I wasn't tied to the tree any longer.'

'What happened?'

A shrug. 'I don't know. Perhaps one of them untied me.' He glanced at Lara, before blinking away. 'Perhaps *He* was unhappy they only had seventeen . . .'

'. . . *It's all about faith . . .'*

Keira.

'What did you do when you realised you were free?' Andrew asked.

'I ran for it. I couldn't really feel the pain in my hand but grabbed some big leaves to try to stop my fingers bleeding. I ran and ran, then hid under this thick bush on the edge of the woods. I could hear them shouting but didn't move. By the time the sun started to come up, I went to the only other place I knew – Lara's.'

'How did you get there if you were covered in dirt and bleeding?'

Nicholas looked at him as if he was stupid. 'Have you *seen* half the people in this city?'

Good point.

'I didn't know if they might be watching her house,' Nicholas continued. 'I went in through the back. At the time, she didn't even know I was missing.'

Andrew turned to Lara, who was still rubbing at her face. 'I wanted him to go to the hospital but then he said it was everyone we knew who'd done it. I did what I could to patch him up—'

'Is that why you dropped out from your medical course?'

'Sort of. My mum was a qualified doctor, though she never did it as a job because it didn't interest her. There were textbooks all around the house and I used to read them. I thought it'd be fun when I was younger. I used them to help fix up Nicholas, but the whole thing felt a bit too real after that. That was a pretty good indicator I wasn't cut out for it.'

'Your mum was qualified as a doctor?'

'So?'

'We looked into your parents but never saw that.'

'Why would you? She never worked as a doctor, nurse, or in any medical role. She ran the business with Dad. If it wasn't for the textbooks around the house, I wouldn't have known and I wouldn't have been interested in studying medicine.'

Andrew focused back on Nicholas. 'So where were you hiding all this time?'

'Here and there. We figured they'd come to ask Lara if she'd seen me, which they did. They didn't want to let on about the whole sacrifice thing, so couldn't tell her everything. It wasn't safe there anyway. I got by through a combination of Lara's shed and a few abandoned houses. None of that was safe, which is why she applied to come into halls. People might have been watching her house but they'd never be able to monitor somewhere this big.'

'How did you know you'd be able to hide in the walls?'

'I didn't. That was a bit of a bonus. The general plan was for me to stay here. There are so many people coming and going with hoods up and the like that you'd never know who was who.' He held his left hand up, indicating the room. 'Lara moved in during the summer and said there was a bigger space between the bedroom and the bathroom, so she fought to get this spot. We figured it was somewhere I could duck into just in case. Usually, I sit around here but, at first, people were always knocking, asking if Lara wanted to go out, so it was handy. Gradually, I started going out more.'

'What happened with Kristian Verity and the rest?'

Nicholas reached for the knife. 'What do you think? The ritual wasn't complete, so they were going to come for me if I didn't go for them. It was for my own safety.'

'How many?'

He didn't answer at first. 'Put it this way: there aren't many left.'

'If there were seventeen to begin with but hardly any left, how come none of it's been in the news? People don't just get killed and that's the end of it.'

Nicholas smiled, and for the first time, Andrew felt the enormity of what the teenager had done. He wasn't sorry for it. 'They didn't want it getting out, so the other members of the circle covered things up. You must have found Wicker's body before anyone else. They wouldn't have liked that.'

Andrew remembered that Richard Carr had called him that night, which now made even more sense. If that was the first body the police had found, he would have been panicking.

'How did you do it?'

There was another nervous glance between Nicholas and Lara, who was clearly less pleased about matters than her boyfriend was.

'You don't need to know that.'

Andrew left it at that – he could fill in the blanks and wasn't sure he wanted to know anyway.

'It was self-defence,' Nicholas added.

Andrew didn't know what to say. Perhaps it was, but he could hardly let things continue as they were, knowing that Nicholas planned to kill his father, among others. The situation was a complete mess.

As Nicholas stood, Andrew's phone started to ring. He fished it out of his pocket, staring at the screen as the two teenagers froze. 'It's my assistant,' Andrew said, holding his phone into the air, asking for permission to answer it.

Nicholas nodded, so Andrew pressed the button. 'Jenny?'

'Hello, Mr Hunter.'

Richard Carr's voice sent shivers along Andrew's spine. There was none of the sorrow from when they'd first met, only menace.

'Have you found my son yet?'

Andrew glanced up to Nicholas, holding up a single finger. 'No.'

'Your little friend here tells me differently. If you want to see her again, I suggest we meet in the woods. You bring Nicholas – he'll know where. And don't call the police.'

42

Nicholas needed no persuasion to go, tucking the knife into his trousers, pulling up his hoody and telling Lara to check the corridor.

Andrew felt like he was on autopilot. In many ways, he didn't care about the bizarre rituals of whatever the Circle of Eighteen was. He was also struggling to feel much sorrow for the members Nicholas had apparently killed. He didn't know the names of most of them and likely never would. What he did know was that Richard had gone out of his way to trick him into finding Nicholas and had then kidnapped Jenny. It was no wonder Nicholas had turned out the way he had when you considered his father.

The corridor was empty, the stairwell quiet as the three of them made their way to Andrew's car. For the first mile, nobody said anything, but then Andrew couldn't take it any longer. He glanced in the rear-view mirror trying to catch Nicholas's eye but the young man was gazing into nothingness, bobbing his head as if listening to music, ready for a night out. Then something else caught Andrew's attention, and he flicked his gaze to the rear-view mirror twice in quick succession.

'Something wrong?' Nicholas asked.

Andrew met his eye with another glance in the mirror. 'No.'

The journey to Alkrington Wood was largely uninter-rupted. A narrow crescent moon hung over the trees, casting a sliver of white light across the bitterly cold evening. Andrew almost hoped there would be doggers out to save the day but it wasn't a night for dangling your bits in public, unless you wanted frostbite.

Six cars were in the car park, headlights off, no one around. Outside the car, there was a scurrying from the undergrowth. Surely not more rats? Andrew couldn't see anything but there was more movement high above in the trees, with birds – or worse, bats – skimming around ominously. Nicholas was already a dozen steps along the path when Andrew called him back.

As a trio, they walked deeper into the woods, listening as their breaths swirled into the night. Lara hadn't spoken since they'd left the flat but seemed to be going with whatever Nicholas wanted to do.

Andrew wanted to try one final time. 'Nicholas.'

'What?'

'What are you going to do?'

'I don't know.'

'You must do.'

'Just go with it, man.'

'I can't . . . Jenny . . .'

The young man didn't reply.

The ground was a mixture of squelchy mud-filled puddles and frozen crusts of wintered ground. Andrew allowed Nicholas to lead him deeper into the darkness, as twigs continued to crack underfoot, with the rustling of leaves above. Andrew wondered if there were people around them, or if it was just animals. Would it matter? Unless it was a SWAT team or a bunch of ninjas, he was knowingly walking into a trap anyway. If only Jenny had gone home when he'd told her. Deep down, he'd known she was probably going to stay late. She beat him into the office most mornings and often needed persuading to go home. That's why he'd asked her to call Richard Carr, rather than doing it himself – and this is where it had landed him.

A gentle orange glow was fluttering at the top of the ridge where Andrew had been with Rory the pug the previous week. Nicholas bounded up as Andrew helped a still-silent Lara. In the moonlight, she looked wraithlike, a spirit ghosting through the trees.

Nicholas stopped at the top of the ridge, waiting for Andrew and Lara to catch up. The three of them stopped, peering down to the shallow hollow below, where six people wearing long brown robes were standing in a circle. There were six torches planted in the ground, sparkling, fizzing flames spouting from the top, catching on the chilled air and dancing a jig.

Only one of them had the hood down: Richard Carr. There was no sign of the friendly dad jumper or loose trousers. Instead, he opened his arms, welcoming the trio of visitors. Nicholas moved ahead first, edging slowly down the decline, Andrew and Lara a little behind. The circle opened, revealing Jenny on the ground in the centre, arms bound behind her, legs tied together. Andrew tried to catch her eye but there was too great a distance between them.

Nicholas stopped a few metres away from the circle.

His father reached into his robe and pulled out a knife much like the one Nicholas was carrying. He knelt, pressing it to Jenny's neck.

'First, we'll take whatever you've brought.'

Nicholas reached into his back pocket and tossed his blade onto the ground, standing with his arms out. One of the hooded figures beckoned him forward before four of them swarmed, frisking him until they were certain he wasn't carrying anything else. When they were satisfied, one of them pulled his arms back, tightening three cable ties around his wrists, before they stepped away.

'Sit,' Richard commanded. Nicholas did as he was told.

Next Lara went through the same process. Her phone and wallet were taken before she joined Nicholas on the floor, wrists secured.

Andrew held his arms out as he felt the flurry of hands skimming through his pockets, tugging at his clothes and patting his body. He was close enough to see Jenny properly but she was staring at him as if this was a normal Tuesday evening. They could have been sitting down for dinner or watching television and her expression would have been the same. Her lips were pressed together, eyes impassive, unworried. That concerned him more than anything. Was he the only one who realised what was going on? Nicholas was sitting on the ground, palms flat to the earth, gazing at his father. Andrew really hoped one of them had a plan because he didn't.

Somebody bigger than him wrenched his arms backwards. He could feel their warm breath on his ear, their rough skin holding his arms. He thought about fighting but it was a little late. He grimaced in pain as the first cable tie ground into his wrists. The second one hurt even more, cutting into his flesh, before the third clicked into place. He tried wriggling his arms to release the pressure on his shoulders but there wasn't much give.

Finally the hooded figures withdrew, tossing his wallet and phone next to Lara's belongings and Nicholas's knife on the ground.

Andrew joined Lara and Nicholas on the sodden earth as the circle closed around them again. He could feel the mud soaking through his trousers, not that it was high on his list of things that weren't going well.

Richard stood again, removing the knife from Jenny's throat.

'I'm glad to see you've returned, Nicholas. It's what He would have wanted.'

Andrew found himself replying. 'Who's He?'

'Just He.'

'Isn't your ritual supposed to be an eighteen-year-old every eighteen years?'

Richard laughed, waving for the others to join in, before his face hardened into a snarl. 'You know nothing of our rituals. That is but one of the sacrifices He demands.'

'Did *He* tell you to choose me? You could have asked anyone to do your dirty work.'

Richard turned slightly to stare at Andrew instead of Nicholas. 'You're a hunter.'

'That's just my name. It doesn't mean anything.'

'On the contrary, names are everything – aren't they, Lara, my love?'

Lara didn't flinch, her voice hoarse. 'I'm nothing to do with you.'

Andrew couldn't help but wish his father's name had been Mr Knownothing. It would have saved him all of this.

He peered around the circle, spotting Elaine for the first time. Her face was bowed, lips moving in a silent prayer or chant, not looking at her son. It was hard to reconcile that with the mother who was apparently desperate to find him, but then she was frantic for another reason: she knew Nicholas was coming for them.

Andrew tried to wriggle his fingers and suddenly someone was pulling him to his feet as the circle closed tighter. He tried to struggle but whoever had him was bigger and stronger than he was. As he flailed, the sharpened edge of a blade appeared next to his windpipe.

'Be sensible,' a male voice whispered.

Andrew straightened, allowing himself to be held. Next to him, other hooded figures had Lara and Nicholas too, blades at their necks. Jenny was still at Richard's feet, sitting perfectly calmly. The person with the knife to Andrew's throat was whispering in a strange monotonous tongue, the words barely comprehensible.

Richard raised his arms higher. 'After the interruption of our previous ritual, we no longer have eighteen members to complete the circle.' He used his knife to indicate the trees around the rim. 'But we do have the three sacred pillars – and three young people to offer our Father.'

He dragged Jenny to her feet by her neck as Lara and

351

Nicholas were yanked backwards towards the edges of the circle. Richard pointed his knife in Andrew's direction.

'And our Hunter can watch.'

Lara was biting and kicking but neither Jenny nor Nicholas were fighting. They had only been dragged a couple of metres when there was a loud gasp.

Everybody stopped and turned. Halfway down the slope a single figure stood, arms by his side, freezing breath disappearing into the atmosphere.

It was Stewart Deacon.

43

Andrew thought he'd seen a familiar vehicle in his rear-view mirror but assumed he'd been mistaken when it didn't follow them into the car park at the edge of the woods. Now Deacon waited a little above them standing side-on, staring between the hooded figures, plus Lara, Jenny and Nicholas. His eyes practically leapt out of his head when he spotted Andrew.

'Who are you?' Richard asked.

Deacon stepped forward, eyes twitching towards Andrew.

'I was, er, following him. He's caused me a lot of problems.'

His voice was trembling, the brash confident image of the man with the knuckle-duster who burst into Andrew's flat long gone – exactly as his wife said he acted when he wasn't the biggest dog in the kennel. The two remaining hooded members of the group took a few steps in Deacon's direction. He flinched, turning in a semicircle as if there was somebody behind him.

There wasn't.

The figures kept moving towards him, no one daring to speak. It was only when the knives flashed from their pockets that Deacon came to his senses. At first he recoiled as if to escape but when his pursuers started to run, he stumbled backwards, reaching into his coat and pulling out a pistol.

Instantly, the atmosphere changed. The two men with knives began backing away, weapons disappearing into their pockets. The knife at Andrew's neck disappeared, with the hand holding onto his arm loosening. Lara had stopped fighting too, as everyone watched the man with the gun.

Deacon's arm was wavering, the pistol aimed somewhere in the middle of Andrew and Richard. He clearly didn't know what he was doing.

'What's your name?' Richard asked, tone slightly lighter, though still firm.

'It doesn't matter.'

'But you're here for Mr Hunter?'

'I suppose.'

'And he's wronged you?'

'Yes.'

'I have no idea who you are but I can see that you're trembling, that you're scared. You didn't mean to come here tonight. You can walk away and pretend that you didn't see anything.'

Deacon's eyes flicked across until he was watching Andrew, but it was hard to read anything beyond the fear. Andrew tried to piece it all together. Violet Deacon had come to see them the previous day, saying she wanted to divorce her husband. He'd either found out, or she'd told him. He must have followed Andrew to the student halls, no doubt wondering what on earth was going on as he trailed them towards the woods. What was clear was that he had a gun.

Silently, Andrew willed him to get help or to use the gun and shoot Richard. Do whatever the hell he had to. As long as he saved Jenny, he could do whatever he wanted. Richard still had an arm across Jenny's chest, the knife close to her throat.

Surely anyone, even Stewart Deacon, could figure out who the good guys were?

Deacon looked away again, focusing on Richard. 'Who are you?'

'How about we agree not to ask each other that? You forget us and we'll forget you? Deal?'

Deacon took two steps backwards, turned, stumbled, corrected himself and then continued backing away towards the rim of the circle. 'Deal.'

In a flash, the gun was back in his pocket and he was running for all he was worth.

Nobody moved. One second, two seconds, five seconds. Ten. Then Richard Carr nodded to the two hooded figures and they set off after him, knives at the ready.

Some truce that was.

The fingers tightened around Andrew's wrist again as he was thrust to the ground. Meanwhile, Lara, Jenny and Nicholas were each pulled to one of the three respective trees. Andrew tried to catch Jenny's eye but she was watching the others. He wondered if she'd been drugged because she seemed so unbothered. Next to Richard Carr, she looked like a child. There was a large tear in her tights, with scuffs of dirt on her hands and face. She didn't look hurt but didn't seem scared either.

Then it struck him: she didn't get frightened. Whether

it was a vicious, hissing cat, monsters under the bed, or standing in front of Stewart Deacon's revving car, she didn't care. Her old teacher thought she had a problem with empathy for others but it wasn't that at all, or at least it wasn't *just* that. She didn't know what being scared meant. That made it hard for her to sympathise with people because she didn't understand what they were going through. He wondered if she even knew the danger she was in.

Andrew watched as Richard made her stand against the tree, knife against her ribs. He twisted to see Nicholas and Lara in a similar position, arms behind their backs, knives to their throats. Over the brow of the slope, the two hooded figures returned, each out of breath, arms held out to say they hadn't caught Deacon. Andrew heard them come to a halt behind him, standing and whispering.

Above, Richard was triumphant, one hand holding Jenny by the scruff of the neck, the other clutching the knife.

'Oh Father, forgive us for we have sinned.'

He lurched into a language Andrew didn't understand, the murmur growing as the other five joined in. It was a strange mix of chanting and singing, with an underlying rhythm to the words. Andrew didn't know if he was imagining it but the air felt heavier, colder. He tried to breathe but there was nothing there. The mantra continued to build until it seemed as if it was everywhere, not just six people in a circle but six hundred in front, behind, above and below. The words were everywhere.

'. . . *I saw things too that I couldn't explain. You think it's all chanting and being immature but there's more to it than that. Words are powerful . . .'*

Andrew forced his head up, trying to watch Jenny, but it was so much effort, as if someone was standing on his shoulders, forcing him into the ground. He continued to fight until he could see Richard. The robed man's eyes had rolled back into his head, the whites burning bright under the moonlight, mouth bobbing open and closed to the tempo of the chant.

Then he raised the knife.

44

'Stop.'

The man's voice boomed across the clearing and, in a rush of icy air, everything felt normal again. Andrew was blinking rapidly, trying to clear his thoughts, wondering if he'd imagined what had just happened.

Standing at the top of the circle was Stewart Deacon, his gun pointing directly at Richard Carr.

Richard's eyes were facing the front, hands out to the side, Jenny standing unaided.

Deacon's arm was steady this time. 'Drop the knife.'

Richard did as he was told.

'And the rest of you.'

Around the rim, there was the sound of metal thwacking into the ground. Three more blades landed behind Andrew.

'I want you all to lie down, else I'm going to use this.'

There was the same confidence in Deacon's voice as there had been in Andrew's flat. Richard fell to his knees, hands behind his head. Andrew turned, expecting the five figures to have done the same but, instead, four of them were bolting for the trees. The only one who remained was close to Lara: Elaine Carr. Her hood was now down as she howled after the people who were running.

Lara was bobbing awkwardly, unable to use her hands to steady herself.

'Are you all right, sweetheart?' Deacon was calling to Lara, apparently unconcerned by the escaping cloaked figures.

She didn't speak but started to waver her way down the slope towards Andrew, who pushed himself up. The ties were still cutting into his wrists and he was finding it awkward to balance as he staggered to his feet. Nicholas appeared by his side, tossing his cable ties to the floor. Poking through the glove of where his three fingers would have once been was a thin, sharp blade. He skirted behind Andrew and sliced through the binds and then did the same to Lara.

Andrew's skin was raw but he couldn't stop looking at the blade. 'Why didn't you use that earlier?' he whispered.

Nicholas didn't reply, strolling forward, up the gentle bank towards his father. Jenny was now sitting on the floor, watching everything.

Deacon was still aiming the gun at Richard's head but his eyes kept darting towards Nicholas.

'Hey, kid, what are you doing?'

Nicholas continued walking.

'Kid, stop. I'm going to call the police.'

Nicholas halted a couple of metres short of his father. 'You didn't think I'd come unprepared, did you?'

Richard didn't respond as his son kicked the knife further away.

'Where's your Father now?' Nicholas said.

Deacon was floundering, unsure where to look. 'Kid, shut it, I'm going to—'

He didn't get a chance to finish his sentence before Nicholas lunged forward and grabbed the pistol from his grasp. In a flash, he had thrown it deep into the darkness of the woods. Deacon was so shocked, he stumbled backwards, ending on his backside staring up.

'If your gun was genuine, there was no way you'd have been able to hold it so steady for so long. Real ones are heavy.'

Deacon didn't argue, scrambling backwards. Only one person was now in charge of the situation and it wasn't him.

Andrew turned at the sound of scuffed feet, watching as Elaine slipped down the slope, eyes on her son.

'Nicholas, sweetie, you don't have to do this. We can all go home and go back to the way it used to be.'

Richard turned to Nicholas, arms out wide. 'Son . . .'

Nicholas either didn't hear them, or didn't care. He turned to his father, face blank. He opened his mouth – *'Ele exigiu um sacrifício'* – and then slashed his arm forward, the blade in the centre of his hand slicing straight across his father's windpipe.

THURSDAY

45

Andrew sat in his office chair and closed his eyes, enjoying the silence. Well, relative silence. The sounds of a
Manchester morning rippled in the background: cars
beeping their way around the streets, the clatter of footsteps on pavements.

At least it was better than the sound of twigs cracking
in the freezing night.

His eyes popped open as he heard someone climbing
the stairs and then Jenny was in the doorway, rosy cheeks,
broad smile and a box of teabags in her hand.

'We're almost out,' she said.

She began to fuss with the kettle in the far corner,
humming under her breath.

'Jen.'

'What?'

'Can we have a chat?'

'Sure, I just—'

'Before you brew up.'

She twisted in a smiling flurry of flared skirt, crossing
the room to perch on his desk. 'You all right?'

'I was going to ask you the same thing.'

'I'm fine.'

He couldn't believe she was grinning. 'This job isn't
supposed to be dangerous. You shouldn't be tied up and

shouldn't spend an entire day being questioned by the police.'

'What are you saying?'

'I think we should go our separate ways. It's one thing for me to endanger myself, another one entirely to put someone else at risk.'

She scrunched her lips together. 'Pfft.'

'And that's not a good enough reason for this to continue.'

'I'm fine!'

'But you might not have been.'

Jenny spun around again, turning her back to him and heading for the corner. 'I'll put a sugar in your tea if you're going to be so grumpy. I'm all right, you're all right: let's get on with it.'

'It's not that simple.'

'It really is.'

Andrew huffed out an annoyed sigh, not knowing what else to say. Apart from firing her, there wasn't a lot else he could do. Not yet, anyway. Jenny was humming cheerily to herself again. Life was perfectly normal, except that it wasn't.

She spoke over her shoulder, still fiddling with the mugs in the corner. 'Any word on the four who escaped?'

'Not yet. The police said they'd let me know if and when they find them. They have the names from Elaine Carr. Hopefully it'll only be a matter of time.'

'What do you think will happen to Nicholas?'

'His mental health is being assessed, so he'll probably spend the rest of his life locked up one way or the other.

It's not as if he doesn't have a case – his parents tried to kill him and chopped his fingers off.'

'What about Lara?'

'Who knows? One of my sources in the police told me that Nicholas took the blame for everything and said Lara didn't know anything about it. She might not even be charged. I would have called to fill you in last night but didn't know what was going on. I was with the police for almost ten hours. There's going to be a scandal because Richard was a councillor. No one thinks there was any connection but it looks bad.'

Jenny crossed the room and put a mug down in front of Andrew before heading to her own desk and rummaging in the bottom drawer. 'Rich Tea?'

'No thanks.'

'Jaffa Cake?'

'No.'

'Toffee Pop?'

'A what?'

Jenny held up something that was round with a caramel centre.

'No.'

She dug out a biscuit for herself and started eating. 'Did they tell you what happened to Stewart Deacon?'

'He couldn't cope with what he saw. After Nicholas told him to call the police, he didn't move. When they interviewed him the next morning, he said he'd been there to threaten me with the gun. They recovered it and confirmed it was fake but that's not really the point. If it wasn't for him, we wouldn't have been saved in the first place, so maybe they'll take that into account? Who knows? What a mess.'

Jenny double-dipped the Rich Tea into her drink, which proved that she wasn't afraid of anything. Few would risk a back-to-back dunk when it came to Rich Teas. Miraculously, the biscuit emerged unbroken and she sucked it down.

'Jen.'

'What?'

'When Richard Carr kidnapped you, what happened?'

She shrugged. 'I don't really remember.'

'Did he give you something?'

'He was here and I made him a brew. I had to nip to the loo, so he could have done. One minute I was here, then I was in his car.'

That was a relief at least: Andrew found it hard to believe that she had no concern at all for herself. Who could be like that? If she'd been drugged, it would explain why she was so pliable. He tried to tell himself that was true but there was still a tingle in the back of Andrew's mind wondering if fearless was simply the way she was.

'Do you remember being in the woods?'

'Yes.'

'Were you scared?'

She polished off the biscuit first, scooping up a stray soggy crumb with her thumb. 'I don't know. I knew I'd be okay.'

'How?'

'I just did.'

'But Nicholas had no intention of saving you. He'd kept

the knife hidden to save himself and then go after his father. The only reason we're still here is because of Stewart Deacon and his fake gun.'

'It worked out, didn't it?'

'That's what I'm trying to say. It did, but not because of either of us.'

'Pfft. We're fine.'

Andrew watched her as she blew on her tea, unable to tell what she was thinking. He could fire her and leave her to her own devices, or do what he really wanted and continue working with her. Did she really care for herself? Or others? He wasn't going to find out by sending her away.

She caught his eye and grinned, eyes wide, dimple set. 'I'm fine!'

'I know.'

That was what worried him.

'What's going to happen to us?'

'How do you mean?'

'With the office and everything?'

Andrew blew on his own tea. 'I don't know. The police will check our statements to make sure they match. They might decide we hampered their investigation but I really doubt it considering everything that happened and the fact they spent nine months not finding someone. If Nicholas confesses to killing all those Circle members, then they're going to look pretty incompetent too, so we'll be the least of their worries. Honestly? I don't think any-thing will happen. A new client will knock on our door at some point today or tomorrow and life will go on.'

Jenny's eyes crinkled into a wider grin. 'Promise?'

'No.'

'Good. I don't like people who promise too much.'

She sipped her tea as someone rapped loudly on the door. They both turned at the same time to see a dusky silhouette beyond the rippled glass.

'Do you want to do the honours?' Andrew asked.

Jenny put her mug down. 'Come innnnnnnn.'

The door swung inwards with a creak, allowing a gust of Manchester air to flood into the office. Standing in the open space was a woman with a blonde bob, bag over her shoulder, crumpled business card in hand.

Keira glanced from Jenny to Andrew, smiling wearily like someone who had seen the news that morning. 'Can we have a word?'

COMING SOON

SOMETHING HIDDEN

The second book featuring
Private Investigator Andrew Hunter

Everyone hates Fiona Methodist.

Her war veteran father shot a young couple in broad daylight before killing himself. With all three dead, no one knows the motive, other than that the engaged pair witnessed a robbery and were due to give evidence.

But Fiona knows her dad didn't do it. He couldn't have – he's her father and he wouldn't have done that. Would he?

Private investigator Andrew Hunter takes pity on the girl and even with stolen Bengal cats to find, and an ex-wife who's not quite so 'ex', he can't escape the creeping feeling that Fiona might be right after all.

ISBN 978-1-5098-0663-8

LOCKED IN

Jessica Daniel Book 1

They think they are safe at home. Someone knows better.

When a body is found in a locked house, Detective Sergeant Jessica Daniel is left to not only find the killer but discover how they got in and out.

With little in the way of leads and a journalist that seems to know more about the case than she does, Jessica is already feeling the pressure – and that's before a second body shows up in identical circumstances to the first.

How can a murderer get to victims in seemingly impossible situations and what, if anything, links the bodies?

ISBN 978-1-4472-2564-5

VIGILANTE

Jessica Daniel Book 2

A killer behind bars is still killing . . .

Dead bodies are piling up for Detective Sergeant Jessica Daniel.

Usually when a serial killer is on the loose, the pressure would be building to find the perpetrator but the victims are all hardened criminals themselves.

The national media can't believe their luck with an apparent vigilante on the streets, while Jessica's new boss seems grateful someone else is doing their job for them.

But things aren't so straightforward when forensics matches blood from the apparent killer to a man already behind bars.

ISBN 978-1-4472-2566-9

THE WOMAN IN BLACK

Jessica Daniel Book 3

Severed body parts. A woman in shadows.
These are the only clues.

Someone has left a severed hand in the centre of Manchester and the only clue Detective Sergeant Jessica Daniel has to go on is CCTV footage of a woman in a long black robe placing it carefully on the ground.

With a lengthy missing persons list and frantic families wondering if the body part could belong to their absent loved ones, she has plenty to deal with – and that's before a detached finger arrives for her in the post.

By the time a second hand is found and a local MP's wife goes missing, Jessica is left struggling to find out who the appendages belong to, how they are connected and just what the mysterious woman in black has to do with it all.

ISBN 978-1-4472-2567-6

THINK OF THE CHILDREN

Jessica Daniel Book 4

One boy is dead. A killer is free. Who is next?

Detective Sergeant Jessica Daniel is first on the scene as a stolen car crashes on a misty, wet Manchester morning. The driver is dead, but the biggest shock awaits her when she discovers the body of a child wrapped in plastic in the boot of the car.

As Jessica struggles to discover the identity of the driver, a thin trail leads her first to a set of clothes buried in the woods and then to a list of children's names abandoned in an allotment shed.

With the winter chill setting in and parents looking for answers, Jessica must find out who has been watching local children, and how this connects to a case that has been unsolved for fourteen years.

ISBN 978-1-4472-2340-5

PLAYING WITH FIRE

Jessica Daniel Book 5

Those who play with fire are going to get burned . . .

Seven years ago Martin Chadwick set fire to a building, not knowing a teenager was sleeping inside. With the media hyping the man's impending release from prison and the victim's father hinting at revenge, Detective Sergeant Jessica Daniel is given the task of keeping an eye on the former prisoner.

Graffitied threats are just the start of what seems to be an escalating campaign of intimidation as the apparently remorseful man is left fearing for his life. At first the culprit seems obvious – but with Martin's son connected to the death of a young girl and a private investigator making a nuisance of himself, Jessica is caught squarely in the middle. Meanwhile, someone in her midst seems intent on burning everything to the ground . . .

ISBN 978-1-4472-2341-2

THICKER THAN WATER

Jessica Daniel Book 6

When Cameron and Eleanor Sexton arrive home to find their babysitter missing but their child and property otherwise untouched, Detective Sergeant Jessica Daniel is sent on what she thinks is a fool's errand to find out what happened.

But Jessica is left confused as the teenager's body turns up in the bath of a different house, seemingly at random – a puzzle which only deepens when a journalist points out that someone placed an obituary for him days before he went missing.

With one colleague leaving while another returns, plus a local businessman taking an unhealthy interest in her, Jessica turns to home to find the one person she can rely on. But is that trust misplaced?

ISBN 978-1-4472-2342-9

BEHIND CLOSED DOORS

Jessica Daniel Book 7

Detective Sergeant Jessica Daniel has barely left her house in months, isolated away from friends and colleagues. She may have given up on herself but one man is sure she still has something to offer.

DCI Jack Cole gives her a chance at redemption: an opportunity to help a neighbouring force by discovering what is going on with a reclusive community living in a stately home in the middle of nowhere.

People are going missing, turning up dead with only a vague link back to the house. But can Jessica beat her own demons in time to find out exactly what's going on behind closed doors?

ISBN 978-1-4472-4785-2

CROSSING THE LINE

Jessica Daniel Book 8

Nitric acid, baseball bats and HIV-filled syringes: People are being attacked publicly by a masked figure in the centre of Manchester, and Jessica Daniel doesn't know how to catch the person responsible.

Not that she'll get much help from the media – it's been twenty-five years since the notorious Stretford Slasher was caught, and those who can remember are feeling nostalgic.

With the city held in a wintry grip, Jessica has a caseload stacking up and an old friend to look after – and all while she's wilting under the shadow of secrets a quarter-of-a-century old.

ISBN 978-1-4472-4787-6

RECKONING

The Silver Blackthorn series Book 1

One girl. One reckoning. One destiny.

In the village of Martindale, hundreds of miles north of
the new English capital of Windsor, sixteen-year-old Silver
Blackthorn takes the Reckoning. This coming-of-age test
not only decides her place in society – Elite, Member, Inter
or Trog – but also determines that Silver is to become an
Offering for King Victor.

But these are uncertain times and no one really knows
what happens to the teenagers who disappear into Windsor
Castle. Is being an Offering the privilege everyone assumes
it to be, or do the walls of the castle have something to
hide?

Trapped in a maze of ancient corridors, Silver finds herself in a warped world of suspicion where it is difficult to
know who to trust and who to fear. The one thing Silver
does know is that she must find a way out . . .

ISBN 978-1-4472-3530-9